I0761108

BY ANNA QUINDLEN

...

FICTION

More Than Enough

After Annie

Alternate Side

Miller's Valley

Still Life with Bread Crumbs

Every Last One

Rise and Shine

Blessings

Black and Blue

One True Thing

Object Lessons

NONFICTION

Write for Your Life

Nanaville

Lots of Candles, Plenty of Cake

Good Dog, Stay

Being Perfect

Loud and Clear

A Short Guide to a Happy Life

How Reading Changed My Life

Thinking Out Loud

Living Out Loud

...

BOOKS FOR CHILDREN

Happily Ever After

The Tree That Came to Stay

MORE THAN ENOUGH

More Than Enough

A Novel

Anna Quindlen

RANDOM HOUSE • NEW YORK

RANDOM HOUSE
An imprint and division of
Penguin Random House LLC
1745 Broadway, New York, NY 10019
randomhousebooks.com
penguinrandomhouse.com

LIBRARY OF CONGRESS CATALOGING-IN-PUBLICATION DATA
NAMES: Quindlen, Anna, author.
TITLE: More than enough: a novel / Anna Quindlen.
DESCRIPTION: First edition. | New York, NY: Random House, 2026.
IDENTIFIERS: LCCN 2025031672 (print) | LCCN 2025031673 (ebook) |
ISBN 9780593734605 hardcover acid-free paper | ISBN 9780593734629 ebook
SUBJECTS: LCGFT: Fiction | Novels
CLASSIFICATION: LCC PS3567.U336 M67 2026 (print) |
LCC PS3567.U336 (ebook)
LC record available at https://lccn.loc.gov/2025031672
LC ebook record available at https://lccn.loc.gov/2025031673

Printed in the United States of America on acid-free paper

2nd Printing

FIRST EDITION

Book Team: PRODUCTION EDITOR: *Mark Birkey* •
MANAGING EDITOR: *Rebecca Berlant* • PRODUCTION MANAGER: *Sandra Sjursen* •
COPY EDITOR: *Caroline Clouse* • PROOFREADERS: *Megha Jain, Vincent La Scala*

Title-page image from AdobeStock/steli[o]rama

Book design by Barbara M. Bachman

The authorized representative in the EU for product safety and compliance is Penguin Random House Ireland, Morrison Chambers, 32 Nassau Street, Dublin D02 YH68, Ireland. https://eu-contact.penguin.ie

For my father,

Robert V. Quindlen

Always with me.

I am out with lanterns, looking for myself.

—*Emily Dickinson*

MORE THAN ENOUGH

I'D SAID I WOULD TELL THEM EVERYTHING.

"Everything," Jamie had said. "Everything." That's Jamie's conversational tic, that she repeats everything for emphasis. Everything.

"I promise to tell you when I get the results," I'd said at the time, whacking off a wedge of cheese. The lingering hormones in my system make me ravenous, then nauseous, then ravenous again, and emotional for no reason I can reliably predict. I cry at subway delays and TV ads. I buy impulsively at white sales. I have a small apartment and seven decorative quilts.

"I think we all need to remember that we gave Polly this DNA kit in the first place as a joke," Sarah had said. "It wasn't serious. We didn't give it to her to pressure her into anything."

"I'm fine with pressuring Polly," Jamie said.

I'd said I would tell them everything, but that was a month ago, when we had my birthday celebration at Helen's apartment. A party hat, a chocolate cupcake, a small square package with foil wrapping and ribbons, then a larger one as well. "I'll report back," I'd said then about the DNA test. Ethnicity, genetic makeup, long-lost family members. While Jamie rolled her eyes and Helen mentioned someone at her law firm who had taken the same test and discovered she was part Russian, Sarah, always looking out for me, had said again, "No pressure at all. Just for fun."

I can feel the folded sheet of paper in my tote bag now, and it doesn't feel like fun. It feels incandescent, as though the three of them will be able to see it glowing like a lightning bug under a leaf stuck beneath my course notes, a folder of essays, my computer, and the fancy needlepoint clutch in which I keep my tampons, because despite all our efforts, Mark's and mine and the doctors', I am not pregnant.

I don't know why I printed out a paper copy of the test results. I guess it was that it would make them feel more real, when part of me wanted them to simply disappear, to go back to the evening in the bathroom when I stuck that stupid swab in my mouth and rotated it inside my cheek, just behind where my girlhood dimples used to be before they turned into the divots of forty. The paraphernalia from that little just-for-fun gift box had been stacked on the side of the sink the same way all the pregnancy tests had been, and the ovulation predictors. I take more tests than my students at the Windsor School do.

Sarah and Helen and especially Jamie want me to tell them everything, everything that's on that sheet of paper in my tote bag. But I'm not ready to do that, not yet. Which is why, a month on from that birthday celebration, I'm standing frozen at the door of Sarah's apartment listening to the faint sounds of the three of them talking inside.

It sounds like a symphony of conversation, Helen low and melodious, Sarah interjecting from time to time in her high, sweet voice, and then Jamie, loudest, sharpest. Timpani, maybe? I know enough about classical music to appreciate it, but not enough to assign instruments to my friends heard at a distance. I don't know what they're talking about, but it's probably the usual—Helen's law practice, Sarah's philanthropic causes, Jamie's annoying husband and annoying counseling clients. We've never really figured out whether Jamie has a good marriage or a bad one, loves Bert or merely tolerates him, since she talks about everyone else as though they're annoying, too. Even sometimes the three of us.

But I know for sure they're not talking about me, or if they are, it's not mean talk. We're not that kind of group. If we want to talk about one another, we do it face-to-face, with a decent white wine, although I almost never drink anymore. But the others do. Not chardonnay. Jamie hates chardonnay. Not expensive. Sarah thinks it's a crime to spend a lot of money for a bottle of wine when there's so much need in the world, even though she's positioned to buy expensive wine better than any of the rest of us.

"We know, we know, we know," Jamie will say when Sarah mentions how many families are homeless in the city. "Jamie," Helen will say, trying to rein her in, although that's clearly impossible. There's a kind of equipoise to our group, so that we'll veer here and there and somehow always come back to center, and peace. Twelve years we've been meeting. These three have been with me through a career pivot, a divorce, two years of mostly celibacy and total misanthropy, a succession of terrible dates, and then Mark. Once we got rid of Rachel, the chemistry was ideal. And that one, Rachel, that was Helen's fault. Helen had finally stopped apologizing for what she called "the Rachel misfire," even though we'd all forgiven her years ago. I love Helen. I really love Sarah. I even love Jamie. I'd told her that once, but only as she was climbing into a cab. "Me, you too," she'd whispered in my ear.

We meet once a month, and so here I was, standing eye to eye with the peephole in Sarah's apartment door. From the sound of their voices I can tell the three are already sitting in her living room ranged around the glass coffee table. The apartment door leads to the long gallery which leads to the living room and the living room windows, with their view of the paths and trees of Central Park. Sarah keeps binoculars on one of the window seats; sometimes at night you can watch a raccoon family waddling across the grass as they pass beneath one of the park lights. It's the apartment of someone with plenty of money but no affectations. Sarah always says that all she really needs is the view of the park outside, pale green to deep green to gold and red to bare and black, spring to summer to autumn to winter, and then around again.

I don't think Sarah ever uses the peephole. To get up to her apartment you have to get past the doorman, and to get past the doorman you have to get past the call up to the resident. "All Visitors Must Be Announced" it says on a sign at the front desk. When the delivery man comes on his bicycle with the Chinese takeout, one of the doormen takes the bags up to the apartment.

The door to the apartment isn't even locked, I know, and yet still I stood there staring at the peephole. What was I, six or seven, when Garrison, my older brother, told me that I should never stand in front of one of those peepholes in an apartment door because when an assassin inside saw the shadow of someone in the hallway with their eye to it, that was how they'd know you were standing there and would shoot you.

"Why would somebody want to shoot me?" I'd asked. "I'm not even tall enough. You're not even tall enough."

"You never know what's going to happen, Polly," Garrison had said. Which is something Garrison still says to me sometimes.

So I finally turned the knob to Sarah's apartment and walked inside.

"There you are!" Jamie called down the length of the gallery.

"Hey, honey," said Sarah.

"Don't get up," I said, putting my tote bag and jacket on the bench by the door, next to Jamie's and Helen's totes and jackets, and sinking down into one of the big upholstered chairs. Sarah's furniture is somehow like Sarah, always ready to give you a hug. There was a faint odor in the room from the street, a combination of exhaust fumes, pot smoke, mown grass, and flowering trees, that was oddly pleasant. Sarah is one of the only people I know in New York City who opens her windows. Air-conditioning May to October, heat November to April: That's the rule for most people in most places. The inside separate from the outside. Which, come to think of it, is true of most New Yorkers, including me. The inside quite separate from what you see on the outside.

"Was it a long day?" Helen said.

"Senior project presentation day," I said.

"Which one of them is curing cancer?" Jamie said.

"They're pretty amazing," I said. "Although sometimes their ambition scares me."

"Why should they be ambitious?" Jamie said. "They already have everything."

"Continue, Polly," said Helen, looking sidelong at Jamie.

"These were four history projects," I said, putting an egg roll and a fried pork dumpling on one of Sarah's little hand-thrown plates. "There was one on Seneca Falls that was practically a doctoral dissertation. Her parents were levitating, they were so proud."

"Which is why you're wearing makeup," Jamie said, leaning forward and narrowing her eyes. "Even foundation?"

My mouth was full and there was no need to respond. Almost all of Jamie's questions are rhetorical. She already knows the answers. Except the answer on the piece of paper folded deep inside my tote bag, as though I could bury it beneath the stuff of my everyday, ordinary life.

"Anything to report?" Helen said.

"Give us the whole shebang," said Sarah.

"Who under the age of ninety says that?" Jamie said. "The whole shebang? What's next? Pardon my French? The bee's knees?"

"I never understood the bee's knees."

"Happy as a clam?"

"Jamie, you're losing the thread," said Helen. "Polly, we want to know what you find out when you find it out. Unless you don't want to tell us for some reason."

"To hell with that," said Jamie. "We want to know everything. Everything."

Looking down at my plate, mouth still full, I shook my head. I've always found it easier to lie with physical gestures than with words. Words are my bond. My face, not so much. It's been that way since I was a little girl. Penelope Isabelle Goodman, did you spit your peas in the sink? Head shake. Once we got a garbage disposal it was so much easier, especially since by then our mother was hardly ever home for dinner. I could dump the whole thing—chicken breast, rice, peas—into the disposal, and like magic it was gone. Even the chicken bones, although they made a lot of noise. "Is there a fork in there?" my father would call from his den.

"I would imagine a real DNA analysis takes time," said Helen.

"It's been a month," Jamie said. "A whole month."

"As I said," said Helen, and I felt the document in my tote bag whispering, It doesn't take long at all, not that long—Polly knows, she just doesn't want to discuss it yet. Or ever.

"I forgot to bring my copy of the book for tonight," I said, changing the subject.

Sarah reached around to one of the side tables and held up a thick book with an oil portrait reproduced on the cover. "*Maria Theresa of Austria*," she said. "The *Journal* says that this biography humanizes her more than ever before. She had sixteen children!"

Jamie put her wineglass down with such force that I was afraid the stem would break. "Did you read it?" she asked.

"Oh, for pity's sake, calm down," Sarah said. "I read the review before I sent out the books. Did you even open yours?"

Jamie shook her head. So did I. "Mine's on the coffee table," Helen said. "I love the portrait. She looks like she'd kill and eat you. Which makes sense. Apparently she ruled half of Europe."

"You read it!" Jamie said.

"I read the flap copy," Helen said.

"I think that's cheating," Jamie said.

"I'm getting fizzy water," I said. "Does anyone else want some?"

"I would love some," said Helen.

"I'll get the brownies," said Sarah, which I knew wasn't why she was following me into the kitchen. She'd clocked the fact that I wasn't taking even a sip of wine. She didn't know whether to be concerned or ecstatic.

"Are you all right?" she asked.

"I'm fine," I said. "My stomach is funky, but not for the reason you think."

"I'm sorry," she said.

"I'm fine," I said.

"Really," I whispered in Sarah's ear when we all three said goodbye at the door, gathering up our things. Helen was responsible for the next book. She said she thought it would be that new novel set in Afghanistan that was getting such good reviews. "Now that's a beach book," said Jamie.

"I don't think you can complain about a book you're not even going to read," I said.

"Ah, I can complain about anything," Jamie said, and Sarah laughed.

In the lobby of my apartment building, there was my husband, waiting for the elevator. Almost six years married, and I'm always still so happy to see him. "Did you have late meetings at school?" Mark said, taking my tote.

"Book club. What about you?"

"The pregnant zebra."

"How is she?"

"Still breech, at least for now."

"Did you try to turn it?"

"Not yet."

"Can you turn it?"

"I don't know yet. Maybe."

In the elevator he kissed me. Mark always kisses me in the elevator, not a sloppy, inappropriate kiss like Benedict used to go for in the old days, that embarrassed and thrilled me. Mark's was just a fast love-you kiss. "Did you tell them about the test results?" he asked.

"Not yet," I said. "I will."

"I wish they'd never given you that thing," he said as the elevator doors opened outside our apartment. "I don't believe most of them are even accurate. If someone wants to find out if they're really one hundred percent Irish, that's one thing. If they want to find out if they carry the genes for a serious illness, they need to see a geneticist."

"And if they want to find out whether they have a family member they know absolutely nothing about and can't imagine how they might be related to?" I asked.

"I don't believe most of them are even accurate," repeated Mark, who is always trying to protect me from unhappiness or anxiety.

In our tiny foyer I looked at the small table and the hooks I'd put atop it for our keys, our bags, our shoes. Mark's backpack was where he always left it, beneath the table's gatelegs, where it had been when he left for work that morning, forgotten yet again. He saw me looking at it and shrugged. "I didn't really need it anyway," he said. Living with Mark is like a constant scavenger hunt with murky clues. His wallet? His coat? His backpack? All of them were apparently somewhere, although his somewhere was never entirely certain. Once, I had been late to book club because he'd taken three veterinary students out to a Thai restaurant and called to say that he didn't have his wallet. He'd hugged me as I restored it to him at the door of The Lotus House.

I hung my keys on a hook, watched as he put my bag on the table, then went into the kitchen and sat down. "I almost said something near the very end," I said. "I got a fortune cookie that said, 'Trouble not shared is big trouble.'"

"You're the only person I know who gets fortunes that actually mean something," he said. "The last fortune I got said something like 'The wind blows across the desert.'"

One night six years before, at a restaurant in Chinatown, the skeletal remains of a Peking duck littering the table, I had opened a fortune cookie that said, "Happiness is right in front of you." It had been the fourth time Mark had asked me out. Or maybe it counted as the third time. Our third date I sat at the bar of a place in SoHo for an hour and then left, furious, despondent, because I'd thought he was different, even good, not the kind to stand me up. He had called me at eleven o'clock, the sound of what seemed like mooing in the background. "Polly, Polly," he said. "I didn't forget we had a date on Wednesday. I just forgot that this was Wednesday!" Given the dark place in my heart where men were concerned, it had been almost impossible to believe. Now I knew that Mark's ability to forget what day it was was a real phenomenon, and so was he.

At the table at that Chinese restaurant he had held up his chopsticks and said, after apologizing for the SoHo no-show, ordering food, then apologizing again, "Sometimes I think the human brain is a house, and the lights only come on in mine one room at a time."

"That's incredibly poetic," I'd said.

"Is it? Really?" And his face lit up.

The fortune in his cookie that night, which he handed to me, had said, "The moon lights the way to the future."

"Who writes these things?" he'd said, and then reached for mine. And read aloud: "'Happiness is right in front of you.' There you go," he said, handing it back. I had stopped believing in happiness, and in men, and then happiness was apparently in this man right in front of me. I tried to hold on to that every time I looked at Mark, the idea that happiness was still right in front of me even when the sadness sunk its talons into my chest. That fortune cookie fortune lived in the little cedar box where I kept my jewelry.

"Does a breech foal ever turn spontaneously?" I said.

"And she's trying to change the subject, ladies and gentlemen," he said. "What about your brother? Have you talked to him about this DNA test? You have to talk to him."

"Next week," I said.

"OH, THAT FACE," MY BROTHER SAID AFTER THE WAITER HAD taken our orders. "Polly, I know that face. Do you want me to walk you through the times I've seen it?"

"No," I said. I'm pretty sure I remember them all without being reminded by Garrison: the time in high school I got pulled over with five friends and three six-packs in the car; the time in college when it looked as if I were going to fail my science requirement and thus not graduate; the two times in those same years when I thought, incorrectly it turned out, that I was pregnant, which seemed horribly ironic now. The time I had decided to divorce my irresistible, terrible, brilliant, cheating snake of a first husband and sobbed, blowing my nose, wiping my eyes, in Garrison's living room surrounded by a garden of balled-up snotty tissues. It had taken me ten minutes that day to finally choke out my decision to leave Benedict, at which point Garrison had cast his eyes toward the ceiling and said, "Thank you, God."

"You don't even believe in God," I'd cried.

Garrison had never made any secret of how much he hated Benedict. My brother had tried to get me to fly with him to Prague the night before the wedding, promised me a suite at the Four Seasons on the river overlooking the bridge in lieu of getting married. "Or Paris," he'd added. "Or Florence. We can drink Brunello and look at the statue of David." He had gotten drunk at the small family dinner after the ceremony. "You'd better not mess her up," he'd said to Benedict in the hallway, brass knuckles in his voice, vodka lending him an uncommon thug aspect. "I will mess you up if you mess her up."

"Get a grip, Gary," Benedict had said. You only needed to meet Garrison once to know that he would hate being called Gary. I'd watched his fingers curl into fists.

"What on earth is wrong with your brother?" my mother had said.

"I'll talk to him," my father said.

"I do appreciate that you always come to me," Garrison said now, as the waiter brought our drinks, and "I always appreciate that you listen," I replied, and we clinked ice teas. Because I'd rarely been able to go to our father with bad news, since he thought I never did anything wrong, or to our mother, who I was sure thought the opposite.

"Well, here's the thing," I said. "Do you think there's any possibility that you have a son or daughter?"

Garrison threw back his head and laughed. He has a resonant laugh, somewhere between alto and tenor. It's a little studied, but still charming. I've been at parties when he did it around cater waiters, and he got lots of passed hors d'oeuvres afterward. And who knows what else.

"I know, I know," I said. "But we've both known gay men who fought it when they were younger, or who weren't sure and had relationships with women, or who just took a wrong turn one night with a female friend."

"Yes, we have. But I'm not one of them. All of my sexual experiences have been with other men." The waiter, who had been about to put our food in front of us, pivoted, and then, after a pause, returned. He smiled at Garrison. My brother is very handsome. Older people say he looks like Gregory Peck. "That's your brother?" one of my students had said in a tone filled with marvel when Garrison met up with me one day outside the Windsor School. When someone remarks that we might be twins I consider it a great compliment, although it's not true. He's prettier, and like our parents, his eyes are a cocoa brown. Mine are blue. It's unusual for two brown-eyed people to have a blue-eyed child, but not impossible.

Ever since I'd gotten the DNA test results I'd thought about eye color a lot.

"But the more pressing issue is why you would even ask me this question," Garrison said.

So I told him while he ate his tuna tartare, while my Cobb salad, no blue cheese, sat untouched. How the women in my book club—"I love your book club," he interjected—had given me one of those DNA kits for my birthday, how I had followed the instructions and sent it off, how I had checked the boxes for ethnicity and genetic predispositions and then casually checked the box for relatives who had enrolled with the company after taking a test themselves, all the while thinking that while our parents seemed untethered to their ancestors, there might be distant cousins it would be interesting to know about, and finally, how I had gotten back a form saying that a second-degree relative had taken one of the tests as well. "Aunt, uncle, grandparent, grandchild, niece, or nephew," I recited to Garrison. "We have no grandparents living, right? Neither of us has grandchildren, obviously. So I thought niece or nephew, and the only way that works is if you've had children."

Of course there was a lot I left out. Like the fact that the book club had given me the kit not only as a kind of goof, according to Sarah, but because, according to Jamie, I'd become a little obsessed about various conditions and ailments. True, given what was going on in all of our lives. Sarah's breast cancer: genes. Jamie's father's Parkinson's: early warning signs. What I knew of my own family. What I didn't know of my own family.

And then there was the continuing drama of my pelvis. All the women I know are used to hating parts of their bodies—their wide hips, their thick legs, their knobby knees. I knew one woman in college who was obsessed by how ugly her feet were and wouldn't wear sandals or even normal shoes. Always boots. Cowboy boots, rain boots, Wellingtons. When we were all padding around barefoot, dressed for bed, boxer shorts, T-shirts, her feet looked like feet to me, no better, no worse. It doesn't matter how beautiful or successful they are, every woman I know undergoes this terrible self-assessment. Jamie can do ten minutes of stand-up about her nose, which is Roman and suits her face completely. Helen says since early menopause struck, she has a roll around her midsection, which none of the rest of us can see. Only Sarah doesn't complain. She lost both breasts to cancer and got away "scot-free," in one of her grandmotherly turns of phrase, with her life. Her hair grew back and she can mostly feel her fingers and toes again. "I was always an A cup anyhow," she said to me once. I'm not sure that's true, but there are so many not-quite-true things we all say to soothe ourselves.

I'm not immune, even with what I've learned from watching Sarah, about simply being grateful to be alive. There are those patches just below my butt cheeks, dimpled like the outside of an orange, that I've been looking at in mirrors over my shoulder since high school. But that was all about the outside, what the world saw, what guys saw, what we saw in shorts or bikinis if we ever wore shorts or bikinis. I never thought, when I was younger, to pass judgment on my insides. I never thought, I'm unhappy with my lungs, my intestines, my appendix. But now I hate my uterus. I imagine I can feel it, like a rock inside.

The women in my book club knew some of that, knew not to grin now when I passed on wine the way they first had five years ago. They knew some of what we'd gone through, Mark and I, to try and have a baby. ("The triumphant second husband," Garrison had called him at that wedding, no European trip dangled in front of me to avoid a mistake this time, no overdoing the drinking, no threats to the groom. "I swear, if he played for my team I'd marry him myself.") In the same way the four of us could read how far to go with questions during Sarah's surgery and chemo, so they had also been good at reading me. But they still gave me the kit from Roots & Branches, with its motto on the green-and-gold box: "Who are you? We offer the answer."

"You don't even have to use it if you don't want to," Helen had said.

"No-no-no-no," Jamie said. "We need you to do it and tell us everything."

"Really, it's just a joke," Sarah said. "The real gift is in the bigger box." A cashmere scarf, fuchsia and green. Beautiful. "That's a great print on you, Polly," the head at my school had said when I wore it for the first time.

"Roots & Branches?" said Garrison as the waiter hovered. "Isn't that the really random one? I think they were under investigation by the FDA or the CDC or someone."

"Sarah said they didn't even bother to get the really good one because it was just a joke."

"But you took the test anyhow."

"I don't have any of the bad genes," I said. "Which probably means you don't have any of the bad genes."

"Pol, I love you, but did you take bio? We could be fishing at completely opposite ends of the gene pool. And you could be relying on a test kit from a company that has results done by people who are fulfilling a quota for positive medical results and family connections. It's a mistake."

"That's what Mark says, too."

"And he's a doctor."

"A veterinarian," I said.

"Look," Garrison said, "if you're obsessed with this—"

"I'm not."

"You are. I know you. I can tell when you're obsessed. So either do it again, or do it with one of the pricey outlets. Although I'm not sure they're any more reliable. I do not have children. You do not have nieces and nephews."

"Sperm donor?" I asked.

"Dessert?" our waiter asked.

"We are going to split the lava cake," Garrison said, and, as the waiter walked away, "I am going to have to give this guy the biggest tip with what he's overheard. And no, I was never a sperm donor. And we know neither one of us was adopted."

I raised my hand in the air, palm out, because I knew exactly what he meant. One morning, when we were children, I had been playing in our parents' room, which we were not supposed to do, and handling our mother's perfume bottles, which I was really not supposed to do, and of course I was playing with the one that was a perfect sphere, tinted lilac and filled with something French, when I dropped it and it rolled under the bed. Garrison had heard me berating myself softly and dropped down next to me beneath the bed skirt.

"Are you sure it went under here? Because I don't see it." All we saw was a fancy leather book, and Garrison, being Garrison, pulled it out and started to page through it. When we saw the pictures, we could tell why it was hidden under there and not with the other photo albums in the den. We had both seen the two sets of pictures taken in the hospital, our mother in bed looking exhausted despite her ever-present Coral Reef lipstick, the doctor on one side, our father on the other. In one set of photos, a tiny bundle with a blue stocking cap. In the other, a baby in pink.

The ones in the album under the bed were obviously the pictures that had been taken slightly before those tidy posed shots. Same dad, same doctor, same bundles, but this time the babies were on their way out, head, head and shoulders, and then held up for display, wet and unswaddled and naked, as shiny under the lights as red patent leather. In one set a boy, in another a girl, with a part of our mother we had never seen, had never wanted to, and knew without question she did not want us to examine looming large. We had both been speechless. I put the perfume bottle back. Garrison left the room. Ten years later, me leaving for college, he just graduated, we split a bottle of wine and a joint in the backyard, and he turned to me and said, "That photo album."

"Oh my God," I had replied.

"Is it still there?"

"Why would you even ask?"

"Just curious," Garrison said.

But it wasn't.

We had never spoken of it again until now. Actually we didn't speak about it now. There was just my raised hand and Garrison's nod. Not. Adopted.

"I suppose it could be Uncle Brian," Garrison said, tapping a spoon on the table. We went through what we knew. Our mother had had two brothers. One lived in Idaho and was named Brian. He and my mother exchanged Christmas and birthday cards and had seen each other four years before, when Brian and his wife spent two days in New York City on their way to Maine. They came to our apartment for dinner and talked about how they had seen a man sleeping on the sidewalk outside their hotel. "You don't see that in Twin Falls," my uncle said. Our mother's other brother, Daniel, had died in Vietnam. When we visited Washington on a field trip in sixth grade and went to the Vietnam Memorial, I had found his name on the long black wall and done a rubbing of it onto a sheet of paper and given it to my mother. I had been surprised to hear her begin to breathe as though she'd been running. "Dear God," she repeated. "I'm sorry," I'd said. I thought I'd done a good thing. Even then my mother and I were like two people speaking different languages. She will treasure this. She will be appalled by this.

Our father had had one sister, who had died of cancer when we were very young. We both remembered a babysitter who let us watch television all day, which was strictly forbidden, while our parents were at the funeral. "Do we know what kind of cancer Daddy's sister had?" I asked, but Garrison ignored the question. "You met Uncle Brian," said Garrison. "Was he the kind of guy who might want to take one of these tests for the sake of genealogy stuff?"

"Maybe," I said. "Maybe that's it. That's probably it. He's probably one of those people who's working on a family tree, figuring out who fought in the Civil War, all that. He would definitely qualify as a second-degree relative."

"And he has kids, right? The cousins we've never met?"

"I think he just has one son, but I don't think he'd be classified as a second-degree relative," I said, finishing the last of the lava cake. "You're right, it's probably Uncle Brian."

We walked out to the street together, I to go home because it was the upper school field day and I had no classes, he to the office because he's always at the office, where he works as an investment banker, apparently with great success, since he has a lovely apartment, beautiful clothes, and is always trying, and failing, to lend me money to upgrade both in my own life. I wish Garrison would find true love, but instead I gather that he has hookups with people as attractive as he is. "Did that waiter write his phone number on the check?" I said.

"I believe he did," said Garrison. "I believe he did."

"The other possibility is that either Daddy or Mother had a child and gave the child up for adoption. Or in Dad's case, maybe he didn't even know. Maybe he got someone pregnant who didn't even tell him. And it's the child of that child who's also on the Roots & Branches site."

"Polly," Garrison said, "take the test again. They made a mistake. Or write to Uncle Brian and see if he took one himself. Go home to your fabulous husband. I'm glad he and I are on the same page about this."

"He has a zebra with a breech baby," I said. "He's trying to turn it so it'll come out headfirst instead."

"I love him," Garrison said. "I love you. I'm all you've got. Live with it."

"Oh, Gar," I said, hugging him, "you're so much more than enough."

"Exactly," my brother said.

I STOOD IN FRONT OF MY STUDENTS, THE LAST OFFICIAL DAY OF classes before summer, and felt the familiar tug and grab and downward thrust in my midsection that meant my period was coming again, the way it had every month for thirty years. Sometimes I wondered if I were in sync with some of my students, if something inside of me responded to how young and fresh and full of estrogen they all looked, with their flushed skin and their unruly hair, if somehow my body tried to talk back to theirs. But that was nothing but a fantasy, that imagined hormonal conversation. The difference in a woman between eighteen and forty-two was a long highway. At best my body was whispering what they were singing.

My senior English honors class was my favorite. The first-years were still a little mean, carrying with them the spats and betrayals of middle school, but by senior year, when all the students saw on the horizon was a separation from girls they'd first met in kindergarten, it was endless hugs. In the morning they came down the street, navy-blue pleated skirts and white polo shirts, their arms around one another. "I love you," they said to one another unselfconsciously, making the second word last in their mouths as a sign of devotion, elongating the vowel.

"So what are the lessons we've taken away from Austen's *Persuasion*?" I asked. "And, by the way, your papers were all very good. I know second semester of senior year, once the college choices are done, can seem like a skate, but none of you appear to have skated in the least."

"So, Miss Goodman, I'm so sad that this was Jane Austen's last novel," said Amanda, who wanted to be an English major.

"And it's such a sad book," said Jessica.

"Why sad?" I asked. "Doesn't it have a happy ending?"

"It's formulaic," said Josephine flatly. Josephine was my best student, but I wondered often about her inner life. Some of my students were from very wealthy families, and some were on scholarship, and sometimes I can't tell the difference, and sometimes—a comment about the long subway ride from Queens, the tan after a skiing vacation in Aspen—I can. With Josephine it was more that she was both brilliant and hard, a diamond of a girl. Despite her youth, I didn't sense there was any romance in her.

"Austen does the same thing in every novel," Josephine added. "The heroine has sketchy taste in men. She rejects someone who is obviously the right man for her, has a passing flirtation with someone who is obviously bad, and then has her eyes opened and winds up with the first man. I'm not sure I ever buy it. I don't think in *Pride and Prejudice* that Elizabeth Bennet would have been fooled by Wickham for a minute."

"A point you made very powerfully in your paper," I said. In my classes, Josephine had never gotten anything but an A. Given her grade point average, this seemed to have been true in every class, even calculus. "She's been heading to Harvard since she was in second grade," the assistant head had said when I handed her Josephine's college recommendation. "I think the parents bought her the sweatshirt when she was still in middle school."

Jane Austen's love life is a bit of a mystery, I'd already told them, if love life it could be called, and she never married. I'd seen some of the polo shirts with the school crest rise and fall as a few of them sighed. So sad. I'd wanted to say, Perhaps what's worse is if you marry a Wickham. That's what I'd done.

Benedict had been in my PhD program. He was British, had taken a first at Oxford. The accent alone was seductive, not to mention the eyes, one green, one brown, and the technique. A man who was mesmerized by your mind, until one day he wasn't. By our first anniversary I had dropped out of graduate school with just a master's degree. Only Garrison was persuaded by the argument that I loved literature and hated deconstructing it. "Defenestrating is more like it," I'd said. "They suck all the juice out of George Eliot and Virginia Woolf. They're contemptuous of Dickens."

"Well, Dickens," Benedict had said dismissively, making both my point about the doctoral program and Garrison's point about why he loathed Benedict.

I had left Benedict after my only real friend in the graduate program, Colin, met me for breakfast and said, "He refers to you as his jejune wife." I was embarrassed to admit that I didn't know exactly what jejune meant, even laughed and said that it sounded somehow French and all, like a compliment. "Dull is what it is," Colin said. "He laughs and says you're thinking of taking a job teaching English at some girls' school."

"I am."

"He sleeps with Abigail in your bed," Colin said.

Afterward it felt like something that had barely happened, like a French film or a short story, except that it remained lodged inside me, like one of those splinters you can't get out no matter how much you dig with the tweezers. The fact that there was almost no shared property to divide said it all. I took everything from the kitchen—the dishes, the silver, the food processor. The couch was secondhand, the bed polluted forever. To her credit, Abigail crossed Broadway when she saw me coming one afternoon, although that didn't make me hate her less. "She calls herself a feminist!" I'd said to Garrison. "Real feminists don't sleep with other women's husbands!"

"She did you a big favor," Garrison said.

The main thing that lingered was the sense of being snookered, an expression that Sarah liked to use. I tried to console myself with Austen heroines, how they'd been fooled by a handsome face, broad shoulders, a great line of bullshit. But it wasn't much consolation in real life. At least I'd already left the graduate program and didn't have to run into Benedict or Abigail. Apparently she was now teaching at UVA, he at Eton. For two years I was chaste, celibate, quietly and persistently enraged, suspicious of all men, from teenage boys on the subway to friends of my father's at the golf club. They all pretended to be nice. They were all surely hiding betrayal. Finally, after I told Garrison that it would be a cold day in hell when he could give the nice, single financial analyst in his section my number, my brother sat me down and said, "The men-are-scum era is officially over. The idea that you're letting that guy shit on your life by remote control is unacceptable."

"Men," I spat at Garrison.

"No, Polly, him. You were the only person who couldn't see what he was. On a shit scale of zero to ten he had eleven written all over him. The world is full of nice men."

When I brought Mark to dinner with Garrison for the first time, my brother leaned in before they'd even brought our main course and said, "Told you, girlfriend!"

"Can I call you girlfriend?" Mark had asked.

"He can, right?" Garrison said. "You are, right?"

"She absolutely is," Mark had said, taking my hand.

The cramping in my belly now was deepening. I looked at the classroom wall clock. Twenty minutes until I could make it to the bathroom. There was a time when I would have seen this as an inconvenience. Now it was existential. I felt like myself was running out of me, like I was becoming hollow, would sink to the floor like a punctured balloon. I blinked. Concentrate, Polly, I thought.

"But then are you saying Jane Austen isn't a great novelist?" Amanda had asked Josephine, with whom she had been in an intellectual rivalry for as long as anyone could remember.

"Of course not," Josephine said. "She's one of the greatest. Many of the greats are predictable. Hemingway. Fitzgerald. Dickens."

Well, Dickens, I thought to myself reflexively.

"What about *A Tale of Two Cities*?" said Amanda.

"That's just Dickens trying not to be predictable," Josephine said.

I smiled despite myself. My God, they were all so smart, some of them a whole lot smarter than I am. The thing about being a teacher is that you stay in place year after year, in front of this room, behind this desk, and they move on. Almost eleven years I'd been teaching here at the Windsor School, and already one of my first students was preparing to publish her first novel, and three others had become doctors. At the reunion last year two of them already had babies, had brought them with them, one a limp sack in a front sling, the other a flushed screamer who had to be hurried out into a distant hallway. Both the girls, women now, naturally, looked so tired that I almost couldn't resent them. When the screamer returned, fed and drowsy, I held her so her mother could circulate among her friends. "Want to take a turn?" I'd said to the assistant head, and she said, "Thanks, but no thanks. That's so not my thing. It's incredibly kind of you to do it, though."

We don't know, do we, what people want, who they are? Incredibly kind? I was one kind impulse from a kidnapping or a crying jag.

Thinking about them now, all the girls who had come and gone, knowing it was the last day for this class, I said aloud: "You are all so impressive. It has been an honor teaching you." My voice broke a bit as I said it, and some of them looked panicky: Oh my God, guess what, Miss Goodman started to cry at the end of class. Hormones, I wanted to say to calm them, but it wasn't true, and it wasn't something a teacher could say in class, even at a girls' school, even as an explanation. It was just that I wished someone had taken note of my worth when I was their age, and I hoped they'd hang on to it. In spite of myself I wondered if my phantom maybe-niece was the same age as they were. "There's no niece," I heard Garrison repeating. Maybe I just wanted there to be one, to have something still unknown that was a part of me.

The girls left the classroom: a noisy gaggle, a lonely solo, a pair, another smaller gaggle. The alchemy of their groups always became clear to me over the first few weeks: the socials, the loners, the thinkers, the feelers. I closed the door as I left. For most people the year ends in December. For me, it's June.

Next year, I thought. My tiny office was just down the hall, crowded with a big white Parsons table passed on when one of the mothers redecorated, a fiddle leaf fig grown enormous in the light from the one window, a chair for me, a chair for any student who was told to come in to talk, or who came in on her own. I called up my calendar and, next to today's date, put a red circle, once again charting my cycle, and as I did, for what seemed like the thousandth time, my eyes began to fill, my body once again at odds with my heart. I heard a cough and, looking up and blinking hard, saw Josephine.

"Last day," I said, what I hoped would pass as an explanation for the tears.

"I know," she said, looking down.

"Do you want to sit?"

"No. I just wanted to say thank you. Thank you for everything. Truly."

"It was my pleasure, Josephine. Truly."

She nodded once, twice, three times, then turned. "You'll never know what it meant," she said. And I thought to myself as I walked home across the park, We don't. We never know what's living inside the people around us. We only guess.

Inside our apartment I hung my things in the hallway and put on the kettle for tea. On the bedroom bureau two stuffed animals had suddenly appeared, a tiny zebra and a bigger one, a message via two plush toys. A mother and a baby, somehow arrived, breech or no breech. I started to laugh as I listened to the tea kettle whistle. That was Mark all over, not just the words, but the gestures.

Benedict had been all words, so many words, the first person I'd ever met who used in conversation words I'd only seen in print. "So handsome," my mother had said at dinner after a judge, one of her law school classmates, had married us in her chambers, a beautiful arrangement of peonies and a bottle of Dom Perignon on the mahogany sideboard. "So erudite."

"That was an impressive venue indeed," Benedict had said to my mother, refilling her glass.

"The federal bench has very showy chambers," said my mother, who is a judge in state court and, I suspect, has always aimed higher.

"And the state court has very showy judges," Benedict had replied, and Garrison had looked over at me and murmured, "He is flirting with our mother."

"What?" our father said.

"Nothing, Daddy," I said. "Just Garrison's nonsense."

"Oh, that," our father had said.

"You'll learn to like him," I'd said to my brother as we put on our coats.

"Your brother doesn't like me," Benedict had said in the cab uptown from the restaurant, his hand on my leg beneath my off-white skirt, higher, higher.

"The driver," I gasped.

"Let's give him a show," Benedict whispered in my ear.

"Would it be okay if I kissed you?" Mark had said in the back of a cab after that Chinese dinner date.

"I thought you'd never ask," I'd said. He had such a serious look on his face, all pink cheeks and big eyes. Something about the way he looked had constantly reminded me, in the beginning, that he was just thirty-two, four years younger than I was.

"He's four years younger than I am," I'd said at book club. "This is going nowhere."

"How's the sex?" Jamie had asked.

"Jamie!" said Helen.

"I have a good feeling," Sarah had said later. I wondered if she was proprietary about Mark because I had met him at her apartment at a fundraiser for the Museum of Natural History. She hadn't known him; he had come with a group. By happenstance we'd found ourselves shoulder to shoulder during the speeches, or at least that's what I thought. Later Mark said he'd come across the room to stand next to me. We stood at the windows, the lamps in the park glowing white against the bare branches of the trees and the deep darkness of the paths. Sometimes, at moments like those, I'm stunned by the city and by the fact that I live in it. Behind us some people were discussing whether the museum would return human remains to Native tribes. To one side two men were talking about the header the market had taken that day. Outside people passed in and out of the park entrance, shadows in the shadows.

"I'm a large-animal vet at the Bronx Zoo," Mark had said when the small talk had moved from getting me another glass of wine to how we'd wound up at the party to what we did, that last almost always in the top three at any New York City event.

"Does that line usually work with women?" I'd said, my old post-Benedict hostility coming out to play like a phantom limb I couldn't stop feeling.

"I guess? Maybe? Probably not. I don't know."

"Seriously," I said.

"Seriously what?"

"What do you do?"

"I'm a large-animal vet at the Bronx Zoo," he repeated. "Would you like a tour of the zoo sometime?"

That was our first date, the tour, although I'm not sure I saw it as a date at the time. The gorillas appeared to greet him with hand signals. We had hot dogs and a box of Raisinets on the bench outside his office.

"He hasn't even kissed me yet," I had said to Sarah as we stood on the sidewalk.

"Don't tell Jamie," Sarah had said, and we both giggled and then full-on laughed, and Sarah laughed and laughed until she started to cough, and I held her in my arms until she stopped, feeling the whole length of her spinal column under my hands like some obscure musical instrument, thinking only that she needed to stop skipping breakfast, suspecting nothing more. She smiled, then started to cough again.

The next day I called her. "He kissed me," I said as soon as she answered. "In a cab."

"Yippee!" she said.

"And then he said, 'I'm going to marry you someday.' Who does that? I just met him! He's crazy!"

"I want to be the flower girl," Sarah said.

"Why is our hostess holding a basket of rose petals?" my mother had asked in Sarah's living room just before the ceremony.

"I told you," Sarah said as we stood together afterward by one of the apartment windows, our reflections looking back at us.

"I was afraid," I said.

"We're all afraid, Pol," she said. "We're all afraid of something." I wasn't sure exactly what she meant until two weeks later, when she told me she was having surgery the next day, to be followed by chemotherapy. It all happened so fast, the hospital, the drains, the head scarfs, Sarah penciling in her eyebrows and going to some woman to have false lashes glued on one by one. It took two hours, she said, and she slept through most of it because she was so tired.

I felt like I should have known, feeling Sarah's spine beneath my fingers.

"You made a wedding for me, knowing that was happening to you," I'd said.

"Under the circumstances, making a wedding was the best thing that could happen to me, Polly. Don't make it sound like a sacrifice. Nothing could have made this easier for me than you and that wedding and your happiness. It was a great wedding. Everyone said so."

It was true. "A beautiful thing," my father had said, kissing me on the forehead. "Really lovely," my mother said.

"What a great party," Helen had said. "Also, your new mother-in-law is terrific."

"Your husband is cool," Jamie said, eating cake. "He knows a lot about capybaras. People overlook them. I love capybaras."

"Give me your bouquet," Sarah had said as Mark and I headed out together.

"I want to keep it!"

"You will," she said. "Trust me. You'll get it back." Now it was right there on the bureau behind the zebras, a bell jar with my bouquet of trailing ivy and yellow roses somehow frozen in time inside, the ribbons arranged to fall gracefully from the bow. On the silver band encircling the wooden base was engraved, "I'm Going to Marry You Someday." I hadn't told Sarah what Mark had said after the wedding, with what was left of the cake in a box on my lap, his tie, with its pattern of tiny lions, balled up in his fist. "Let's have some kids," he'd said. "Let's start tonight."

"Let's take a break from all of this," he'd said last year, after the sonogram showed that the third embryo had been as unwilling to take root as the first. The second time around had been the worst, the one with the tiny beating heart, my imagining it fluttering like a hummingbird in my belly, and then, three weeks later, blood in the bathroom. We'd both wept, sitting on the cold tile floor next to what was left of that dream.

I sat down at my computer and called up my calendar, seeing the red circles polka-dotting the year so far, the monthly notice that I had failed once again. If I scrolled back there would be many, many more. It had been four years of my keeping track: ovulation, menstruation, injections, implantation, all the rest. The eggs that were harvested but deemed unusable. The embryos that came from good eggs but weren't, apparently, good themselves. One piece of bad news after another. Everything that was failing, failing me, failing him, although it had only made me love him more over the years we'd been married. We had started out gleefully with the usual thing, that didn't work, gone to the halfway measures, that didn't work, and then to the full-on routine of shots and doctors' offices and samples from him and eggs from me and lab reports and mood swings and the bright light overhead that shone through my closed lids like a red storm sun as I lay on the table with my feet in the stirrups and my knees up. That didn't work. He had been with me for it all, not reluctantly but whole-heartedly. He was a whole-hearted man, my husband. That second time, his face alight as the tech ran the probe over my gelled belly and picked up the thumping sound from the beating heart of the embryo, he'd said, "We're pregnant!" I'd always resented men who said that, but he had earned it.

And then we weren't.

He and I shared a calendar so that we could always keep track of each other. Maybe that said it all. He knew where I was, and I knew where he was, and it didn't feel intrusive, just collaborative. He would see the red circles, and he would know. He might bring flowers home, or eclairs, or some funny little fridge magnet. "Step Aside, I'm Hangry," the most recent one said. Or a pair of stuffed animals that told a story, a story my husband had wanted to share with me about how he had spent his day.

There was a text from him. "Not to overshare, but there was A LOT of pulling involved," it said, and then a photograph of a zebra nursing its gangly baby.

There was a posting from the Bronx Zoo public account: "Meet our newest foal!" Mark was in one of the photographs, gloved up.

And there was an email with the unmistakable graphic: a brown trunk leading to golden branches and green leaves. "This is Roots & Branches," it said. "We will always protect your privacy! There is someone enrolled who believes that they have matched with you and would like to hear from you about a possible family connection. If you want to be in touch with them directly, please respond to this email."

"HEY, DADDY," I SAID, SITTING IN THE ROCKING CHAIR NEXT to him on the broad veranda overlooking the perfect golf course of a lawn at Edgemere, where my father has lived for the last three years. I wondered if, in some small synapse, Jack Goodman occasionally looked at that long stretch of green and wondered about a tee time, thought he was waiting for a foursome at the country club, not whiling away yet another day in a nursing home.

"Hey," I repeated. "It's me. It's Polly." That's what they'd taught me. Introduce myself every time. It's me, your beloved daughter, the girl you once told that no man would ever be good enough for. But now I think you were wrong about that. You told me, too, that someday I would be the world's best mother. And now I wonder if you were wrong about that as well.

Slowly my father's head turned, his neck a long stem in the collar of what had become a too-large shirt. Gingham shirts and khakis were once my father's uniform. Garrison's uniform is the beautifully cut dark suit, a striped dress shirt with a white collar and cuffs. Mine is black pants and a white blouse. Our mother's is a ceremonial robe, always a dress beneath it, an artifact of the time when women didn't wear pants in court.

Gingham shirt and khakis, loafers with no socks: That's what my father was still wearing when he came to Edgemere three years ago. Now he wears striped open-necked shirts with no buttons, the executive version of a T-shirt. He still wears khaki pants, but they're pull-on, with an elastic waist. Getting him into dress shirts and zippered pants had become too challenging for the staff, and for him, too, and over time his old uniform had become a new uniform. My brother is sensitive to detail—sensitive in general, too, although his studied sophistication often belies it. He'd bought the new clothes for our father, and the new shoes, too. Not loafers, bedroom slippers, but Garrison makes sure they are leather, expensive, as close to loafers as slippers can be.

My father's clothes had changed to acknowledge circumstances, and so had he. The anger of the first six months had faded to resignation. The discursive anecdotes about his boyhood, the old neighbors, the client who hadn't been a client for decades, began to disappear. Paragraphs became sentences. Sentences became phrases and, sometimes, silences, water running down the drain.

He lifted his eyes to mine, blinking. One, two, three. Everything he does now seems like slo-mo footage: Here's Jack Goodman, sports fans, trying to figure out who this woman sitting next to him might be. Watch him bring his big brows together as she notes that the aides are not shaving him thoroughly, and there's a faint whiff of old people sweat from his body, now slightly folded in upon itself. There's a metal-and-plastic stool in his tub where he sits when they shower him with the handheld nozzle. "I always make sure to condition his hair," one of the aides had told me. "He's got such great hair. Better than most of the women, honestly."

"Uh-huh," my father said, nodding. Then, as though on a five-second delay, he smiled. I love that smile. It was the sunshine of my childhood: Polly-O, you are a princess. "Here she is," said my father, as though he had simply been waiting for this moment for me to appear. "She's here. Never fails."

On his other side is a woman named Claire. My father sometimes doesn't remember his wife now, and sometimes does and becomes agitated or enraged at her absence. Claire doesn't remember her husband, and he has mostly stopped visiting her. In the beginning her daughter was rattled by the relationship between Claire and my father, but I think now she feels as I do: whatever makes them happy, whatever happiness means to the two of them now.

In warm weather my father and Claire sit here on the veranda for hours holding hands, occasionally speaking in tiny truncated sentences, as though they were only allotted a certain number of words in life and at this juncture they have to use them sparingly. The staff talk about them fondly. It must make a nice change from the ones who wail or try to leave or take off their clothes. There was one man who would sneak phones from the bags of visitors and call 911, reporting his kidnapping, another who would try to feel up the female staff and make graphic suggestions. Jack Goodman is a prince, the staff agree. My father was always good-humored, well-mannered, and sweet-tempered. He still is. So is Claire.

"Look at the sun," he said, nodding toward it.

"It's warm," said Claire.

"It is warm," he said. "It's good. It's a beautiful day."

I try to come at least twice a month, but there have been a few times when I wasn't sure he knew exactly who I was, although he knew I was someone he liked. The nurses say some days he doesn't talk at all, and some days he talks with them and mostly makes sense, at least until he gets tired. In the beginning, three years ago, he retained a memory of all three of us: Garrison, my mother, me. He occasionally thought his parents, dead for decades, were still around. He wanted them to bring bagels from that place on the corner, wherever that long-ago place was. He sometimes said he wanted to take me to swim class and take Garrison to Little League. And he always said he wanted to go home. "Take me home, Mary," he would say to my mother over and over again. "I want to go home now." When I came then, he would ask if I had a car. No, I lied, and his face would fall. I was afraid I wouldn't be able to hold out, that I would put him in the passenger seat and take him back to the house.

I thought back to the years when he had first started to repeat himself, had decided to retire, had seemed a little vague. "I'm losing a step," he had said more than once, as though if he admitted it to himself, it wouldn't be such a big thing. Aging, I had thought, driving away the idea of anything more, because he was only in his sixties then. But then it had risen like the tide, swamping his history, his memory, leaving only a few things on the shore, until if you asked him about the people across the street he would be unable to remember who they were, or he would remember the people who had lived and died there decades before, when we were kids, when he was young.

"Is it Alzheimer's?" I'd asked my mother.

"The doctors said they could run more tests to pin it down more specifically," she had said. "I didn't see the point. If I had to remove the mirror in the hallway because he thinks his reflection is some stranger who has broken into the house, does it really matter what we call it?"

It's a nice drive out from the city to this part of New Jersey, some of it on back roads thick with maple trees, dotted in summer with nascent hay and cornfields. I can almost make the trip on some internal autopilot; it's not far from the house where I grew up, the high school I attended, the Y where my father used to take me to swim class, closing his office early because what could be more important? Now this trip is my crying spot, there and back. At the tunnel I start; at Edgemere Place, where my father lives, I stop. When I pull out of the lot after my visit I start again. It's my routine.

"Daddy, do we know anyone who lives in Vermont?" I asked.

"I'm hot," he said. He was wearing a vest over his shirt, which is sometimes part of his uniform, and I helped ease it over his shoulders and arms. "That's better," he said. Claire is skeletal, and she always wears a sweater. She smiled at me. "That's better," she said. It's in the last year that she's developed a tendency to repeat everything my father says. She also sometimes climbs into bed with him. The staff had pulled me aside. "They're just sleeping, no more," the floor manager had said. "Let them be," I said.

"Let me introduce myself!" said the message Roots & Branches had forwarded to me. "My name is Talia Burton, and I live in a small town near Bennington, Vermont, but someday I hope to live in a big city, ideally New York. I love listening to music, hiking, sushi, and animals. I have three cats named Winken, Blinken, and Nod. I have a dog named Charlie. I would like to become a fashion designer. I make my own clothes and even some for my friends and family. I would make something for you if I met you! I'm excited to have other family members since I'm an only child. It would be great if you could tell me how we're related and something about the rest of our family. That might be a lot to ask, but if you would write back and tell me about who you are and where you live, it would be so exciting for me! XOXO. I hope nothing in this message makes you not want to do that."

"Do we know somebody named Burton?" I asked my father. "Somebody in Vermont?"

"That's an old name," he said.

"Who?" Claire said.

"It's a Welsh name," my father said. Where did that come from? Is it even correct?

I think sometimes my father is a little wary of me. When he was first moved here he was more sentient and verbal. But that was when I was in the midst of getting hormone injections to, as the pamphlets said, "stimulate robust ovulation" so that the doctors could knock me out and suck up eggs from my ovaries with a needle and introduce them to Mark's sperm in a glass dish somewhere so they would turn into embryos. The terrible distance I felt between that process and how I had thought I would get pregnant, not to mention the side effects of the hormone injections, made my moods unreliable. Actually, my moods were reliably terrible. I learned breathing exercises so I wouldn't snap at my students, but I hadn't used them when my father asked where my mother was and when they would go home, over and over. I certainly hadn't used them with my mother, nor she with me.

"You have the luxury of visiting this house whenever you want,

Penelope," my mother said three years ago when she had decided to have my father move to Edgemere. "I don't. I'm here all the time, dealing with him day in and day out."

"And so is Sonya," I'd said. Sonya had been with our family since I was in middle school and my mother was first trying cases, Sonya cooking and cleaning and being there when Garrison and I got home each afternoon. Sonya had stayed even when the two of us were gone, taking care of the house, and then, when he began to forget where and who he was, acting as my father's home health aide. She had heard his stories a hundred times, about carrying his grandmother down three flights so she could sit in a lawn chair in front of her tenement building, of winning a baseball scholarship to college in Ohio and having to stay home instead and go to City College, of meeting my mother at a party for his uncle's restaurant. My parents were a prototype or a cliché, depending on your point of view: grew up hardscrabble in Brooklyn, moved to the suburbs after they had their first child, my brother. Some of their friends moved east, to Long Island. Some went west, to New Jersey. They were part of the second group. My parents still owned the white center-hall colonial with the sharp eaves that they'd bought before I was born, the two of them cobbling together a down payment. Over the years they'd added a sunroom, a guest wing, a pool, so that the house had gone from lower-middle-class to upper-middle-class, just as they had. They thought they'd live there forever, or however long forever lasted. Now my mother planned to live there alone. Or maybe not. If my mother decided to sell the house where I'd grown up, she would tell me after she'd already signed the contract on a condo.

"Sonya is a godsend, but she's not here in the middle of the night when he gets up and says he wants to have dinner, or when he picks up the phone and calls the number of his old office and gets upset when the receptionist doesn't answer. The last time he went out in the car, he ran out of gas because he drove around for three hours trying to get back home. He wound up in Paterson. Thank God I had a tracker in the glove compartment, but I had to drive over there with a gas can."

"He shouldn't even be driving."

"Well, since you're his darling daughter, you tell him that. He said I was being a tyrant. I had to tell him I'd lost the keys and was having a new set made. He still went out and got in the car in the middle of the night last month and started beeping the horn when he couldn't get it started. I went out in my bathrobe, and the Gressners were outside standing on their front steps."

"You could get a nighttime person so the man can stay in his own home."

"Or he could come and live with you. Or you could move in with us and deal with him at night."

"In sickness and in health?"

"Oh please, the smugness is so unattractive. He doesn't know where he is much of the time. On any given day he thinks I'm his mother or his sister or you. Besides, Sonya wants to spend time with her grandchildren on the island. She's worked for us for almost thirty years. She deserves her retirement. Edgemere is lovely. It's like a country club."

"And you have work to do."

"And so do you. But only mine is cause for rebuke, correct? Please."

"That's a nice place, where your mother and I will be living," my father had said, easing himself into one of the leather recliners in the den after they took the tour and my mother signed the papers.

"It's really nice," I said. "You won't have to worry about getting the lawn mowed."

"I didn't think of that, Mary," he said at dinner, looking across the table at my mother. "I won't have to worry about getting the lawn mowed."

"You can come here every weekend," my mother said, and he looked puzzled. But he hadn't done that, the home visits, after the first two weekends, when he'd tried to get out of the car when it was time to go back to Edgemere, when he'd wept. "It's too much," my mother had said. "For whom?" I said.

My mother brings out the worst in me. "You should try couples therapy," Jamie had said to me once. That's what Jamie does for a living, couples therapy. Helen, Sarah, and I are all boggled by the notion, because within our group, she's the kind of person who can argue about how to tie a scarf, and she makes her marriage to Bert, who is a psychoanalyst, sound like long spates of bickering and the occasional first-degree insult. But apparently when she's sitting with two people whose bond is frayed or broken, she's aces. A woman in our building who had seen Jamie and me together said she had a friend who tried to get in to see Jamie and there was a long, long waiting list. When she said it, I wondered if the friend she was talking about was that same alleged friend who, in college, was worried she was pregnant or had an STD, the friend who was actually you yourself but was too ashamed to admit it. She and her husband stood in the elevator together as though they were trying to prove how large a distance two people in a small space could create between their shoulders. They felt like magnets pushing each other away.

"You wouldn't believe how many women come in for therapy with their mothers," Jamie had added. "I have a colleague now who does nothing but mothers and daughters."

"Does it work?"

Jamie shrugged. She has a pretty vivid shrug.

"Depends," she said. "It might be worth a try."

I held my father's hand on the veranda at Edgemere, tracing the bulging veins beneath the thin skin. His bloodline. My bloodline. "Vermont?" I said again.

"There's that college in Burlington," my father said. How is it possible that he doesn't remember that his parents and his sister are all dead, and yet he can remember something like that. He probably means Bennington, but even that near miss is a triumph nowadays.

I stroked his hand. He takes blood thinners so he won't throw a clot, taking care of his heart while his brain goes walkabout, and his hands and arms are covered with dark bruises, blood that erupts beneath the skin at the slightest bump or scratch, purple and blue and red. His hands look like my belly after all the hormone injections.

There was a rumble of thunder past the low green hills that surround the expanse of lawn. "There's a storm coming," my father said. "I like a storm."

"I like a storm," said Claire.

"Who's paying for that place?" I had asked my brother. "It must cost a fortune."

"You can't have it both ways, Polly," Garrison had said. "I know you don't want him in a place like that, but you don't want him in a crap place like that. It's clean, the staff are good, there's plenty of them, the food is decent. Our parents both have long-term-care policies." My brother gets weary from my constant upset, my worry about my father, my antipathy toward my mother. I don't know why, exactly, but he seems to take it for granted that the relationship between parent and child will be difficult, and that it doesn't need to matter so much that it is. Or maybe he just pretends that's true. Jamie told me men are like that. "We girls, not so much," she'd said. "Not so much at all."

Garrison is the executor of the estate. "It's no reflection on you, honey," my father had said at the time. "It's just his deal, right, financial stuff." They made the will, and the decision, eight years ago, when they were both old enough to think it was necessary but young enough not to sweat it, my mother sixty, my father sixty-six. He was a little vague then, but he'd always been vague. "Where the hell is my briefcase," he'd say, standing by the front door, and my mother would call from upstairs, "It's on the dining room chair where you left it." I suppose that's why I took Mark's absentmindedness in stride most of the time. Asking, "Do you know where I left my keys?" felt familiar to me.

"Drums," Claire murmured as the thunder erupted again.

Slowly my father looked down at my hands on his, then turned to look into my eyes. His own were all at once alit, the sign that he saw and knew me, really knew me for a moment. "Pumpkin pie," he said. The first time the nurse heard him say that, she'd smiled ruefully and then shook her head. She thought it was nonsense. But it wasn't nonsense at all, it was the name my father had started calling me sometimes when I was little. "How about ice cream, pumpkin pie? Soft serve with sprinkles?" An afterthought, he'd call, "Gar? Dairy Queen?"

"No, thank you," Garrison would call from behind the closed door of his room. My father knew better than to interrupt my mother. When I was four she'd be studying for a test in con law; when I was eight she'd be writing a brief. She rose uncommonly fast: By the time I was blowing my father off to go to Dairy Queen with my friends, she was reading briefs so she could rule from the bench the next morning. The Honorable Mary K. Goodman.

"Your mother is a judge?" Jamie had said. "Well, that's an interesting wrinkle, therapeutically. A judge."

"Pumpkin pie," my father repeated, and he lay his big head on my shoulder, his hair silver but still thick and wavy. "That's my girl." I ran my fingers through it, combing it, the way I did when I was a little girl, when it was the same color as my own, milk chocolate with sparks of copper. "Pumpkin pie," he said again. "She'll come see me soon. She always does." I smelled coconut and vanilla, the conditioner the aides used when they helped him shower. "Daddy," I replied. "I'm right here. It's me."

"WELL, YOU'RE IN A BIT OF A PICKLE," SARAH HAD SAID AS WE walked around the reservoir in Central Park tracking a trio of ducks gliding across the gray-green water.

A bit of a pickle. I kept repeating those words as I drove north toward Vermont, heading to a town south of Bennington, close to the New York border. I hadn't told Talia Burton anything about myself, just that I thought we should meet. I would recognize her, she said, because she would be wearing a Fair Isle sweater. ("That's a kind of pattern around the neckline," she'd added, I suppose in case I was fashion challenged.)

In every friend group there's always one person who you think of as first among equals, I guess, although you always feel vaguely guilty about it. Sarah and I went out of our way at book club not to mention the dinners we two had shared, the phone calls we'd had. She would listen to me tell Jamie and Helen stories I'd already told her, and I would do the same. We were lucky ducks, she always said, to have met as we had. Jamie vaguely knew me from college, Helen's husband was a friend of Jamie's husband, Helen and Sarah were on some kind of board together. Jamie and I were both thirty when the book club first started, Helen and Sarah eight years older. Our backstories came out in pieces that first year. Jamie a therapist, Helen a trusts-and-estates lawyer, Sarah a philanthropist.

"Lucky you," Jamie had said when Sarah had first said that, meaning, enough money to give it away and not chase a paycheck. But over the years I'd learned more, although Sarah was sometimes obtuse about her past. Her mother was "a piece of work," her father "a bit of a head case." What happened to them was never explained, and the way she described her childhood made most of it seem forbidden, even to me, her closest friend. Her grandmother had raised her, which is where all her old-fashioned turns of phrase apparently came from. Her grandmother had raised her to accomplish what she herself had not: college, grad school, work as a landscape architect, and one day a commission to overhaul the gardens at the Connecticut country house of a widower thirty years Sarah's senior. Hence her marriage to Richard, the enormous apartment, the place in the country, and the philanthropy. She'd been married to Richard only seven years when he died suddenly, the kind of heart attack they called the widow-maker. He died by the pond at the house in Connecticut. Sarah found him on the grass when it was far too late. He had two sons, both around Sarah's age.

"And they both hate you with a passion?" Jamie had said early on. "The wicked stepmother? The gold digger?"

"They're both really lovely to me. The elder one had me host the rehearsal dinner before his wedding."

The death of Sarah's husband had been the first big terrible thing we'd all talked about together. There have been big good things, too: my second marriage, Helen's surprise pregnancy when her two girls were already six and eight. There'd been small bad things: Sarah's dog's being put down, the dyslexia for Helen's second daughter that made school difficult and took a while to diagnose. And then there were the other big terrible things: Sarah's breast cancer, the dementia of Helen's mother and my father. "We should fix them up with each other," Helen joked. "But they'd forget each other by dinner," I'd replied, and, seeing Sarah's face, I had added, "Life is a tragedy for those who feel and a comedy for those who think. Molière, I think."

"It's not an either-or," Sarah had said. Sarah took bad things to heart, except her own, which she took to heart but refused to wear or even air much. For others she had emotional ESP. It wasn't just that she understood when you were upset; sometimes she understood it when you hadn't even acknowledged it to yourself. "You should have been a therapist instead of Jamie," I had said to her once. "Oh no,"

Sarah said. "I would have held it all inside and imploded at a certain point. Jamie has that ability to let things go."

Sarah walked the reservoir every morning when she was in the city, when she was not in Connecticut deadheading the roses and reading grant proposals, and I always tried to join her when I wasn't working. How to explain when somehow you and another person fit together, not in that sudden lightning bolt fashion that often preceded a love affair—as it had for me with Benedict, or what I had imagined Benedict to be until I knew him better—but in that quieter, in some way more satisfying fashion with someone you recognized as likely to be a lifelong friend. When Mark had been so determined to see me again after we had met at the benefit at Sarah's apartment, I'd been incredulous. "Why?" I'd said to him. "I wasn't even nice to you that night."

"I was standing near you and your friend Sarah, the one who gave the party, when you two were talking," he'd said. "You were really nice then. The two of you were the happiest people in the room. Also, you were the prettiest."

Sarah was the only one who knew the full story of how we'd been on the baby chase, Mark and I. I'd described shopping for the clinic I liked, rejecting the one that was all glossy ash-gray waiting areas and art photography, how we finally settled on the one that felt smaller and friendlier and had only women doctors and staff. "Will that make you feel out of it?" I'd said to Mark in the cab. "Not at all," he'd said. "I've inseminated ibex and okapis, but that's simple compared to this." The driver had looked in the rearview at the two of us, and we started to laugh. "What, no lions?" I said.

At the same time I was having an embryo transferred into my womb, which was supposed to be its comfy home for nine months, Mark had done two embryo transfers on bison. The bisons' took. Mine didn't.

"What do I always tell you?" Mark had said two years after our marriage, taking my hand. "Whatever makes you happy," I repeated. "Let's do this thing," he'd said.

This fertility thing. That's what I called it when I talked about it, not wanting to go into detail. "Oh, you know, the fertility thing," I'd said casually at book club when I was bloated, nauseous, teary. Only Sarah heard the play-by-play, the shots in the belly to make the eggs pop, the dream state when they harvested the eggs, the shots to make the uterus what they termed "hospitable" so the embryo would implant and stay put. I was lucky, I said, I had a husband who had given so many injections professionally and who insisted on taking care of mine, doing the shot quickly, dabbing at my eyes afterward with a tissue. "All done," he always said. When I first saw him holding one of his brother's babies, or watching kids blowing bubbles while we sat on a bench in the park, it lit me up. Now it just brought me down. The man was born to be a father, married to a woman who couldn't seem to be a mother. Inhospitable. That's what they called my body for the purposes of pregnancy.

I'd run Sarah through my DNA test conversation with Garrison, the retest that had showed the same genetic connection, the message I'd gotten from what I figured was my nominal niece. Sarah shook her head and sighed. "I wish we'd never given you that darn kit," she said.

"My brother says I need to ask myself why I'm even pursuing this, why I wanted to do it in the first place."

"You know I love Garrison, but that's ridiculous. Why do we want to do anything? Why do you teach? Why did I marry Richard?"

"Love?" I said.

"Well, of course love, but there are a thousand different reasons we do anything we do. Some of them we know, some we don't, and some we deny. And the most important question isn't what this all means to you. You're the one in the catbird seat, honey. Don't forget that. You have Mark, the girls at Windsor, who all my friends say adore you. Your brother, your parents. I know that doesn't always feel like a blessing, but it is, take my word for it. You're healthy." Automatically she pressed her hand to her sternum. "The question is, what does this all mean to this girl who took the test and then wrote to you? Because we're assuming she's young, correct? Her message sounds very young. Even if your brother got someone pregnant when he was a teenager, she'd be relatively young."

"Garrison swears it can't have anything to do with him."

Sarah sighed. A bit of a pickle, she'd said, and that was my mantra as I drove up the thruway. Either my father had a child he didn't acknowledge or know about, my mother had one she doesn't want to admit to, my brother had a one-night stand with a woman when he was blitzed, or a lab tech at Roots & Branches dribbled chicken soup into one sample that somehow led to another. A bit of a pickle.

I don't know why, but I felt everything in my body so powerfully these days. A bump in the road reverberated from my pelvis to the base of my throat. The Elgar on the classical station thrummed in my chest, and the trees along the verge of the road were a green that made me squint. Maybe this was an uncommon side effect of all the damage I was doing to myself, because although no one liked to talk about it, it must be that all these different medical procedures were changing things inside me, not to mention the adrenaline flooding my body as I thought of meeting Talia Burton, whoever she was.

Half superannuated, half hypnotized, I was so distracted on the highway that I almost rear-ended the car stopped in front of me. A tractor-trailer full of PVC pipe had overturned, so it looked like a pile of bleached dinosaur bones had come to rest along the median. The three-lane highway was down to just one. A honeybee strafed my windshield, and despite myself I recoiled.

Written on my body for all time was that sleepover at Sadie Safer's and the moment we all ran down the big hill behind her house to the pond. I tripped and fell and rolled, laughing, rolled right into the hole in the ground where the yellow jackets had made their home. They were inside my T-shirt and my shorts in an instant, the pain like a burning electric current all through my body, my screams bringing the others to a sudden stop, all three screaming too, that way girls do, a chorus, as I pulled off my shirt and then my shorts and ran into the pond. A few hornets were still clinging to my shoulders as I came out of the water, and Sadie smacked them off with my shirt as her younger sister ran for their mother. It was one of those moments in my past that I can summon in technicolor, on video, in my mind, Sadie saying in the car on the way to the ER, me wrapped in a big bright beach towel, "It could have been worse. There could have been boys around with you in your underwear." And Mrs. Safer saying, when the nurse at admissions asked, "Oh no, I'm not her mother, I couldn't get ahold of her on the phone."

As the traffic started to move again, funneled into the right lane and the shoulder, it crossed my mind that I might be rolling into a metaphoric nest of stingers, but before I could decide to avoid it, evade it, I saw the signs and took the turnoff. Mount Bennett, the town was called. Talia Burton wanted to meet me at a place called Pie Is Infinite. I parked around the corner, edged out of all the spaces on the main drag by the farmers' market, thinking that at the very least I could pick up some produce, some bread, and some goat cheese for dinner. And some pie. I could smell the pie four buildings away.

Pie Is Infinite had an exposed brick wall, an enormous abstract painting on it, bistro tables, and a glass case full of pies. Someone had stenciled the words "Pie, pie, me oh my" on the beams below the tin ceiling. It was so quaint, quaint on steroids, as Jamie might say. In the back corner was a girl in a Fair Isle sweater who looked up as the bell over the door chimed, and for just a moment we stared across the room at each other looking for something, anything, and then the teenager behind the register said, "Welcome to Pie Is Infinite! The pie of the day is double-crust peach!"

"Thanks," I said, and I threaded my way to the back of the place.

What a pickle we are both in, I thought as I approached Talia Burton. It was a damp and unseasonably cool summer day, and the sweater she wore was overlarge, her hands fisted and barely breaching the sleeves. She was the kind of girl people say got noticed by a modeling agent on the street or in a school play, not exactly beautiful but with something about her face that made it hard to look away. She was also very young and obviously Black, her perfect skin a deep dark glossy brown with undertones of copper. I could see in her eyes that my appearance had collided sharply with her own imagination, that she was expecting someone who looked quite different, who looked more like her, and that maybe she hoped I was a stranger headed to the table next to her, until I stopped and said, "I'm Polly Goodman."

"Wow," she said, looking up at me, the disappointment in her voice impossible to mask, the sense that some hope she had had been undeniably and completely dashed. "Wow."

"So," I said, my elbows on my knees in Helen's living room. And I finally told them everything: the DNA test results, the email from Talia, the meeting with her.

There was a lot to cover for Jamie and Helen, while Sarah pretended she hadn't already heard it all—up to my trip to Vermont, which I hadn't had a chance to tell her about yet. I was able to give them all the outline but couldn't really manage the feelings. "Don't focus on plot," I sometimes told my students, but plot was what I was delivering as the three of them leaned forward, listening. I guess that's what makes real friends, right? Listening.

"Do you want ears or mouth?" Sarah asked sometimes. The first time she'd said that, Jamie had said, "That's good. I'm using that. That's really good." Ears or mouth. Listening or advice.

Of course at some point in my story Jamie couldn't keep still. "Please tell me that isn't actually the name of a pie place," she said.

"Jamie!" Helen hissed.

"I will shut up as soon as I get an answer to one question," Jamie said. "What about the genetic stuff? Anything you have to worry about? Anything we have to worry about?"

"Nothing," I said.

"And you're definitely not Jewish?" said Jamie, who definitely was.

"Sorry, no sign of it. You remember how I told you once about my friend who adopted a dog and did a DNA test and found out the dog was about eight different varieties? Corgi, basset hound, dachshund, whatever? I'm apparently kind of like that. Irish, English, German, Polish. Not Jewish. Sorry."

"Continue," Jamie said with a wave of her wineglass.

"But if it is indeed a shit test, that could mean nothing," Helen said evenly. "About there not being anything to worry about."

"Okay, that was not helpful to my mental health," Jamie said. "Continue, Pol."

"I'm also not Black," I said.

"Which honestly comes as no surprise to us," said Jamie.

"But came as a complete and really unwelcome surprise to Talia Burton," I said. "Who is. Or is at least biracial. Her father is white, her mother Black."

Talia reminded me of my students, which was not completely true. My students have a veneer, although maybe that just makes it more heartbreaking, and much more glaring, when they crack. Talia seemed stripped to the skin, the dark skin that so clearly did not match mine, no matter how you thought about the variety in human beings.

"I thought you might be related to my mom," Talia had finally said. "I thought you might be her sister." The weight of disappointment, disenchantment, lay on the table surface between us, between my hands and hers. Her nails were bitten down farther than I thought it was possible to go, and her cuticles had been savaged, a bloody mess. There were silver rings, a bird, a sun, a half-moon, on almost every finger, and that somehow made it worse, the ornamented wounds. She made patterns with her fork in the crust of her peach pie, but she didn't lift the fork to her mouth. My pie sat there untouched, too.

"Tell me all about yourself," I'd said. It's my opening line with new students, too. That "all" makes it sound as though you're truly interested.

Her mother was originally from Ghana, she said, the utter impossibility of our connection landing with another thud between us, and her father from upstate New York. Her father was a civil engineer and surveyor with his own business. Her mother was an artist. "But mainly a mom," she said, as though the art were a hobby or a past life.

"And you?" I said. There was something about her soft knuckles that told me why she was being so cagey about herself. "How old are you, Talia?" I asked, and she hesitated, then muttered, "Twenty."

I remember once listening to the girls talk in the stairwell at school when I was on the landing above them. The stairwell was a good place to overhear what was happening beneath the veneer, to hear the sobs beneath the smiles. The girls were talking about fake IDs to get into clubs, where to buy them, where to keep them so your parents wouldn't find them. "You have to memorize everything," one of them said. "Don't be stupid and think you can just hand it to one of those guys at the door, because if he asks, like, what's your date of birth or how old are you and you hesitate, you are so not getting in. Like, know the answer."

"Also your star sign," another added. "There's that one guy at Buzz who always asks about your star sign. So many girls get busted that way."

"No," I said to Talia. "You're not twenty."

"Eighteen?" she said, and I started to laugh.

"Sophomore?"

"Almost a junior," she said, putting her fork down.

"Which means sixteen. Isn't there a box on the Roots & Branches app that you have to check that says you're twenty-one or older?"

"Is that true?" Jamie asked in Helen's living room. "See, maybe that was the problem."

"Oh goodness gracious," Sarah said. "Really, Jamie, that's completely looney tunes!"

"I said we should have gotten the more expensive kit," Helen said.

"The whole thing was a joke," Jamie said, "because she's turned into such a hypochondriac."

"I'm not a hypochondriac," I said. I looked at Sarah. "I don't know why I've pursued this, but I know why she did. It was all about her mother."

Talia Burton, by her own description: likes school, gets mostly

A's, feels hemmed in by the small town, although, maybe in answer to my lifted brows, she is not the only student of color in her class. Loves to draw, made the costumes for the school musical last year, which was *Into the Woods*. She also played Cinderella although she wanted to be the witch.

"Your parents must be so proud," I'd said, and her full lower lip started to quiver like some small animal before it runs for the shelter of the tall grass.

"Her mother died," I told the book club. "In January. She said her mother had been sick for a long time and she died right after the holidays. That's why she did this. She knows no one in her mother's family, knows nothing about them, and she was hoping I was one of them so she'd have some kind of connection to her mother going forward. My God, she was so disappointed. I was so disappointed for her."

What does that feel like, I'd thought as I drove south, leaving Mount Bennett, crying without being exactly sure why. Was I crying because that poor girl had lost her mother, then lost what she thought might be her last link to her? Because that poor girl was not my niece? Because my wonderful husband could make any mammal have babies except for me?

My mother and I have always had what my former therapist called "a predictably challenging dynamic," but I felt moored by my family, and by Mark's family, too, his warm and thoughtful mother, his practical-joker father, his brothers, his cousins. Talia said she knew everything about her family on her father's side, had photographs and anecdotes, spent a lot of time with her grandmother, who lived about an hour away over the New York border, sometimes saw her grandfather, who was an occasional visitor from New Hampshire. "They're both kind of hippie dippy," she'd said. "Not like my father. He's completely straight-arrow. I really like my father's mother a lot. Grannie B, that's what I call her. I spend the weekend with her sometimes. My grandmother says my father is like the kid in some TV show that used to be on a long time ago, where the kid is really straight because his parents aren't."

I told her about myself, too, maybe so it wouldn't feel quite so much like I was nobody, nothing, not the answer to her prayers. I told her about teaching in a school for girls, about Mark's work, even about the book club and how they had given me the test kit and how surprised I had been by the results.

"Do you have kids?" she asked, and I said, "Not yet," because there had to be some sunshine of hope in this dark morning.

"Do you want to take that with you?" the waitress asked when she brought the check, looking at my untouched pie. I nodded. Mark loves pie, any kind of pie. On his birthday he always wants pie instead of cake. Last year I made him lemon meringue, the year before, cherry. "I wish you had told me this all those years when I was baking cakes," his mother had said. "Ah, I didn't want to disappoint you," Mark had said. "I like cake. Cake is good."

"But you prefer pie," his mother had said, taking her son's face between her hands.

"I really love pie," Mark had said softly, putting his forehead against hers.

At the door of Pie Is Infinite I had hugged Talia. "Can I drop you at home?" I said.

"I have someone," she said, unknotting her messy bun of tousled ringlets, reknotting it again, just the way my girls at school do, and nodding toward the curb, where a boy in a baseball cap was tapping his fingers on the wheel of an old Honda. I wondered who he thought I was. I wondered who he was. Too quickly I'd become proprietary for, it seemed, no reason at all, except that I had taken a liking to Talia Burton, and for a short time she and I had thought we each were someone else to the other.

"It was really good talking to you," I said.

"I'm sorry you came all the way up here for nothing."

"Hey, it wasn't for nothing. I was as curious as you."

"I'm writing to that damn company," Jamie said when I finished telling them what had happened. "How can they make mistakes like that?"

"Maybe it's not a mistake," said Helen. "Maybe, at some time in the past, your genetic paths somehow crossed."

"I thought of that," I said. "I even said it to her to make her feel a little better. But if it was a mistake then the results wouldn't have shown such a direct connection."

"What about her father?" Sarah said.

"She never thought that might be a factor," I said. "It was all about her mother."

"That poor girl," Sarah said, hand on her chest. "That poor, poor girl."

"I know," I said, because I had thought of that all the way home, what Sarah had said to me when we were walking in the park: that when I thought about stirring up a nest of hornets, I didn't think enough about the fact that I wasn't the person who would get stung.

"You have to meet my family," Mark had said only two months after we'd met.

"It's a little early, isn't it?" I'd said.

"I don't think so. I told my mother all about you, and she really wants to meet you. She's a teacher, too. She's really excited. Next time everybody's at the house we'll go. Okay? Will you?"

I did. I do. The house is on Long Island Sound in Connecticut. It looks a little spooky, brown siding, turrets at either end, lots of evergreen trees that make some of the bedrooms dark. You can imagine a movie location scout eyeing it as a haunted house. The power goes out a lot during storms; there are Coleman lanterns at the ends of the halls. "We should get a generator," Mark's father says every time there's the drumroll of thunder, but they never do. There's a shed full of old kayaks and life vests that mice nest in during the winters, and a rotting wooden sign at the end of the driveway: "The Baileys."

No one we know would be able to afford that house today, but Mark's parents bought it forty years ago, when they already had the first two boys but didn't yet have the second pair, before there were four: Thomas, Douglas, Mark, Michael. "I was starting to run out of names," their mother had said at dinner that first time I visited. On weekends somebody is always spending the night, siblings, sons, daughters-in-law, grandchildren, friends, friends of friends. There are seven bedrooms and four inflatable mattresses and a tent in the yard that the kids like to talk about sleeping in until they start to hear the *snap crackle pop* of wildlife at night and they slip into the kitchen and up the back stairs, the little ones sometimes sobbing loudly because the older ones have told them there are bears. There are bears, but the scare bears are made up.

If Mark's mother or father did the Roots & Branches test, the list of people they're related to would go on for pages. Or maybe not. The only ones who appear on your list are other people who've used the test, and maybe everyone in this family would think that a test like that was a waste of time, already know whom they are related to, and how: "So my mother and Lou are second cousins because their mothers were first cousins because . . ." I won't ever make the mistake again of asking how some distant relative is related. "Well, I have to go back a ways to answer that one, Polly," Mark's father once started a sentence in reply to my question, and everyone but me left the porch. Even his wife. Keeping it all straight is a little like higher math, or diagramming complex sentences.

My sister-in-law Emily and I were sitting on Adirondack chairs to one side of the lawn at the tail end of Fourth of July weekend, between her two little girls wading in the shallows and the four Bailey brothers playing badminton on the dry and weedy grass. "Damn it, Mark, are you blind?" yelled Thomas, Emily's husband, Mark's eldest brother.

"It's a game, Tommy, not Wimbledon," Mark said.

"I was so relieved when Mark married you," Emily said. "For years I was the only one who didn't want to play frisbee or flag football or whatever the hell they were doing."

"Right back at you," I said. "I would have felt all kinds of pressure to do it if it wasn't for you. Although Lou never plays either." Lou was our mother-in-law, short for Louisa. "She teaches first grade," Mark told me when we got together, and I knew right away what she would be like. Patient, good-humored, eye contact a little bit more intense than any adult is used to. It had all come true. "So you're the famous Polly," she'd said, hugging me, and I fell for her even though it all felt like a lot.

"It felt like a lot when I first came here," I said to Emily.

"Ya think? How about the Scrabble games? Or the Monopoly games that last all weekend and end with people not speaking to each other?"

"And the way they all tell each other everything." Which isn't exactly true. The husbands tell the wives. The wives tell one another. One of them tells Lou, who tells Skipper, her husband. Skipper asks his sons what's going on. "Nobody ever tells me anything," Skipper likes to say.

"How's your pursuit of parenthood going?" Emily asked, although this is not courtesy of the family whisper-down-the-lane but of a conversation I had had with Emily about doctors she could recommend. Although I know the whisper-down-the-lane is in on it, too, by a certain sympathetic look in Lou's eye. Before I could answer Emily she put up a hand, shifted the timbre of her voice into a harsher gear, and said, "Hold on—Rebecca? Do not go any farther. Your sister is going to follow you, she'll get in too deep, and I'll have to come in there in my clothes, and I don't want to do that today. Do you hear me? Rebecca! Don't ignore me."

Emily sighed. "I'm a great advertisement for motherhood. I mean, no one warns you how 24/7 it is. Every minute of every day. Maybe that was my mother's problem, that she never got a break from us. It turns out that she's a great grandmother, which I didn't see coming."

"As good as Lou?"

"Different. Less cinnamon toast, more museums and theater."

"I love cinnamon toast."

"Everybody loves cinnamon toast. And don't get me wrong, I love these kids. There's just a succubus aspect to the whole thing, like they colonize your entire existence and there's no you left."

"You work," I said. Emily is a psychologist. It's one of the reasons I talk to her. I'd seen a therapist on and off for the last ten years, but I'd finally gotten as exhausted with interrogating my psyche as I was interrogating my ovaries. With what seemed like similar results, or lack of same. Now I just talk to Jeannine, the therapist at the fertility clinic, sometimes about things that have nothing to do with fertility. She doesn't seem to mind.

It had turned out that Jeannine was the antidote to most of the rest of it: the medicalization of our sex life, my insides, our future as parents, if any. When it first crosses your mind that the thing that sixteen-year-old girls are so terribly good at, having sex and missing their periods and throwing up and saying, Oh God, no, you think you're just being impatient. It's only been three months, right? Or six. Or close to a year. And once again your midsection knots and that telltale blot of blood appears and you look at the charts and you realize that the sixteen-year-old you once were, so afraid of this, has become the forty-year-old who wants it and can't make it happen. But even once you sit opposite the doctor, holding your husband's hand, his fingers making a kind of cradle with yours, and listen to the plan, you figure, Oh boy, six months of this nonsense. And a year goes by, and another. I'm embarrassed to admit that every time, at the unmistakable sight of failure, I stare and search, look and look, because there has to be a baby in me somewhere. There has to be. No one can imagine something so clearly that doesn't exist. But there was always nothing, and I always felt hollow after, as though hope was leaving me month by month.

"Does this whole process make some people crazy?" I'd said to Jeannine once.

"Lots," she'd said. "Most, actually."

Together Emily and I looked out at the water of the sound. Finally, she sighed. "Yes, I do indeed work. And while I'm seeing patients part of my lizard brain is perseverating about those two and whether Rebecca is bullying Sophia and Sophia isn't getting enough attention and the big winner is the baby, whose mother doesn't have enough bandwidth to obsess about him, which is probably for the best."

"Where is he?"

"Upstairs sleeping in that old crib, which is probably a death trap by today's standards. Do I look worried?"

"You're a great mother."

"And you? How are you holding up?"

"Do you think the body knows? Do you think there are people who aren't meant to have children and that's why they have problems?"

"Hmm," Emily said, sipping at her Tom Collins. "That's an interesting theory."

"Is anyone but me paying attention to this game?" Thomas yelled, and Douglas, brother number two, started to laugh, which only enraged Thomas. "Are we going to play, or are we going to play?" he shouted.

Emily turned to me. "That's an interesting theory, Polly, but it's total horseshit," she said. "First of all, it assumes that somehow the universe has decided the chemistry of both you and Mark should be skewed against procreation, which is ridiculous. Second, it ignores all those women I know who got pregnant like that"—finger snap—"and are nightmare mothers. Believe me, the world is full of nightmare mothers. They're why I have a job, so I can listen to patients talking about their nightmare mothers. It's the biggest part of my work."

"My mother isn't a nightmare mother exactly. But I wouldn't want to be a mother the way she was. It always felt like she had other priorities. Law school, then practicing, then the judgeship. It always felt like we weren't enough."

"What if you weren't?"

"Doesn't every child want to feel as though they're the most important thing in their mother's life?"

"But not the only thing," Emily said. "Some of the most common problems I see in my practice are the illusions so many people have about family. The Hallmark card version, the fantasy of unconditional love, everybody sitting around the Thanksgiving table, overwhelms the reality. Some families are filled with people who, sitting on a bus together, wouldn't exchange a word. But I constantly see people who feel damaged because they aren't best buddies with their sister or don't have much in common with their parents. This"—her hand swept the lawn, the house, the badminton game—"is an aberration. Hold on—Rebecca, don't do that again, or I'll send you inside." Emily leaned back. The old Adirondack chair groaned. "Sometimes this kind of family happens, but most of the time it doesn't. I can't tell you why. I can tell you that when it does happen, it's seen and felt by the people in it as though it's no big thing. And when it doesn't, it takes on this huge significance. It's like with love, at least for women. Either you hook up with someone in college, and there you are, or suddenly you're thirty and looking for your soulmate, which is an expression I hate. And if somehow all of that doesn't go according to plan, it's this monumental tragedy."

"Well, you beat all that."

Emily raised her glass and smiled. "Oh, honey," she said. "I spent the best years of my young life with a guy that I thought was the sun and the moon. Until he wasn't. He was more like Pluto. Isn't Pluto the one that was a planet, and then they downgraded it? What is it now, a rock?"

"But then after Pluto you met Thomas?"

"Correct. I met Thomas."

Rebecca dragged Sophia toward us by the hand while her sister tried to pull away. "Ow, ow, ow," she moaned.

"Mama, she says she feels like she's going to puke," Rebecca said as Thomas called, "Em, my mother says David's awake upstairs."

"Apparently your father's arms are broken," Emily muttered.

"They are?" said Rebecca.

"I can go upstairs and get David if you want," I said. "Sophia, honey, are you okay?"

"She's fine," Emily said. "Rebecca learned the word puke, and now she just wants to say it all the time."

"Aunt Polly, can I sit in your lap?" Sophia whispered in my ear.

"Of course, sweetie," I said. She was wetter than she looked from wading in the sound, and grubbier from the sand. She pushed my hair behind my ear and, leaning close, whispered, "When Mama was having a baby she wouldn't let me sit because she said she didn't have a lap. And the baby was David. He can't walk yet. And he poops a lot."

Emily stood, stretched, and dumped the ice cubes from her drink on the ground. "You two come with me to get your brother," she said.

"I want to stay with Aunt Polly because she has a lap," Sophia said. "A big lap."

"I'm getting a granola bar from Grannie," Rebecca said. "I don't want to go get David."

Emily turned to me as she reached for Rebecca's hand. "See how wonderful it all is?" she said. "So wonderful."

IT WAS MY NIGHT TO HOST THE BOOK CLUB, AND I'D GIVEN MARK a heads-up. "I saw it on the calendar," he said. "I'm having dinner with Douglas downtown."

"I don't like to drive you out of your own house," I said.

"You are the sunshine of my life," he sang, putting his arms around me. Mark is prone to bursting into song. His mother once told me that the kindergarten teacher asked her if there was a way for him to do it more quietly.

"That makes me feel so special," I said, "especially since I saw some video online of you singing it to the zebra."

"I told them I wanted that cut out, but the publicity people loved it. Apparently a lot of people did, too. You gotta bring in the bodies."

"How can people ignore you? You have penguins!"

"It takes all kinds. They did some kind of survey, and it's amazing how many people like the reptile house. They didn't even include the elephants because of the court case to free them."

"I remember." I remembered my mother saying, at Thanksgiving at Edgemere, "I would have welcomed the opportunity to rule on that." Incarcerated elephants were not, she said, a civil rights issue. "An elephant never forgets," my father had said. It had come as a surprise to all of us, his saying that. "Irony much?" Garrison had said when we were walking out together.

I took Mark's keys and wallet from the tray by the door and handed him both. "Anything you want me to tell Douglas?" he asked. "Or not tell Douglas?"

"Nothing, but really, if you get done early, come home. There are chocolate chip cookies for dessert."

"Save me some, but I'll pass on dropping in. I love Sarah, I like

Helen, and Jamie scares the hell out of me. Plus the last time I walked in, purely by accident because it was after nine and I thought they'd be gone, everyone went quiet so fast I could hear people talking on the street outside."

"Yeah, that night," I said. "It wasn't your average night." Memorably menopause. Sarah had been thrown into it because of the chemo; Helen had started but said she felt fine except that, not only were the waistbands of her pants tight, but occasionally she had to take her jacket off during a meeting; Jamie insisted she couldn't wait so she could buy pricey underpants without wrecking them each month, and I was terrified of it. My doctor had said that she was certain, between my own hormones and the ones I'd gotten loaded into a syringe during all those years of fertility treatments, that I had a long way to go, and that if we needed to pull me back from the brink there were protocols. My whole life now felt like a set of protocols.

"What age was your mother when she went through menopause?" my doctor had asked.

"I'll ask," I said. I didn't.

"It was terrible," Sarah had said that night before Mark walked in and shut everyone down by unwittingly trailing testosterone. "I couldn't sleep, I was sweating through my nightgown, I keep having breakouts. And I haven't had acne since I was fourteen."

"I don't believe you ever had acne," I said.

"I'll be so happy to ditch the IUD," Jamie said.

"I have a friend who thought she was going through the change at forty-seven, and now she has a toddler," Sarah said.

"Okay, two things," Jamie had said. "Who still calls it the change, and why would you tell me that, now that I'm finally getting out from under?" Jamie's twin daughters were entering middle school at Windsor. I anticipated teaching them in the upper school, which, Jamie had told me, would be the worst year of my life. But we all knew, all the teachers, that most of the students that we'd heard were, to quote Jamie, "heinous little bitches," were fine at school. They saved that stuff for home, for their mothers. When we discussed that, I'd wondered how far I had really come since seventh grade. "Why do you let her take up so much room in your head?" Garrison had said to me one night when we were talking about our mother. "How can you not?" I'd said.

On the way back from my meeting with Talia in Mount Bennett, I had driven on automatic pilot to go see my father. It was Saturday and the parking lot at Edgemere was crowded. Sunday, I knew, would be worse. Maybe some people thought of it like going to church, get up, have breakfast, visit the aged. Sacramental.

My father was on the veranda again with Claire, but this time my mother was on his other side, holding his other hand. It was as though he were flanked by the princesses from a fairy tale I'd loved as a kid, "Snow White and Rose Red": Claire's transparent skin with its lilac undertones around eyes and throat, her white, almost colorless hair cut short, her pale-pink sweatsuit, and, by contrast, my mother, dark chestnut hair curved on her shoulders, tanned skin from tennis, flowered shirt and red capri pants.

"Hi, Daddy," I said. "It's Polly. I brought you peach pie." Mark would totally understand if I gave his pie away to my father.

My father tilted his head back like a baby bird, some species with a crest of silver and a sharp beak, and opened his mouth wide. Claire giggled. My father winked.

"I'll get a fork," my mother said. I broke off a piece of crust and hand-fed it, then another. My father smiled. "That's good," he said. "That's good pie." Two full sentences. Excellent. My father used to recite "The Wreck of the Hesperus" and "The Charge of the Light Brigade" from memory, and now I was delighted if there were two words in a row from his mouth. Although Garrison likes to remind me that it was always our mother who talked from one end of the dinner table while he nodded from the other. But for me, my father's few words were love. And so I still cling to them.

"Keep the pieces small, Polly," my mother said as she returned and handed me the fork. "He chokes sometimes."

"He doesn't," said Claire. Another more or less full sentence. I wondered if my mother brought out the words in the two of them, a kind of rebellion.

My mother seemed to accept Claire as part of the scenery at Edgemere Place. Early on the staff would distract Claire elsewhere when my mother arrived, but I think they had finally decided it was unnecessary. Mark had said at dinner one night, Garrison joining us for pizza and a movie, that the fact that our father had a companion might make our mother feel less guilty. Then Garrison and I began cackling. "I think both of you should stop stereotyping your mother," Mark said.

"He's such a nice person," Garrison had said, putting an arm around my husband. "Is he always this nice?"

"Pretty much," I said. It was true. Mark would have insisted I give his pie to my father.

"Good," my father said, chewing the pie slowly, licking his lips so that there seemed something a little lascivious about it.

Claire opened her mouth wide and I fed her some pie, too. I alternated between them until the pie was gone while my mother looked on. "Sorry, did you want some?" I asked.

"It's a bit late now," she said. And then, "No. I'm having an early dinner with some friends."

My mother guards her private life from me, which makes me think she has a boyfriend. "Or a girlfriend," Garrison had said. Her professional life I can sometimes follow on news sites. I got an alert once when I was actually in the waiting room of the fertility center to let me know she'd sentenced some assemblyman to six to eight years, and that in response the assemblyman's wife had hurled herself at the bench, screaming, threatening to kill her. The news report said a pejorative was used, which made me think the woman had probably called my mother a bitch. There was an accompanying photograph of my mother, looking grave and imperturbable, with a court officer on either side of her. It appeared from that picture that she'd recently had her color done, with slightly lighter streaks, but she'd gone back to the darker brown last year.

"Do we have any family in Vermont?" I asked.

"Family?" said my mother, as though it were the first time she'd ever heard the word.

"Cousins?" I asked, thinking of Talia's father.

"Cousins? I don't think so. There was someone in your preschool class whose family moved to Vermont, I think. Or maybe it was New Hampshire."

"What about Uncle Brian's kids?"

"Bri? One boy. Well, man now, actually. Last I heard he lived in Canada, was some kind of forest ranger."

"That's good," my father said.

"What?" my mother said.

"That's good pie."

"I'm afraid you finished it, Jack," said my mother, kissing his cheek.

"I'm leaving, Daddy," I said, patting his knee. "I'll bring pie again next time. That was good, right?"

"That was good," said Claire. "That was good pie."

"Love to Mark," my mother said, pulling out her phone and checking her messages. "Oh goodness, I need to step outside for a minute. Can you wait until I get back?" From the veranda I could see her down on the lawn, putting in her ear buds, looking down at the phone, tapping one foot. When she looked up and saw me watching she turned away. Maybe she thinks I can read lips.

"There's Mary," said my father. "There's Mary."

"She needed to make a call, Daddy. Work, probably."

"Mary comes every single day," he said. "I love her."

MARK AND I FIRST CAME TO THIS SUITE OF MEDICAL OFFICES almost four years ago, first to have a baby, which seemed simple, then to have interventions, which seemed complicated, and then to get pregnant, which has come to seem impossible. I have a physical reaction, not unlike the way I feel when we hit turbulence on a plane, when I see that plaque, copper with weathered greenish letters, Caroline Betz, MD. It's to one side of the lobby doors in one of those lovely solid prewar buildings right off Central Park, a few blocks south of Sarah's building, the entrance guarded by a doorman in a gray suit with a kind of military look, a mosaic tile floor faintly visible within. In Dr. Betz's office there are pinkish chairs, gray carpet, and wall art that is all watercolors. When we started this, when it seemed a matter of months in our minds, we visited one clinic that had black-and-white photographs of babies in the waiting area. Can you imagine doing that: Look, look, here are pictures of what you can't have! It felt to me like a Weight Watchers facility with hot fudge sundae pictures on the wall, or an AA basement with photographs of Jim Beam and Jack Daniel's.

Mark pretends that walking into this office is like going to the dentist for a cleaning or visiting the massage therapist who works on his lower back, because apparently your lower back always gets tweaked when you work with large animals. But I know that there's a sadness in him behind those bright eyes and his ready smile. It's hidden but it's down there, deep, like that spot in the waters of the Long Island Sound right off his parents' house where sometimes, if you dive down far enough, you find an unexpected pocket of water that's much, much colder than the rest. Once, when I was in some mood abyss because of hormone injections, when I despaired of nothing ever working, I tried to tell him he should find somebody else to marry, someone who could give him a clutch of kids. "We are not having that conversation," he said fiercely. Once, he tried to tell me that he would love a child we adopted every bit as much. "We are not having that conversation," I said. "Not yet."

Of course what I knew now was that putting off adoption often had the same result as putting off conception. No result at all. Biology favors the young, and so do most adoption agencies.

Whether Mark wants to admit it or not, Dr. Betz's fertility practice is that cold spot in the sound, but there's one warm place in it for me, and that's a very small office that sits to one side of the hallway leading to the examining rooms. Jeannine sees me in that small office. I always wonder whether it's painted pink because Jeannine wanted it that way. "It's like a little womb," I said the first time I met her, during intake, when a meeting with the clinic therapist was a requirement.

"Hey, Polly," said the receptionist. "She's waiting for you."

I don't need to see Dr. Betz today, or any of the other four female doctors who work with her. My hormone levels are more or less whatever they are normally without the injections, and, since we've already tried and failed with the eggs we'd managed to harvest and fertilize, no embryos await me. In terms of technical matters we are teetering on the edge of a new phase, the phase that feels to me as though I would somehow get sidelined. Donor eggs from someone younger, more obviously fertile. Surrogacy, with someone else carrying what everyone will assure me is my child. Another woman's egg, another woman's body, my husband still in the mix but me, in my mind, as a bystander. I wonder if I'm jealous, which seems both absurd and understandable. I've been given yet another pamphlet about all this, and about all the people who happily do it, holding what one describes as a miracle baby. I wonder if I'm just too conventional, or narrow-minded, or unimaginative. But I'm not ready for that phase yet.

So I'm just here to talk to Jeannine. I'm not sure about what, but talking to Jeannine has been my favorite part of this process, except for the part when they showed me that tiny fluttering heart on the sonogram. Jeannine had lasted much longer.

"I really liked that woman," Mark had said after that first meeting. "I don't really know exactly what she does, but whatever it is I can tell she's good at it."

I'd liked Jeannine from the beginning, and Dr. Betz, too. Dr. Betz twirls her hair around her index finger when she talks, when she's behind the desk wearing one of her oatmeal-colored sweaters and not gowned up, hard at work, her eyes enormous and inhuman behind the magnifying goggles, like fish eyes. She was so different from most of the others, at Great Expectations and Parents Inc. and The Stork. The Stork was the hardest sell, a video of three couples—one same sex, of course—that ended with four babies. One set of twins.

"It feels like you're saying that you can guarantee my wife and I will have a baby," Mark had said in a voice I'd rarely heard, the voice he mainly saves for the super when the super says he can't get to our apartment until the day after tomorrow even though our toilet has overflowed all over the old tile floor.

"I can guarantee you that you two will have a better chance here than any place else," that doctor had said, turning a paperweight of baby feet over and over in his big hands and rattling off statistics.

"I just wonder why that video we watched didn't discuss those couples who have a tougher time," Mark continued, same voice, more so.

"We like people to start out from a place of positivity," the doctor said. "I'm sure you both are familiar with the mind-body connection." He looked down at the questionnaire we'd had to fill out before he'd even agreed to meet with us. "A vet at the Bronx Zoo," he said. "I bet you have to deal with some of these issues."

"We have our challenges," Mark said.

"The rhinos, right? It's gotta be those rhinos."

That was that. "That guy was like a car salesman," Mark said before we were barely out the door.

It'd been different here from the beginning. Dr. Betz didn't try to sell us on anything. When Mark asked about the future, she made no promises: Maybe this would work, maybe that would work. We would have to wait and see. She introduced us to Jeannine. "She's in charge of feelings," she said. Jeannine had sighed as she led us into her pink office and sat in a chair while we took the couch. "I wish she'd stop saying that," she'd said. "But since she did: How are you feeling?" Jeannine was the reason I'd stopped seeing my old therapist, because Jeannine was so much better at the work. I'd talked to her about so many things, about my father, my mother, my marriage, my students. So many things that had nothing to do with why I was here in this office in the first place, and why I continued to come even when my stomach clenched at the sight of the door: because I wanted to have a baby. I wanted to have Mark's baby. More than one, actually. But we had discussed that less and less, Jeannine and I, although I was pretty sure it was the basis of my feeling of connection. She knew me inside and out.

"Is there any genetic reason why people don't conceive?" I asked now. "Are there genetic tests associated with infertility that people can take?"

I'm sure Jeannine noticed that self-protective "people." What I mean is, is there a genetic reason why I can't do this, this one simple thing, this one thing that I want more than anything I've ever wanted in my life. At least, I think that's right, that wanting, although somehow it's turned into something else. After a while the process takes over, becomes estranged from what I suppose you'd call the product. But it's like reading a book you don't really like; you've come this far, and maybe it will get better if you keep going, if you read on. I have to believe in the process because I've been living it for years now.

Blood tests, injections, sonograms that look like some weird art you'd see at a storefront pop-up gallery downtown: Penelope Goodman's Ovaries with Follicles. Every year it's gotten more distant, the idea that all of it ends with an actual baby. Although maybe that happens even if you haven't spent years at this. Jamie told us once that after she got home with the twins, the pediatric visiting nurse showed up and said, "Hi, Mom!" Jamie said she'd turned to her husband and said, "Jesus Christ, I'm somebody's mother!"

When I think of somebody's mother, I think of mine. "Everybody does," Jamie said. "Everybody."

"I've never seen any data on a genetic predisposition to infertility," Jeannine said, handing me a bottle of water. "Once we get past any structural issues, it mostly comes down to age. You know that already. And I feel like that question takes us back to where we began, right? You feel as though you need a sense of control, so you try to figure out what you did that caused this not to happen. You can't accept that you didn't do anything, that this is just the way the universe is sometimes. Oh my God, did I just say that? The universe? Sorry. I went to a yoga retreat with one of my friends, and the universe played a big role."

This is another thing that I liked about Jeannine right from the beginning, that what my therapist had called the therapeutic model didn't seem to apply. She didn't hesitate to make some comment about herself, even a mocking comment. I'd often thought she would fit right into the book club. That immediate sense I had of *here was a woman you could talk to about anything* probably accounted for our first solo conversation about who was to blame for the fact that I couldn't get pregnant, now that they'd shot dye through my tubes and pronounced them open, eyeballed Mark's sperm and said it was swimming just fine.

"Is infertility ever associated with termination?" I'd asked her then.

"Are you asking if you haven't gotten pregnant because you once did and had an abortion instead of a child?"

I'd nodded, suddenly mute. Kept nodding. I'd just met her, didn't even know her last name, and I'd already told her what I guessed was my deepest darkest secret. Two days after my friend Colin told me that Benedict was unfaithful—chronically, I would later discover; Abigail was scarcely the only one—I realized that I hadn't had my period for—well, it seemed like a while. I peed on the stick, watched it bloom, did it again just in case. I took the first two pills under the gaze of a clinic aide who admired my purse, the second two in the windowless kitchen of our tiny apartment. There were two things I remember so well that I get a trace memory every time I smell blood: Benedict hammering on the door of the bathroom where I was bleeding out into the bowl while moaning with the pain, and the soft but unmistakable sound, like the first big raindrop on the surface of a pond, when something more substantial emerged and fell into the water.

"We have one lavatory, Polly," said Benedict, who refused to use the American term *bathroom*. "You cannot set up shop in it."

"Go to hell," I'd said as I pushed past him, fleeing to Garrison's apartment and curling up on his big sectional with a hot water bottle.

Wrong man, wrong time, wrong memory to come out to play just at the moment when I wanted an annunciation instead of a termination. But I can't deny that the first time I'd seen the pregnancy sonogram here at the clinic, with that little bean in its kiddie pool in my belly, I'd remembered that long-ago time as though it had just happened.

I'd never told Mark that there'd been a pregnancy before, and that I'd exorcised it, and that in some little superstition closet of my mind, where lots of people keep their religions, I believed I couldn't have now what I'd not wanted then. I'd never told the book club, either, even Sarah, although I was pretty sure some of them had stories like my own, because so many women did. Of course I'd never dignified Benedict with the news.

But I'd told Jeannine, maybe more than once. She'd told me the same thing every time, that one thing had nothing to do with the other. Statistically, scientifically, I'm sure she was right. But I can't help the compare-and-contrast. That short-circuited pregnancy happened at a time when I was drinking martinis and margaritas and wine, occasionally smoking pot, and having morning coffee from the place at the corner whose coffee was so strong that it was probably bad for your tooth enamel. Now I do everything right. I don't drink alcohol, have one cup of decaf in the morning, stay away from soft cheese and sushi, both of which I love.

At various times I have taken red clover, evening primrose, black cohosh, and something called motherwort, whose label made me feel terrible every time I looked at it. For years I have negotiated with my body: Look, look at how good I'm being. No dice, my body has replied. Last month I was watering the plants on the fire escape landing outside our kitchen window, having some weird tea the acupuncturist recommended, that tasted the way mulch smells, feeding the potted butterfly bushes and miniature roses. I looked down at one big terra-cotta urn that has nothing in it. I've planted three or four different things in it, most recently impatiens, and it's not so much that they die as that they evaporate, disappear. "This pot is like me," I said, watering it despite it all, and then I felt Mark's arms wrap around me from behind, like a second, thicker skin. He was humming, and when I listened closely I could tell it was one of his favorites, the Beatles, "All You Need Is Love." I guess that's the other thing I've gotten through this terrible, endless process, not just the conversations with Jeannine but my certainty about my husband. Not many women get to know that even under the hardest of conditions, they can count on the guy they married. He can't remember where he's left his jacket a lot of the time, but he always finds the right thing to feel, to say and do.

"What else is going on?" Jeannine said. And if it had been anyone else asking casually, I would have talked about preparing for the new school year, the seminar I was creating on women poets, the trip to Mark's parents' place, the four-week session I was running for new teachers of English looking for guidance on curriculum. But because it was Jeannine, I told her what was really going on, about the Roots & Branches test, and my trip to Vermont, and Talia Burton and her mother.

"I have really mixed feelings about those tests," she said, shaking her head. "The police are using them to solve old crimes because some great aunt did a saliva swab and it matches the DNA from a cold case. And you read about all these people discovering they were adopted, or their fathers had a second family."

"I've seen documentary proof I wasn't adopted, and there's no way my father could have had a second family. He didn't travel or go away on long weekends," I said. In this I've actually realized over the years that we were lucky. Home for dinner, movie matinees on Saturdays. He didn't even start playing golf much until I left for college.

"I mainly feel sorry for that poor girl," I added. "Her mother died, and now she's using any means necessary to find her family. I wonder if her father knows what she's doing. Of course she asked if I had children."

Jeannine sighed and shook her head.

"I bet you can guess how many times I've been asked that question," I said. "At curriculum night this year one truly lovely woman with three daughters said to me, 'Don't leave it too long!'" I know both Jeannine and Dr. Betz have children, but there are no photographs in their offices, no fingerpaint hands with a barely legible name printed at the bottom.

I've told Jeannine that that's one of the downsides to living in the city. What Mark likes to call biodiversity means that in New York we're surrounded by all kinds of people, all ages, ethnicities, incomes, although sometimes that feels less and less true for someone who is teaching at the Windsor School. What it means for a woman like me is that there seem to be children everywhere. After I left Benedict, for at least a year or two, I would pass couples on the street and savage them in my mind. No one was happy. No one was faithful. Their smiles were fake. Their linked hands were a show. I can't do the same thing when I see babies on the street, because even funny-looking infants, the ones that look like just-fledged birds with a tuft of cottony hair and big bug eyes, look wonderful to me. The pretty ones, the ones with pink cheeks and creased thighs full of mother's milk, almost level me. I have to turn away.

"I can either let you hold him all the time," my sister-in-law Emily had said after David was born, "or I can arrange it so you hardly ever see him when you're here. Whatever works with how you're feeling at this stage of the game."

Park, subway, deli. You could argue that I put myself in psychic harm's way every day because of where I work, and I admit that even the Windsor kindergarteners, who wear pinafores, can get to me on a bad day. But inevitably it's the babies, staring up from their strollers, heads barely visible in front slings. Even the ones who are shrieking, gas pain or existential angst, stir something inside me. Even the mothers who are clearly at the end of their rope, spit up on their sweatshirts, binkies in their back pockets. "Do you see that?" an older woman once hissed at me in Riverside Park, canting her head toward a bench where someone was nursing an infant so small it barely made an armful and looked as though it might be smothered by the blue-veined breast. Then the woman saw the look on my face and stomped off to find someone else suitably appalled instead of someone enthralled, on the verge of tears.

"It's not easy for you," Jeannine had said then, and she said it again now.

"I'm going to start thinking about next steps," I said, and Jeannine nodded. The long ladder: ovulation chart to intrauterine insemination to in vitro. Then, as Jamie said before I started all this, when one of her friends was going through it, "Shit gets real." That next phase. It all moves further and further away from what you imagined when your husband said, a thrill in his voice, "Let's have some kids."

"How's Mark?" Jeannine asked. I like that about her, too, that she understands that Mark is the kind of husband who is part of the program. It was amazing to me in the beginning how often we would come here and see a roomful of women sitting alone. "He isn't interested in the mechanics," I heard one of them say to a friend who was with her, holding her hand. A female friend. I'd look over at my husband, and he'd squeeze my hand and grin, a real grin, not a pretend-to-be-sympathetic grin, not a getting-through-this grin, but a real you-and-me-babe grin. My accidental savior. What if I hadn't gone to that museum benefit at Sarah's? What if I'd blown him off because he was younger, so eager, so seemingly unprotected emotionally in a way that I found at first suspicious, then scary?

What if I had closed my eyes to the truth and stayed with Benedict?

We walked out of her pink office together, Jeannine's arm across my shoulder. There were three women in the waiting room looking down at their phones. We don't make much eye contact here. Maybe we're all afraid of what we'll see of ourselves reflected in some other woman's eyes. There were only a few times when we'd talked to one another. There'd been a woman one day last year in a flowered dress and sandals, red hair, hazel eyes, carrying a novel I'd heard about by a young Irish woman apparently written entirely in dialogue but with no quotation marks. I'd tried, and failed, not to pass judgment when I'd heard about the lack of punctuation.

"That's the book for my book club this month," I'd said.

"How did everybody like it?"

I'd laughed. "We didn't read it. We pick a book every month, and we all get it. But the rule is we don't read it. That's the rule. You can't cheat even if you want to."

The woman had laughed. "That's the best book club I've ever heard about. So you all just talk about stuff?"

"Exactly."

"How long have you been meeting?"

"Almost twelve years."

She'd laughed again. "That's a lot of unread books."

"We read the first five, and then one of the women showed up and hadn't read the sixth one and said she was never going to read the books, why didn't we just have a bitch fest instead." It had been Jamie, of course, and a woman named Rachel, who was an accountant and lived in Helen's building and had been invited by Helen to join, said, Why would anyone want to belong to a book club that didn't read the book? Helen said Rachel was in two book clubs now, one that was run by a Columbia professor in which all the books were histories or analyses of world affairs, and that she still acted condescending when Helen met her in the elevator, Rachel carrying books with titles like *The State of the Middle East: How Diplomacy Failed in the West Bank.*

"And meanwhile we're all talking about menopause," Helen said.

"And supporting writers," Sarah said. Sarah was the one who had come up with what she called our marching orders: All right, we won't read the books, but we will buy the books. We would even bring them to our meetings. Jamie, of course, hardly ever did. She was always suspicious that one of us was reading behind her back.

I turned to Jeannine. "One more question," I said, pivoting back into her office. "There's a woman I've seen here on more than a few occasions. She has red hair, very curly? I haven't seen her here for a while." I waited for Jeannine to give me a name but of course she didn't. Patient confidentiality and all that. "I was just wondering." Still nothing. "Never mind." Jeannine smiled and opened the office door again. I'd seen that woman again, twice, and both times she'd asked about the book club and what we were not reading. "It's like the unbirthday party in *Alice in Wonderland*," she'd said, which made me think again that it was possible to like someone almost instantly, the friend version of love at first sight. But that had been months ago. I wanted to know whether she'd given up, or gotten pregnant. Each idea was upsetting to me in its own way.

"I'm always glad to see you, Polly," Jeannine said with such warmth in her voice that tears filled my eyes. I left just as one of the women in the waiting room was called into the doctor's office, her face full of light and hope, a look I remembered.

There's such a just-unwrapped feeling to that first day when the girls are back at school. We teachers have been in the building for weeks beforehand, working on a syllabus, checking on books and, in the lower grades, making classrooms bright with construction-paper flowers and hearts with names written on them, so that the little girls can come in and say, Oh, oh, there I am, Chloe, Zoe, Carolina, Kristina. We all have whiteboards now, and the older girls all have tablets, and they don't have to take notes in the same way because what I write on the board appears magically on their screens. But my students still write down much of what I say in class, and sometimes they're simply writing messages to themselves. My second year teaching at Windsor I had a girl who hunched over a journal with a tooled leather binding, writing with such unwavering concentration that one day, journal left on her desk—by accident, by design?—I opened it. I hate this. I hate this. That's what she had been writing over and over again. I told the head of school, who didn't look surprised. The head told her parents. She left suddenly, but one day I ran into her on Madison Avenue. "You're such a fraud," she said, scratching hard at her forearms. How can we know what helps and what harms? I wondered about her from time to time. Someone told me her family had moved away.

They come in waves, moving down the street, an ocean of girls still excited by the possibilities of a new school year, like packages with the ribbons just untied. Fourteen of them flow into my room for homeroom, stowing their things, unrolling their uniform skirts, which reach mid-thigh when they're in the building but barely cover their rears when they're outside. I'd always had new clothes for the first day, and I wondered if Talia did, if she was looking forward to the new school year, if there was some shirt or shoes or accessory that was a must-have at her school. The it bag this fall for my girls is nylon with a geometric print and a long shoulder strap. I know one of my homeroom students this year is spending an hour on the train from the north Bronx every morning and has a mother who works cleaning office buildings, but damned if she doesn't have the bag just like most of the others. I wonder how much it costs and am glad I don't have one. Mark's mother gave me the requisite beige canvas tote with my initials in a nice bright pink, although they're not really my initials, not PIG—did it even occur to my mother, when she gave me the middle name Isabelle?—but PGB, what my initials would be if I'd changed my name after I was married, which I hadn't. But, hey, what a relief not to be walking around with a tote that had PIG on the front. When you teach in the upper school at a girls' school, there is always at least one—and maybe more than one—as mean, in Sarah's words, as a snake.

I teach a Shakespeare seminar that the smartest seniors always want, the Women in Literature senior honors course, which includes Jane Austen, and this year Women in Poetry, which I've already heard complaints about via the head because Elizabeth Bishop and Anne Sexton have been joined by Joni Mitchell: "Little Green," the lyrics written to commemorate the birth of the daughter Mitchell gave up for adoption. "Little Green, have a happy ending." Our Windsor girls don't have unwanted children and adoptions; they have IUDs and abortions overseen by their mothers' gynecologists. But it turns out the two parents who complained don't know the story behind the song. They just think because it's folk music it's unserious. Our Windsor girls aren't supposed to do unserious.

I also teach the introductory English class to the first-years. We don't call them freshmen anymore. They all complain that *Middlemarch* is too hard, are all amazed and thrilled when they discover *Little Women* at the end of the reading list. "You've read it before, but have you really read it?" I always say, which makes the best students nervous. What is the trick, the hidden meaning, to Meg, Jo, Beth, and Amy? I wonder if it's mean of me to make them think there's some impenetrable symbolism embedded in the novel that they'll have to excavate in order to get an A. Some of them read too much for the grade and too little for pleasure.

"Let's begin with *The Taming of the Shrew,*" I said once the seniors were seated. They've been charged with reading the play over the summer, and all the way from the front of the classroom I can see the notes in the margins in the paperback versions we sent out. So many notes. To try to inject some fun into their work, which can be difficult, I'll show them the old movie version of *Kiss Me Kate* next week in all its garish technicolor.

Between Shakespeare and the intro course I have a free period, a bottle of water and an apple at my desk. "You are such a healthy eater," one of the younger teachers said last year, and I didn't say, Yes, and I hate it, I want a Big Mac and Oreos and an espresso, but my body is a temple, at least until I give in and decide it's not. The longer you wait to do something, the more impossible it seems. Like skydiving: I could have maybe managed it at twenty, but certainly not at forty-two. Is that how it would be if I had a baby now?

The head's secretary knocked at my office door. "I got a call from a Brenda Livitz, who said you need to call chambers between one and one-thirty?" she said. "She was a little vague, but she said you knew the number."

"Vague," I said. "That's a nice way of putting it. You mean high-handed?"

"Not the warmest," said the head's secretary, who is obliged to be warm as a condition of employment and is by nature anyhow.

"Thanks. I've got this." I dialed my mother's office number. "This is Brenda Livitz," said the familiar voice, vaguely British by way of Bayonne.

"It's Polly," I said. "I can't call between one and one-thirty. I'm teaching at that time."

"She says it's important," Brenda said. I can hear her typing as she talks. Brenda has been with my mother for twenty-five years and is very efficient. She created spreadsheets of my class schedules when I was in college and grad school and is annoyed that I won't share my teaching schedule at Windsor.

"If it's important I can speak with her now." But I was beginning to worry.

"She's on the bench until twelve-thirty, and after lunch she has a settlement conference."

"I'm available after three," I said.

"Let me see what I can do," Brenda said.

"There's no need to call the head's office. Just leave a message on my cell."

As soon as I hung up I called Garrison. I could tell he was speaking on his cell through the dashboard of his car. It sounded as though he were in a wind tunnel, and in the background I could hear classical music. Tchaikovsky, I think.

"Calm down," Garrison said by way of greeting.

"I don't even know what I'm calming down about. Mother wanted to speak to me about something important but naturally was too busy to speak to me. What is it?" *Daddy Daddy Daddy* is running through my head like a piece of music with only two notes, like Philip Glass. I hate Philip Glass.

"Dad fell and it looks like he may have broken his hip. Apparently it was a bit of a shit show. Claire wanted to go with him in the ambulance, Dad was calling for Mom, the aide who was supposed to be helping him out of bed when he fell was crying, the administrator is terrified because our mother is who she is. I'm on the way to the hospital. It'll all be fine. Either it's nothing, or it's something they can deal with. He's not bleeding, and they don't think he's concussed, although who the hell knows what'll happen at the hospital when they're looking for a head injury and they ask Dad who the president is and he says Kennedy maybe."

I started to cry, tried to speak. "Stop crying, Pol," Garrison said. "You always overreact. He'll be fine."

"I hate this," I said. "Did she send you?"

"The Edgemere administrator called me. I'm first on the call list."

My feelings were hurt by this, but instead I said, "Our mother didn't call you?"

"Pol, I can either deal with you right now, or I can get myself ready to take care of business. I think we both would prefer the latter. I promise I will call you as soon as I know anything."

"I can leave here at three," I said.

"By then we may be on our way back to Edgemere. Hold tight and trust me. Do you trust me?"

Garrison knows exactly how to wrangle me. When I turned up at his apartment crying about Benedict, he sat me down and said, "Why bother discussing a divorce when I can just go over there right now and beat the shit out of the little pissant until his ears bleed?" It had calmed me right down, the mental picture of the bleeding ears.

"You know I trust you," I said.

"Call you soonest," Garrison said, and ended the call.

I called Brenda back. "Tell my mother I've talked to my brother and I'm already up to speed," I said, and hung up, then gathered my books and papers for the first-years. Each term I put a poster on the old corkboard with a quote from a writer. This year it's from Louisa May Alcott: "I am not afraid of storms, for I am learning how to sail my ship." At least a few of the first-years will copy it down, worried that it will make its way onto the exam. Every time I look at it, I will think to myself, Lies, lies, and damn lies. But that's just me, still afraid of storms, and of capsizing.

"Who is George Eliot?" I'll ask them right out of the gate so that I can get a snapshot: the ones who had researched the writer, the ones who hadn't, the ones who didn't know who I was talking about, even occasionally the ones, usually transfers from other schools, who thought George Eliot was male. I loved my job, and I loved Windsor, but I had to start playing intellectual chess day one.

"Animals are smarter than most people think," Mark had said one night when I talked about how much effort it took just to stay even with my students, especially during those times when the hormone shots made me both tetchy and fuzzy. ("Sounds like the planet's only fun law firm," Garrison had said when I described myself that way.)

"But animals are also kind, aren't they? I've watched those videos of elephants helping each other out, of dogs nursing kittens. Animals are nice to each other. Some of my students are affirmatively not nice to anyone. But the weird thing is, they grow up to be people like Sarah and Helen and Jamie, who have kindness cubed, right? I mean, even Jamie, when you dig down, would do anything for me."

"From what you've told me, that's true. What do you think happens between now and then?"

"Life, I guess," I said.

From the outside I guess my life seems pretty simple and easy. I have work I really like at a place that values it, a husband I love and who hardly ever irritates me except when he calls to say that he's sending a car to pick up his laptop, which he thought was in his backpack but wasn't. I have a brother who is way smarter and richer than I am and never acts that way and dresses like a dream but rarely criticizes my clothes. I can't complain about my mother in front of Sarah because at least I have one who semi-raised me, and I can't worry about my father in front of Helen because her father disappeared when he went bankrupt, and they had to sell the house where she'd grown up because there was no money. Although now that I think of it, from the outside both their lives seem simple and easy, too, now that Helen has a nice apartment and a stay-at-home husband so she doesn't have to worry about finding a nanny, and Sarah's hair has grown back, a little lighter and wavier than before.

"That's strange, how your hair is different now," Jamie had said the first time Sarah came to book club without her chemo head scarf. "I think your brows are thicker, too. And I wouldn't think it was possible, but I think you've gotten even nicer after being sick."

In her pretend treacly voice, Sarah said, "Thank you, Jamie."

"I didn't necessarily mean it as a compliment."

We all three burst out laughing. Sarah ran her hand through her hair.

"You must be a completely different person at work," I said to Jamie.

"Everyone's a different person at work, Polly," Sarah said, and in the treacly voice she added, "Oh goodness, you're absolutely right, a copper beech would be wonderful in that spot."

Jamie flattened her expression and leaned toward me. "I'd like to hear more about that," she said in a voice I'd never heard before, a low and somehow warmer voice she obviously kept for the couples she counseled.

"I wear makeup and cover my freckles because I once had a heinous boss who said I looked like Pippi Longstocking," said Helen. "I never wear black because another trusts and estates partner told me it reminds people of death, which they don't want to think about when they're deciding how to deal with their assets after death."

"Come on, Polly," Jamie said. "We're all different at work. You're so half-assed half the time with us, and then when you stand in front of those girls at school you're the damn Delphic oracle."

I remember that I didn't know whether to be insulted by half-assed or happy about the Delphic oracle. I remember walking home and thinking about the different selves I was, the one at school, the one with my mother and my father, even the one with Mark, the only person who made me feel all of a piece.

Maybe all of those different selves was why, despite outside appearances, from the inside my life at the moment felt like a maelstrom, me pinned against the wall of everyday by centrifugal force. My father hadn't really been hurt by his fall, only somewhat diminished further, with a physical therapist three times a week and a walker at all times, even now that he was safely back in his little Edgemere Place studio. Mark and I were supposed to meet with Jeannine to talk next steps, but both of us have found reasons to break appointments: for Mark, a gnu with an eye infection, as well as a beaver kit rejected by its mother who needed to be handfed and then died anyway of something called beaver fever, for me a student who needed a meeting with me because she was convinced she was failing when she was merely hovering in B territory, as well as a mother who wanted to discuss whether her daughter could take the poetry seminar remotely while she was in a facility for what her mother called body image issues.

And then there was Talia, my not-niece. Over the last two months she had sent me drawings of her dress and coat designs, and then two photographs of the finished products. They were good. "I would wear these!" I'd written to her. "What size are you?" she'd immediately written back.

So I wasn't completely surprised one late fall day, the last of the golden gingko leaves twirling like fans as they fell outside my office window, my simple-seeming life a snarl of complications behind the scrim, to receive an email:

> Dear Ms. Goodman,
>
> My name is Stephen Burton, and I am Talia Burton's father. She has told me of her meeting with you, although too long after it happened or you would have heard from me much sooner. I will be in New York City for a professional conference Saturday through Tuesday of next week, and would like to buy you a cup of coffee to fill you in on Talia, since it seems as though she wants to continue some kind of connection with you. I hope it's not an imposition.

The civil engineering conference Stephen Burton was attending was at the big blocky impersonal Hilton, and that was where Stephen Burton was staying as well. It seemed easiest to meet in one of the restaurants there. It was the kind of featureless place—burgundy carpet, dark captain's chairs, landscape paintings in identical frames—where you'd never meet a friend, only a stranger. It wasn't cold, exactly, just utilitarian. "I'll be wearing a red sweater," I said in my message, and he replied, "I'll recognize you. Talia showed me a picture." I wouldn't have recognized him. Tall, thin, with sandy hair, pale skin, and a slightly beaky nose, he bore almost no resemblance to his daughter, as though he had been sent here specifically to show me that the genetic hand we are all dealt is very various.

"This is strange," he said after we both ordered English muffins and decaf coffee. I understood right away what he meant: a man and a woman with virtually no point of connection except for one teenage girl, whom each of them knew in very different ways. The reason it didn't seem strange to me was because that precise calculus, or some version of it, was my professional life, happened all the time: sitting across a table from parents who wanted a window into what seemed like the shut room where their daughter sometimes lived, a room that they suspected I might have penetrated.

"Your daughter seems like a great girl," I said, which is how I often began those meetings.

"I just wanted to apologize for what she did. She is pretty great, but she's having a hard time these days, and she shouldn't have lied to that company about her age and then dragged you all the way to Vermont because of it."

"I enjoyed meeting her," I said.

Stephen Burton's hands were folded on the white tablecloth, tanned, callused, a few small scars, the hands of a man who worked outside in all weather. He was wearing a broad silver wedding band cut with a black zigzag pattern. He saw me looking and said, "My wife made jewelry." The waiter brought our food.

"Talia is looking for something," he said. "That's what the therapist says. Well, hell, of course she is. Her mother died, and even before that her mother was the one looking for something, which really affected Talia. My wife was a great woman. She was smart and creative and warm, but she had a lot of issues. She was adopted from Ghana, of all places, by a nice enough couple, but they were part of a very religious group in the Midwest, Nebraska actually, small-town Nebraska—can you imagine being the only Black girl growing up in small-town Nebraska? I guess there was a lot of talk about what a gift it was, that these people had adopted her, like they'd done her some enormous favor. They named her Margaret. She got out of there as fast as she could, went to France as an exchange student and never really came back. They called her Marguerite in Provence, which she loved. She worked as an au pair in France, then a nanny in Boston, and I met her my last year of college. My mother said the first time she met her, 'That girl is on fire.'"

He looked down at his untouched muffin and said quietly, "That's not necessarily what you need for the long haul, being on fire. You burn out." He looked up at me and raised his eyebrows.

"Anyhow," he said, "Marguerite was always wondering who and what she was. Was there a whole family in Ghana, sisters and parents and cousins, the whole deal? She had absolutely no clue. It was a closed adoption, locked up tight. She wasn't interested in her adoptive parents' family. Half of them wouldn't even look at her, and the other half—well, she had one aunt who always called Africa the dark continent, so that pretty much sums it up, right? I met her adoptive parents two times, our wedding and right after Talia was born, and it wasn't like I got to know them. After Talia was born Marguerite had three miscarriages, and there was something about that, being pregnant and then not, that had a deep, deep effect on her mind. Maybe there was something that was always there, and the losses just intensified it. She just went south every time she lost a baby."

"I'm so sorry," I said. More than he could know.

"What did Talia tell you about her mother?"

There wasn't much to report except that she had said her mother was an artist and had died after a long illness. When I said that, Stephen Burton made a sound like a cough, like a throat clearing, like a barking laugh, all in one, harsh and somehow mean. He looked up from his hands and pinned me with his eyes as though he had to drill the words into me, as though what he was telling me was something he had to persuade people was the truth, or maybe had to persuade himself. "Talia's mother killed herself," he said, and he sounded not sad, but angry, furious. "We took down the Christmas tree and she put on the down jacket I got her for a gift, the one she'd asked for specifically, and she went out for a walk and I said, 'Why don't you take the dog,' and she said, No, she'd leave the dog home."

He drummed hard on the table with a spoon. "She hung herself in the woods. Not in our woods. She went down a hiking trail to some public land so she wouldn't pollute our place with it. At least that's what I assume she was thinking. I heard her stop in the garage and I didn't know why and then later I figured out it was to pick up the rope. She didn't even leave a note, except that she drew a heart on Talia's bedroom mirror with her lipstick. Which is still there. I don't think she'll ever wipe it off."

I didn't say anything. What was there to say? The restaurant wasn't crowded, and there was a kind of atonal background music, all the clicking sounds of silverware being sorted, dishes being put down on tables, coffeepots being lifted from warmers. But in the vicinity of our table there was an enormous silence except for the sound of Stephen Burton hitting the table with his spoon. Finally he stopped and turned to look for the waiter. In my experience that's what men tend to do when faced with great emotion, look for some small task as a momentary distraction. Opening the mail, checking the oil, replacing the smoke detector batteries. "I need a refill on my coffee," he muttered, looking from one side of the room to the other, and that's when I saw his ears.

"None of you ever think about your ears, do you?" I'd said one night at book club. It must have been when we were not reading the Van Gogh biography.

"My ears?" Helen said, raising her hands to either side of her head.

"Why, you mean because of how weird yours are?" Jamie had said, looking at me and scraping the frosting off a cupcake with her index finger, popping the frosting in her mouth, and putting the cupcake back on the plate.

"Jamie!" said the other two almost in unison.

"It's fine," I said. "I mean, it's pretty undeniable." Benedict had mentioned it our first night together, when he'd pushed my hair back to get to my neck. "Oh, goodness," he'd said, "I'm about to ravish Tinker Bell!" From time to time he'd call me Tink, although not in a nice way. One night, when he called me that at a dinner with a group of grad students, he insisted on illustrating. "She has elf ears," he said. And I do. They're narrow and long and come to a sharp point at the very top. Peter Pan. Hobbits. I've heard them all. I don't wear ponytails or tuck my hair back behind them. I just don't, never have. When I was a child I once overheard my parents arguing about getting my ears fixed. "Don't be ridiculous," my father had said. "Her ears are fine."

Stephen Burton had elf ears, too. Mr. Spock, I bet someone had called him in high school, Star Trek man. Beam me up. I could almost hear it.

After the waiter refilled his cup, he exhaled audibly and said, "Anyway. I wanted you to understand why Talia was so anxious to meet you. I think she's finally beginning to accept that you can't possibly be related to her mother, that someone made a mistake somewhere."

"That's what my brother keeps saying," I said. My brother, Garrison, who has brown eyes, like our father and mother. Very unusual for two brown-eyed people to have a blue-eyed child like me, but not impossible, my high school bio teacher said when we studied genetics.

Stephen Burton's eyes are blue. Lots of people have blue eyes, I say to myself. Sarah has blue eyes. Aloud I said, "What about your parents?"

"What about them?"

"I mean, for Talia," I lied. "That must help, having grandparents."

"She and my mother are close. My mother is kind of a type, sort of an earth mother, spiritual but not religious, if you know what I mean. Marguerite was a little like that. My mother makes jewelry, too, so there was that. It's been hard on her, on my mother. I don't think she's ever been depressed a day in her life, even when money was tight in our house, when I was a kid. She's a positive person. Annoyingly so, sometimes. She tries to be understanding about what

Marguerite did, especially when she talks to Talia. But I don't think she understands any more than I do."

"Where does she live?"

"My mother? She's up in the Catskills. She has a big farm up there."

"Where's she from originally?"

Stephen Burton put down his coffee cup with a clunk. "Is this because of the genealogy results? Because if you're thinking you're my mother's secret love child, given up for adoption and never mentioned again, I can shut that down right now. If my mother had had a baby and given it up, she would have told me about it when I was a toddler. She's one of those women who talks about everything to everybody. Breast cancer, home birth, other things I don't even want to mention, but trust me, she will. When she found out Marguerite was adopted, and from Ghana, she talked about it endlessly. She and my wife got on really well, but even Marguerite said, 'Sometimes your mother is exhausting.' My mother puts all of it on her blog now, but even talking to thousands of people she has absolutely no filter."

"Your mother has a blog?" My mother habitually mentions that texting is for people with short attention spans and no power of real thought. She says she adopted email under duress.

"A website, so I guess it's technically part of the website, a section called 'Thoughts from the Fields.' You can look it up if you're really curious. The website is Warm As Toast, all one word."

"Holy shit!" I said, then clapped my hand over my mouth.

Stephen Burton rolled his blue eyes. "I should have known you'd recognize the name," he said.

"His mother is warm as toast," I said after we had all assembled in Sarah's living room two nights later.

"So you went and met her?" Sarah said. "The girl's grandmother? You liked her?"

"No. Warm. As. Toast."

There was a pause until Jamie's eyes widened and she slammed her copy of a new British thriller on the coffee table. "The incredibly expensive sweater people?" she yelled. "Holy shit!"

"That's exactly what I said."

"I love those sweaters," Helen said softly.

"I have no idea what you're all talking about," Sarah said. "And if I used the expression 'warm as toast' you would mock me, Jamie."

"Not if you were buying me a sweater I wouldn't," Jamie said.

I'd never actually visited the Warm As Toast website before, because I'd known I was never going to pay a thousand dollars for a sweater. And those weren't even the really expensive sweaters, the long cable-knit cardigans, the patterned pullovers. Like the one Talia was wearing that day I met her: That one is even pricier. I think I've seen it on one of my students. I know I've seen some of the others on the mothers at school pickup. They're really nice sweaters, the products, I discovered, of a four-hundred-acre farm in the Catskills where alpacas roam free. The alpacas are the stars of the website, one photograph after another, which makes sense because they are really great looking in an improbable kind of way, with long necks, hypermobile lips, and the kind of eyelashes you draw on people when you're drawing faces in elementary school.

"Are alpacas nice?" I asked Mark.

"Yeah, they're very pleasant. They spit occasionally, but only if you really piss them off. Otherwise, they're cool. I hear they're good around kids, and they're very clean. You have to trim their teeth, which is a bit of a job. They don't grind them down naturally the way other animals do. Why?"

"Talia Burton's grandmother has an alpaca farm," I said.

To its credit, the home page of the Warm As Toast website is all alpacas, not sweaters. You have to click on "What We Make" to get to the sweaters, and you have to seek out "Thoughts from the Fields" to get to Barbara Burton, who is Talia Burton's grandmother, Grannie B. There she was, just as I imagined when her son described her, a corona of silver curls, an Indian-print dress, dangling earrings. No sign of her ears beneath the hair. She was a familiar type, the kind of woman who once followed the Grateful Dead, who knows what each tarot card means, who did yoga when it was for centering the mind and not for bathing suit season. She may have actually been at Woodstock; her age is right, her persona, too, and her alpaca farm isn't that far away. Her page is full of affirmations. There's a lot about being good enough. According to various philosophers, yogis, and thinkers, I am. I see what Stephen Burton meant when he was talking about his mother's attitude toward life.

She also writes well, although her love of nature sometimes makes her prose what I would call a little overheated. She rhapsodizes about purple loosestrife in the fields, the smell of fresh hay, the supermoon, the summer sunsets, and, of course, the animals. Watching a baby alpaca being born. Shearing the coats. Even the tooth trimming. All the alpacas seem to have names. Twelve of them are named after the signs of the zodiac. One is named Tally, and I wonder if it's a tribute alpaca named for or by her only grandchild. Or what I assume is her only grandchild, because what do I know anymore.

Walking the reservoir with Sarah, avoiding any mention of my ears, I had said, "Everyone seems to agree that this genealogy site made a mistake. Garrison keeps sending me stories about their failure rate, about people who thought they had family members they didn't, or I guess worse, thought the family members they had weren't actually related to them. They've got a bunch of lawsuits pending. But Talia Burton keeps sending me emails. I liked her. It feels cruel to blow her off."

"Given your work, it would be surprising if you didn't resonate to her, or her situation."

"Teenage girls just feel as though they're completely unprotected, like they're bound to be burned by life. And that's before their mothers hang themselves in the woods. Can you imagine?"

"No," said Sarah, although I'm fairly sure that her own family situation was, if not tragic, at least tragedy adjacent. "And even under the best of circumstances, I wouldn't be that age again on a bet."

"Agreed." I'd run into Josephine on the street the week before, home from Harvard for a cousin's bat mitzvah. The area beneath her eyes was a dull purple, and she picked at her lower lip. "How's college?" I'd asked brightly. "It's different than I expected," she said.

"You'll do great!" I said, an exclamation point in my voice, and then back in my office I'd rued the unexamined enthusiasm. "Email Josephine," I wrote on the pad of paper next to my computer. My own first semester at college had been miserable, my working endlessly to make papers sound intelligent and succeeding only in scrubbing them of any zest or juice. "Relax," my adviser had said, which is the sort of direction that makes you tense.

"The smartest ones have the hardest time," the head of school said when I mentioned Josephine. "We're a small pond. Suddenly they're no longer big fish." She'd sighed. "Hostages to fortune," she'd said, and I'd nodded.

"The website says you can visit the Warm As Toast farm on Sunday afternoons," I told Sarah. "I'm thinking of going. Is that crazy? I feel as though everyone thinks I've gotten a little crazy since I took that DNA test."

"Does Mark think it's crazy?"

"Actually, he doesn't." Actually, when I had told him about Stephen Burton's ears, he had looked thoughtful and said, "That's kind of interesting." If there is a person in my life who knows genetics, it's Mark, who knows the family trees of wolves, antelopes, great apes who are certainly not monkeys, don't try his patience by calling them that. I had combed Barbara Burton's website for photographs of her with her hair pulled back, but while there are pictures of her speaking to schoolchildren, shoveling dung, hammering silver, riding on a tractor, and holding stork pose, there are none that reveal whether she, her son, and I share the same odd ears. And what would that even mean, given the fact that I was quite certain I had once been appalled by pictures of my own mother actually giving birth to a girl baby that, in more decorous shots, was said to be me.

My mother, the honorable, and Stephen Burton's mother, the mystical, existed in different maternal galaxies. At least one previous blog post suggested that Barbara gave birth in a kiddie pool outdoors, and another that she would have nursed indefinitely except that her son began to bite. The posts were warm as toast, too. This month's "Thoughts from the Fields" was about pumpkins; apparently the alpaca love them, and the beta carotene brightens their coats. They eat the whole gourd, every bit. Pumpkin, Barbara reminds us, is a fruit. "So is everything with seeds," she writes. "Cucumbers—yes, it's true! Eggplant, too."

At Windsor we have a veteran biology teacher, Dr. Shanevsky, whom the girls both lampoon and revere for his almost aerobic enthusiasm for his lessons. Some of the drama girls imitated him perfectly at an upper school assembly: "Photosynthesis"—each syllable rolled around his wide mouth like hard candy—"the process by which ORGANISMS use SUNLIGHT to create ENERGY!" And then, in a whisper, "It is . . . a miracle."

It's the way Barbara Burton talked on her website about the pumpkins and the alpaca. "The recycling of nature," Barbara called it, "glorious in its efficiency and needing the work of no woman to be fruitful. Unless the female in question is Joan Baez." Joan Baez is the name of the largest of the female alpacas, and apparently she is the most enthusiastic pumpkin eater. ("I will refrain from saying Peter, Peter," Barbara wrote. "Except there—oh dear—I said it.") Joan Baez has a bristly brush of pale hair, not unlike the singer in her later years. The largest male is named Bob Dylan.

The silver jewelry, designed and occasionally made by BB, as she sometimes calls herself, but more commonly fashioned by the apprentices she finds in disadvantaged communities, was the kind of thing the arts majors wore when I was in college, the hammered bangles, the necklaces with zodiac charms, the rings that I'd already seen on Talia's fingers. I wondered if Talia's mother's jewelry had wound up on her mother-in-law's site.

"I can come with you to see the alpacas if you want," Sarah said. "It'll be like a field trip for grownups. Although now that I know about this, I've looked at the sweaters, and I worry that I would buy one. They're gorgeous sweaters, but the price tag is sinful. What do you know about the husband?"

A chilly gust lifted my baseball cap almost off my head. Time to switch over to the winter wool watch cap. Although maybe there was a Warm As Toast beanie. If so, it would probably cost as much as I usually paid for a sweater.

"What husband?" I asked.

"The mother's husband. Goodness me, this gets complicated. The husband of the woman who has the alpaca farm."

"There's no husband. Maybe there never was, or maybe they're divorced." I'd asked Stephen Burton near the end of our breakfast, after I'd heard him explain how his mother had turned a small flea market silver jewelry stall into a big-ticket online phenomenon, how she'd done it almost without meaning to, and how she plowed most of the profits back into alpacas, apprenticeships, and arts programs for local kids. "Did your father play a role?" I had said, and he laughed that kind of barking laugh again, but with less heat. "My father is what you might call a rebounder," he said. "He came. He left. He came back. He left again. My mother says he's a free spirit."

"I'm sorry," I said again, and he'd shrugged.

"I probably couldn't pick him out of a police lineup today," he said.

"I HAVE A CAR," GARRISON SAID ON THE PHONE. WHAT HE MEANS is that he has arranged for someone to drive us, which means he wants the option of drinking, which doesn't surprise me. We were going to a country club in New Jersey, and Garrison had a car for all three of us: him, me, Mark. My mother was being honored by the Women's Bar Association, which is the kind of thing she always insists she hates—hates being called a woman judge because, she says, it's a qualifier that makes it sound like if you threw her into the common pool with all those guys with the red ties and gray suits beneath their robes, she'd sink, or at least founder. Which, believe me, is not true.

"There's no need for you to attend," she'd said when Garrison had heard about the dinner from one of his high school classmates who was the managing partner at a firm that had purchased a table. "We're coming," he said he'd told her. "Before you even asked me?" I said. "Yes, Pol, before I'd even asked you. Because I knew you'd try to get out of it by saying you had some school thing that night."

"As it happens, I do."

"No you don't," Garrison said.

Mark was, of course, not only happy to come but convinced that his parents should come, too. The only thing close to an irreconcilable difference we have is when we approach family obligations. A month before we were married Mark insisted we go to a state park where his parents were running a 5K in the over-60s class. They were easily beaten by a seventy-two-year-old marathon runner, although Mark's brother Thomas said his father could have placed if he hadn't insisted on running alongside his wife, who had to walk a couple of legs of the race. But when they finally crossed the finish line, Skipper holding Lou's hand, an enormous cheer erupted because, unlike the runners who had only a few friends there, or the runners who had come alone, Mark's parents were greeted by a phalanx of family, their own cheering section made from scratch. Of course Thomas had muttered, "One of these days he's going to have a coronary doing this," and Emily had said, "Honey, I love you, but you could make a christening seem like a drowning waiting to happen."

"I feel like we should have brought something," Mark said in the dim light of the car's back seat. "Flowers or something. Well, not flowers, but something."

"Polly is wearing a color instead of black and white," Garrison said. "That'll be a gift."

"It just seems like an event that should come with a gift," Mark said.

"She'll get a plaque," Garrison said.

"Or they'll give her a paperweight," I added. "Something crystal with her name engraved." My mother has a dozen of those in the office in our old house, lined up on the bookshelves in front of *Black's Law Dictionary* and all those commemorative copies of the Constitution.

"I guess your dad coming was out of the question," Mark said sadly. He'd mostly known the vaguer Jack Goodman, the one who occasionally got a blank look when he saw Mark with his arm around me on the sofa, but even then Mark had really liked my father. And he knew how I felt.

"I asked her about bringing Dad," Garrison said, and that was that. Because I imagined we both knew what our mother would say about bringing him to an event like this one, him shuffling in, bent and sleepy-eyed, nodding off during her remarks or, even worse, replying to them aloud: That's right, Mary. That's good. You always get to the heart of things.

But then Garrison added, "She was afraid it would upset him."

"Right," I said.

"Polly," Mark said, taking my hand. He had never bonded with my mother exactly, but he always says he appreciates the fact that I'm warm, empathetic, understanding. He doesn't like that I'm not that way whenever my mother comes up. Given his family dynamic, it's like I'm speaking in tongues, the kind that suggest someone is possessed. Mark had once idly said, when I found a piece of paper in the pages of his copy of *Doctor Doolittle,* a little pencil drawing of a mouse, that it was just one of the notes his mother put in his lunchbox. I didn't entirely believe him until I'd actually met his mother. Once, driving home from Edgemere, I had said to him, "You have to stop assuming that everyone has a mother like your mother."

My mother had never been the kind of mother who would put a pencil drawing in my lunchbox. The only time she had ever done the kind of mothering my friends described, and complained about, was during the six months after I had decided to exit graduate school as well as my first marriage. She called several times a week, twice came to the city to take me to lunch, three times insisted I come home for some family occasion that turned out to be takeout with her and my father. In lieu of larger concerns she focused on how, exactly, I was managing to pay my rent. As she circled the issue while we sat at the table in the breakfast nook, my father stared out the window, not looking at her, not looking at me, not looking at the beaver dam of pizza crusts in the center of the table. Neither he nor I were willing to say that he had pivoted from paying my grad school tuition to paying for the tiny studio on Ninety-second Street with a view of a neglected backyard, a single plane tree improbably thriving amid a hostile surround of cracked concrete and rat burrows.

"I'm getting by," I finally said.

"I just don't understand how you can stand to be idle," she'd said, as though I would never again be a contributing member of society because I had stepped off the path for a few months.

In the car I squeezed Mark's hand on one side and Garrison's on the other.

"I don't want to upset you by saying this," Mark said, "but there's more of your mother in you than you like to admit."

"Oh my God," Garrison said. "Have you lost your mind?"

"I don't mean in terms of presentation, though in some ways that's similar, too, but because you both act like you do because of your jobs. Your mother is certain of herself and, okay, judgmental, which makes sense because she's a judge. That's her job. And you're personally engaging and teacherly because, duh. But inside you're both people who are strong and smart and dependable."

"Honey, I can assure you that she was judgmental before she ever got appointed to the bench," I said.

"So there are two possibilities here, both of which are scientifically valid. Each of you was a certain kind of person and found the kind of work that was consonant with that. Or each of you wound up in a certain profession and your personalities evolved accordingly. It's all adaptive, the way carnivores have pointed teeth to rip and tear, and herbivores have blunted, square teeth for chewing plants."

"So our mother is a meat eater and Polly is a veg?" Garrison said.

"Sometimes it's like playing ping-pong with the two of you. Psychologically."

Garrison reached across me to pat Mark's knee. "He is a treasure," Garrison said. "A goddamn treasure. Don't ever let him go. He's one of the only truly good people I know. Even our mother likes him."

"But does she?" I said.

"Oh, lighten up, Polly," Garrison said.

"Do you think she really doesn't?" Mark said, turning to me.

"She's being a wiseass," Garrison said. "It's one of her many charms."

"I'd like to disabuse you of the notion that you are the only woman in the world who doesn't like her mother," my therapist had said three years before, when my mother had first decided that my father needed to live at Edgemere instead of with her, in his own home.

"It's not that I don't like her," I'd said.

"You could have fooled me."

"I don't think she likes me," I said.

"That can't be right," Mark had said once when I said the same to him.

"I don't understand why you can't move past this," Garrison had said when I told him the same thing.

I'd also told the therapist that I didn't feel I really knew my mother, and that was never clearer than on the rare occasions when I went to events like this. Just inside the carved double doors of the Morton Hollows Country Club was an easel with an enormous photograph on it, with curlicue letters: "A Tribute to The Honorable Mary Kerr Goodman." Even allowing for airbrushing, the woman in the picture staring into the distance in three-quarter profile, her pale face floating above her black robes, was what I suppose people would call handsome. She had grown into her face, too fierce and angular for elementary school, not soft enough for wedding pictures, but perfect for a woman jurist of a certain age. "Your mother is certainly a good-looking woman," Mark's father had said after the meet-the-parents dinner. "She must be just brilliant," Mark's mother said. We'd been in the den at their Connecticut house feeding logs into the fire, and when Lou turned from the woodpile, Emily, soon to be my sister-in-law and friend, had raised her eyebrows and I had nodded, both of us reading "just brilliant" as "not the friendliest person I've ever met."

Garrison and Mark and I were all seated together at table one, according to our place cards, and surrounded by a knot of acolytes the moment we entered the banquet hall. "You're Polly!" a young woman in the kind of black dress you wear when you want to seem older said, with an enormous smile and a determined head tilt. "I'm Lauren. I'm so glad to finally meet you! I feel like I know you! I'm clerking for the judge this year, and every time I pass the pictures of you on the credenza, I think, Someday I'll meet her in the flesh. And here you are! She'll be so glad."

"How is the clerkship going?" I asked. I knew the answer because I've asked the question in the past. But I have to hear it again because it's always so improbable to me. The first time was years ago, and I'd waited for the hesitation, the carefully couched words, the equivalent of "just brilliant." It never came.

"It's amazing," Lauren said, clasping her hands together. "It's as though a week as her clerk is equivalent to a year of school. I'm learning so much every day, and she lets us participate so much more than the judges some of my friends are clerking for. I mean, it's not easy. She can be tough, but not in a harsh way. She just always wants you to do your best. I feel so lucky. Everyone you talk to here will say the same."

"That's great," I said.

"But you already know that." She looked around. "Let me find her for you."

"Thanks, but I'll track her down." I could already see my mother across the room through a break in a wall of dark suits. She was wearing a red dress. I'm wearing a red dress. I can already hear my husband thinking, Told you so.

"That color is good on you," she said when we finally saw each other, taking our seats for dinner.

"You too."

"You really didn't have to come," she said.

"I wanted to," I lied as she kissed Mark on both cheeks.

One of her former clerks, now a partner at her former firm, was seated to my left. To my right was the president of the Women's Bar Association. Over salad and salmon I had the opportunity to hear about how my mother was a wonderful mentor, a champion of women, a role model for members of the bar. Eventually I tried to steer things back toward some semblance of the woman I know.

"Isn't she tough in court?" I asked the former clerk.

"Incredibly tough. I mean, be prepared, or you're going down. One of my partners will say, I'm appearing before Judge Goodman, and I just tell him, Best of luck, buddy." I looked to the left of his plate. There was a tumbler of scotch and wines both white and red. In vino veritas. The Bar Association woman, by contrast, was drinking sparkling water. Of course I wondered if it was because she was pregnant, but her skirt suit suggested not. "Of course she's tough," she said. "She's a judge. That's her job. No one even asks the question about male jurists." She sighed deeply. She had eaten her fish and her string beans but not her potatoes. "I don't even know why they bother with a starch on the plate at these things," Jamie had said once when she persuaded us all to sit at her table at some women's event for Central Park.

"Excuse me," the Bar Association woman said, and I thought for a moment she was so offended by my toughness question that she had to abandon her seat, until I saw her move toward the podium and at the same time watched my mother reapply her lipstick using the flat of her butter knife as a mirror—which, I have to admit, is a good trick I've adopted.

And thus, the introduction, during which much was always made of the fact that Mary Kerr Goodman had gone to law school some years after she'd graduated from college, after she'd already started a family. I saw Mark looking at me across the table—he'd been on one side of my mother, Garrison on the other—and I could see that he was worried about how I would respond to that phrase, "started a family," because it suggests that Mark and I are only a couple, nothing more. But instead I was annotating in my head all the times with my father solo in the seats at school because of a moot court event, an answer to interrogatories that needed filing, a trial that went on longer than expected. I could almost hear the president of the Bar Association replying, Male judges miss their family obligations all the time, and no one says much about it, do they?

Her clerk Lauren had said, "You must be so proud of your mother." And I was proud of the Honorable, in theory. In practice I had wanted more of a standard-issue mother when I was a kid, not a role model. And maybe we never lose that, the wanting or the kid. Or maybe it's like everything else in life. One night at book club Sarah and I were rhapsodizing about Jamie's exuberant head of curly hair, and Jamie dismissed us with a hand semaphore and said, "Yeah, yeah, yeah, the ones with straight hair want curls, the ones with curly hair want it straight, it's the secret of life, and it doesn't just apply to hair, it applies to everything. Every damn thing." The thing is, when Jamie is dismissive, she's almost always right.

The Bar Association woman looked up and put her arm out in what seemed like a weirdly theatrical gesture, and then there she was, taking the stage, the honoree, her dark hair blown biggish, the faint sparkle of her gold seashell earrings, the ones my father gave her for her fiftieth birthday, picked up by the lights overhead. First she hugged her introducer, and then she looked down at our table and she . . . winked? Did she just wink at us?

"When I was a child I wanted to be an archeologist," she began. I looked at Garrison and he looked at me, both of our faces held perfectly still because we didn't want to react, to communicate with lifted brows, big eyes, curled lips, that this was a new one on both of us.

"Archeologist?" we both said as soon as we were in the back seat and the car doors were closed.

"It all made sense," Mark said.

And it had. Maybe it was even true. But, more important, it was a good opener for a good speech about how the law, the process of discovery, the trial, is all a question of excavating, looking closely, sifting material, deciding what matters and what doesn't. It was smart and interesting and just the right length, and even her faint rebuke—"this process knows no gender"—was leavened with exactly the right caveat—"but perhaps we women are used to digging deeper and looking more searchingly." Maybe the standing ovation would have been inevitable anyhow, but the speech was good enough to deserve it.

"I'm picturing her in a pith helmet," I said in the car.

"Oh, pith off, Polly," Garrison said, slinging an arm around my shoulder and tugging gently at my hair.

I'd had my picture taken with my mother, my brother on the other side, her holding the award, each of her children touching its base. It was indeed a piece of crystal, shaped for some reason like clasped hands. But there was a large coterie of people wanting to talk to her, young ones looking to clerk, older ones currying favor. The name partner of her old firm had greeted me as though we were old friends, and his wife said, "What a wonderful speech," and I said, "It was, wasn't it." We three slid out while the judge was having her picture taken with her many admirers.

"Sometimes I feel like I don't even know who she is," I said, sitting between Mark and Garrison.

"Yep," said Garrison.

"Yep, you feel the same?"

"Not exactly, but hold that thought if you find it comforting."

"What's that supposed to mean?"

"Nothing," he said. "We did our duty, and now it's done. I know you won't believe it, but she was really grateful we were there. Especially you."

"And what you said before," I continued, turning to Mark. "The way we all are in our professional lives should be different from the way we are personally. I'm her daughter, not someone making a courtroom appearance and getting chastised from the bench for not being forthcoming. I don't treat you the way I treat my students. I have a different way of engaging with the people I love, and so should she. If we have children—"

"When we have children," said Mark.

"—will you be staring into their ears and palpating their abdomens?"

"Yep, probably. Probably I will."

"This is a profound conversation," Garrison said. "I can't have a profound conversation right now. I had too much to drink."

"You did seem as though you had a lot to drink," I said. It always intrigued me that Garrison insisted that I was the one who was ridiculously anxious in situations like this with our mother, but he was the one who always, always wound up getting hammered.

"The only way around is through," Garrison said.

"Which means?" Mark said.

"It means he had a lot to drink," I said. "So you feel it, too, the not knowing what she's thinking and feeling. It's not just the mother-daughter thing."

"The mother-daughter thing is definitely a thing," Garrison said. "But there's also the mother-son thing, not to mention the mother–gay son thing. Which reminds me, some big fat dude who was also a judge, at least I think he was unless his parents named him Your Honor, introduced himself and said, Oh, you're the gay one, I admire that. I almost followed him into the men's room to see exactly how much he admired it. Never mind, just let me sleep."

"Almost home," Mark said, squeezing my hand.

We drove out to see my father the Sunday after Thanksgiving. "Evening up the mother-father score?" said Garrison, who sometimes can't help being snide and who knows me better than anyone. Saturday had been the zoo staff party, which was always a lot of fun. No one was exactly sure who first came up with the idea of having turkeys wandering around the party, and there's no question that it gets messy. Turkey scat, as I learned to call it from hanging around Mark and his co-workers, looks more like cat than bird, and by the end of the day, which was part picnic, part dance party, you really had to be careful where you stepped.

"I really love that party," I said to Mark as we drove toward Edgemere.

"They're a good bunch," he said.

"No nastiness, no undercurrents."

"Don't get carried away," he said. "We have our share of backbiting. Of course, that's mainly the baboons."

"That's what I mean. The whole party was like, animal jokes. The deejay even played 'Wild Thing.' Twice."

"I appreciate that he does that, but it's a bad dance song, right? So is 'The Lion Sleeps Tonight,' though I do love to sing along." For a moment, in the car, he did. Aweem away, aweem away.

"'Crocodile Rock,'" I said.

"That one works."

The parking lot at Edgemere was only half full, and I wondered if the good family members had come on Thanksgiving Day proper to eat turkey croquettes in the dining hall, croquettes being the necessary alternative given how little chewing and how much choking took place among the residents. The dining hall was all white and gold with big long windows, so pretty that a year or so ago a young couple had had their wedding reception there for the sake of her grandmother, although they had had to move on later to a more conventional venue because the administration had said no way to a dance band and two hours of the electric slide. Apparently some of the residents had gathered in their chairs on the veranda and showered the departing couple with confetti. There was an enlarged photograph of the moment in the lobby, which made Edgemere seem like one big party.

It had gotten too chilly in the last few weeks for the residents to sit outdoors. There had been heat lamps and horse blankets at the zoo party, although once the dancing started we hadn't needed either. Most of the Edgemere residents existed in a vaguely shivery state all year round, anyhow, throws over their laps at noon, sweaters in midsummer. The heat had already been turned up high, and I took off my coat and my cardigan. My father and Claire were in one of the common rooms, the one that's called the library. There was a fireplace with a gas fire behind a solid glass panel, because sometimes one of the residents will forget that fire burns and that touching it is not as good an idea as it seems.

"Mark's here, Daddy," I said, the two of us in the big leather chairs facing the pair of wheelchairs. It's easier for the staff, the wheelchairs.

"Mark!" my father said, almost as though he actually remembered him. "Good to see you, Mark!"

"Hey, Jack, it's been too long," Mark said, and then he launched into a long story about transporting a male leopard from Cincinnati to mate with a female leopard at the Bronx Zoo. My father just nodded. Tranquilizer darts. Horse trailers. Neighboring cages. Gradual introduction. Check. Check. Check.

"You know," Jamie had said at our book club meeting, apropos of the husband in the novel we were not reading, who was apparently so boring that his wife was having an affair with the custodian at the kid's school, "this reminded me of Mark."

"Okay, first of all, that's a terrible thing to say, and second of all, why would you even say that, because I know you didn't read the book. Helen might sneak read, but you wouldn't."

"I have never sneak read," Helen said.

"But getting back to why the boring husband in, what's it called, *The Terminus*—" I said.

"Terrible title," Helen said.

"—reminded you of my husband."

"The only reason I know he's a boring husband is because I read the *Times* review, and it said he and the wife are both lawyers," Jamie said. "And it made me think that maybe the best marriages are when your husband has a job so weirdly different from yours that you don't get bored by it. And if anyone has a weirdly different job, it's your husband."

"Agreed," I said. "He's trying to get two leopards to warm up to each other so they can have more leopards. Although by your reasoning, he should set up one of the leopards with a lion."

"But see, that's what I mean," said Jamie. "You'll ask Mark about that, and you'll have something to talk about."

"I like leopards," my father suddenly said to Mark. Really?

"I do too," Mark said. "They're beautiful animals."

The stone mantelpiece in the Edgemere library was engraved with the phrase "Joy in the Morning." Looking at it, then at my father, I wondered if he could still read. There's been a book about the history of Guadalcanal on the chest of drawers in his room for months now, and it looks like it was laid flat, open to the same place a third of the way through, for all that time, as though the book finished with him rather than the other way around. If he can read the fireplace quote, does it feel like an indictment to him, to Claire, to the other residents? Their morning is so far away, although I've always noticed that they seem to recall it—the school days, the weddings, the births of the now-grown, now-old children—better, more vividly, than they do what they had for dinner yesterday or what they did last year. They remember the beginnings of their days, but their actual lives now are perpetual evening.

"Gradual introduction is an issue with a lot of species," Mark was saying to my father while Claire looked down at her folded hands. "For instance, if you're putting a new queen bee in a hive, you do it with her in a little box called a queen cage with a plug of what's called queen candy at the end. The hive gets used to her over a day or two while they're eating the candy plug."

Maybe Jamie was right. I've never heard of any of this before, and it's pretty interesting. In the car going back to the city I'll ask Mark about bees, although given that he's a large-animal vet I have to wonder about the source of his bee knowledge. On the other hand, he does seem to know a lot about not-so-large animals. He once assured the owner of a bearded dragon who was walking it on a leash in Central Park that it was perfectly normal for it not to eat for days at a time during the winter months.

As Mark had been describing the behavior of a new queen in the hive, my father had been nodding, but now he had nodded off. There was a kind of vest, not so different from a life vest really, that went from the back of the chair to the front of its occupant for those whose spines had curved past the point of ever being vertical again. But it was also useful when someone fell asleep in a wheelchair so they didn't just keel over.

"I think I'll take him to his room," I said to Mark.

"I can take Claire," he said, and looking over I saw that, like so many other things, they'd fallen asleep in tandem.

The elevators don't ding when they are called, when they arrive at the correct floor. The dinging makes too many of the people who live at Edgemere nervous, reminding them of late-night phone calls and hospital sounds. My father's room was on the third floor, light, bright, painted a butter yellow, framed photographs of Garrison, our mother, and me on the bookshelves. When he first came to live here my father would say good night to the photographs, to the three of us, when I left late in the evening: Night, Gar. Sleep tight, little girl. When he first came to live here he was more himself. He had fought the idea most of the time, and for the first few months after he moved into Edgemere, he complained to his friends when they came, and to me after they stopped coming, that his wife was trying to get rid of him. Then one day it was as though he had given up. "I decided to stay here," he said to me. "The food isn't bad. The house is a lot to take care of. It'll be easier." In the first year there were still times when he seemed to think my mother was living at Edgemere, too. He stopped saying good night to her picture, and I thought that was why, until one day I asked.

"What about Mom, Daddy?" I'd said.

"I'm angry at her right now," he had said. "She took my car keys."

Now sometimes he stared at the pictures, and there was a look in his eyes, searching, wondering, that made me think he was trying to figure out who those people were, who they were to him. Me at middle school graduation. Garrison knee-deep in the surf at the beach. My mother sitting on a stone wall somewhere in the country, wearing a short polka-dot shift and sunglasses.

I stepped outside to look for an aide, to ask whether I should just leave my father in his room, in the chair, or get someone to move him into bed. The place seemed deserted today. Usually there were other visitors, the other daughters, the other sons, the spouses. We smiled, nodded, said hello, but we didn't really talk to one another. What would we say: How lost is the person you love? How much worse? Over three years I had gotten used to seeing the same faces among the residents and the visitors. Then it would suddenly occur to me that the tiny woman with the long braid, the daughter who always wore bright red lipstick, had gone missing. It would occur to me, and then I would file it away, somewhere deep, because the whys for the disappearance were too hard to think about. I tried not to look into the future too much at Edgemere.

There was only one person in the corridor, and when she turned

I saw it was the director, wearing jeans and a sweatshirt, as though she had been spending a quiet day at home and then been called in for some emergency.

"Oh, I'm so glad you managed to get here," she said, as though I were the emergency, and as though I scarcely visited, which twanged both my terror and my guilt strings.

"He seems fine," I said.

"Oh no, no, he's not why I'm here. It was something else entirely, in another wing." The other wing is C. A is for those whose families no longer want them to live alone but who are perfectly capable of eating and chatting and complaining over meals in the dining hall, watching movies in the library, going once a week on shopping trips or excursions to museums. B is where my father is. C is dire. I won't ask, but if the director has been called in to something in C, it was probably because someone had died, or is about to.

"But since I'm here, I'm glad to have the opportunity to connect with you. I assume your mother filled you in on her visit on Thanksgiving, and our conversation."

I shook my head and set my jaw. Mark and I had spent Thanksgiving at his parents' house on the sound. The kitchen had been so crowded that at one point Lou told us all to take a walk, please, get out of the way, I've got this. Twenty-six for dinner, including the children, who had their own table and spilled constantly—cider, gravy, cranberry sauce—until Emily had yelled, "If I have to mop up one more thing I'm sending you all outside." Their plates still mostly full, they put on their coats and trudged in a line onto the strip of beach, Sophia keening about the cold although it was unseasonably warm that afternoon in the sun. Emily's parents had come, and one of her sisters and her family.

Garrison was in San Francisco for a friendsgiving, and my mother had said she was having Thanksgiving with neighbors. Maybe she even had, after she came to Edgemere for croquettes.

"She was here for about two hours," said the director, "and she said your father scarcely spoke. She also wanted to walk around the grounds with him, it was such a temperate afternoon, but one of the staff let her know that he was having a lot of trouble with his balance. Even with the walker he's finding it difficult to get around. We told her we would recommend that he use the chair from now on. We don't want to take a chance on another fall."

I nodded.

"It's nothing to get too concerned about. We can still manage him here, and he seems contented. But as you both know, the illness is progressive, and he seems to be heading into a less responsive and self-sufficient time with us here. Have you been here long today?"

"About an hour, an hour and a half. My husband is with me."

"Did he speak with either of you?"

"He called my husband by name."

"Well, that's excellent," she said, and it was all I could do not to reply, "Also, he says he likes leopards." When my father first arrived, he used to go to movie nights in the library. Mainly comedies, which I guess made sense. "That Steve Martin," he would say the next time I visited, "he's a funny guy." And I would think, Yes, that's true, Steve Martin *is* a funny guy, Jack Goodman's still got it. And then fifteen minutes later he would tap me on the knee and say, "Boy, that Steve Martin. He's a funny guy."

He hadn't gone to movie nights in a year. Maybe more than a year.

"Did he recognize my mother?"

"That was another concern she had. As you know, he's sometimes angry at her. Not as much as in the beginning, but there are still the occasional complaints about her putting him here. But there was none of that, and he didn't use her name as he often does. I think he asked for you once or twice."

"Thank you for letting me know," I said.

"Even if he doesn't seem to recognize you, visits are important," the director said. "We don't know exactly what his interior life is like, whether he's silent and unresponsive and yet thinking to himself, My daughter is here."

When I went back inside the room, the sun had started to go down outside the windows, so that the top half of my father was in shadow, as though dusk was swallowing him up, taking him over. The visual metaphor was so glaring I could barely stand it. I moved his chair so more of him was in the waning daylight. He was still asleep, snoring slightly, a snail trail of spit running into the deep lines from one corner of his mouth to his big square chin. "I'm going, Daddy," I said. "Mark says goodbye. I love you. Sleep tight. Don't let the mosquitoes bite. If they do use dynamite." I put a hand on his. "I won't let them put you in C," I whispered. The dull light shone on the frames of the photos on the shelves and then made a prism out of the piece of crystal next to them, the piece of crystal my mother had been given to honor her at dinner. It made a faint rainbow on the back of the bookcase.

"HOW'S YOUR FATHER DOING?" SARAH ASKED IN THE CAR.

"More or less the same," I said.

"The same is good," she said, looking out the passenger window as we drove to Earthshine, which is what Barbara Burton had named her alpaca farm. A bright, silvery Sunday afternoon in December, and the cornfields on either side of the gravel road looked sad and diminished, yellow-brown stubs of the summer stalks, an occasional gnawed cob along the pitted roadside. Winter was on its way.

"I always wonder if I should move to a place like this," Sarah added.

"You already live in a place like this," I said.

"The Connecticut house? Oh, Polly, I love that place to death, you know I do, but you've drunk the country house Kool-Aid. Where I am in Connecticut is like a diorama. Cocktail parties, fundraisers. All the grass is mowed. All the gardens have stone borders. The farm stands get their produce from places like this. Real farmers can't afford to live there. This is where the real farmers live."

She sighed. "Every time I drive through a place like this I think it would probably be easier to live here. And all the people who live here probably think it would be easier to live the way I live." Farther along the road we passed two trailers side by side. Someone had added front decks to both of them, with plastic chairs to sit and watch the road, which seemed to provide a view of nothing much, at least to me. I had no doubt that the residents would jump at the chance to live in the kind of house Sarah had in Connecticut.

I have to admit, I never think of living in a place like that, or this. I understand the appeal, the quiet, the trees, the fresh air. I've heard so many friends over the years say they're done with the city. Gave up on it, couldn't handle it, couldn't afford it, abandoned it. But not me. Not us. It would be nice to spend weekends or summers in a place like this, but we don't make enough money to afford a country place, and I guess a weekend every now and then with Mark's parents satisfies the yen. Sarah once asked us to stay at her place in Connecticut to take care of her elderly springer spaniel when she was going to London, but once we were there for a day or two we realized it was basically an act of charity on her part. The spaniel, an artifact of her marriage whose name was Persnickety ("Don't tell Jamie," Sarah had said), Perry for short, slept most of the time, and Estelle the housekeeper was scarily efficient, so fresh towels appeared the moment either of us had showered, and meals were magic, on the table with no sign of preparation except a series of wonderful smells—bacon, melted cheese, roast chicken, pie. I was sure Sarah had told Estelle about Mark and pie.

We had had a wonderful time eating on the patio, reading on the screened porch, walking for miles in the parkland that bordered the back of the property. The gardens Sarah had created were, of course, beautiful, wild enough to look natural, brick paths and rock borders and fruit trees and shrubs that apparently flowered in succession. When Mark disappeared one afternoon, he came back with goat cheese and seeded bread and said he'd talked to the one vet in town who handled large animals, mostly the horses at the stables and the cows at an organic farm. "I'd make twice as much as I make at the zoo, and he's thinking of retiring," he'd said.

But it didn't feel like us. Both of us were people who'd grown up in what the local news called the tri-state area, grown up squinting toward the towers of what we, like everyone else around us, called "the city," as though Houston and Baltimore and Chicago didn't exist, as though there was only one. The thing about living in New York City is that you feel either perpetually untethered or unwaveringly embedded. I knew about the first after Benedict, when I rented that tiny studio and felt, in the lobby, on the street and the train, like a raindrop running down a windowpane, searching for a puddle so I could be among others like me.

But here, with Mark: Boy, were we embedded in the city. I know lots of people feel hemmed in by the buildings, the crowds, the unending movement of the place. But I always felt instead like the city was hugging me: love you, Polly, more than trees ever could. Even though we couldn't afford a dining room or a second bathroom to go with the second bedroom. We knew every face in our scruffy prewar rental building, and most names. We sighed in the elevator along with the Newmans and their kids when we saw the notice that the water would be shut off on Thursday, offered to take Mrs. Shapiro's recycling down with our own. We panicked as a group when the rumor spread that the building was going co-op, since most of us couldn't afford to buy, and heaved a sigh that almost seemed to inflate the brick walls of the building when the rumor turned out to be just that.

When we first moved in, there was a woman two buildings down who sat on the sidewalk in front of an old six-story tenement with a fire escape crawling up its front, bent over a cat with a bell on its red collar. "Oh no, oh no," she would repeat, holding him fast as the cat followed with its topaz-yellow eyes the dumb strut of the pigeons on the sidewalk. Three years later (a little before I started the hormone shots) and she suddenly wasn't there. Spring days, warm enough for the thick coat sweater she wore, the same black as most of the cat, and she'd vanished. Her building was too small, too run-down to have a doorman, but one of our doormen, Hector, said the lady had died. "What about the cat?" Mark said.

Now sometimes I see the cat at the window of 3B in our building, one paw raised as though he's waving, though his eyes never leave the pigeons. The Newman kids had named him Hunter.

"How could we move?" Mark said. We had looked into a larger apartment in the building when we thought we would need one, and we'd figured out how to afford it. But last year a three-bedroom came up, and we didn't even bother.

We were lucky. The roundelay of treatments to have a baby if it doesn't come naturally are really expensive. Mark and his brothers, the four Bailey boys, each had a trust from Lou's father. Thomas used it to buy a house, Douglas to start a business, and Michael, the youngest, to bankroll an organic farm in Maine. Mark had spent his on me—on medication, implantation, and many, many blood tests. I tried not to total it up in my head: Emily and Thomas had a house with a wraparound porch in Croton; Douglas was, in the words of his older brother, minting money; and Michael had developed a frost-resistant peach.

Mark, I thought when I was feeling low, had me. And a two-bedroom rental.

"I like living where I live," I said to Sarah in the car.

"So do I," she said, sighing. "Both places. Never mind my wool gathering. December's not my best time. I think I have seasonal affective disorder."

"You could come to us for Christmas." I say that every year, even though the first part of our Christmas, the size of the tree and the size of the company, is constrained by the size of our living room, and the second part, at Mark's parents', is a mob scene.

"The boys are coming to me." Sarah says this every year, too. Her stepsons are both married, and one has two boys of his own. I can just picture them peering up the chimney rising from the big stone fireplace in her living room, and I feel a tremor and a pang. Christmas is another season that's hard for those of us who want to be out buying alphabet blocks and dollhouses, and not buying them for other people's children. Sarah has never seemed to mind that she didn't have her own, once or twice made reference to her childhood as the kind that would make any right-minded woman avoid motherhood. But she had embraced the secondhand role. Richard's two little grandsons considered her their grandmother.

"Anyhow, I'm glad we're doing this. I don't know anything about alpacas. Are they like llamas?"

This, we discover, is that comment that should never be made, the observation that, for an alpaca farmer, is not unlike the comment teachers hate, the one about having summers off, the one that makes a teacher who signs on for summer school to support her grocery habit grit her teeth. It's like the comment to lawyers that you can't understand how they can represent guilty people, which I've shuddered hearing someone say to my mother because I know how cold and harsh her voice will become. "Everyone feels that way until the day they get indicted," she will say.

"Are alpacas the same as llamas?" a little girl asked Barbara Burton as we stood in a clot of down jackets and wool hats along the fence line, and while Barbara's voice did not become harsh, her face hardened a bit. It was clear that there was an alpaca-llama divide, and we were squarely standing on one side of it.

"I like a llama as well as the next person," Barbara Burton said from the alpaca side of the fence, running her long fingers through its curly off-white coat while the alpaca next to her chewed on a carrot and nudged her shoulder when the carrot was gone. "You've had enough, Saturn," she said. The alpaca blinked. It had a tongue the color of bubble gum.

Turning back to the girl, Barbara Burton continued, "But llamas and alpacas are quite different. Llamas are much larger and, in my opinion, less intelligent. They can be stubborn and sometimes spit. Alpacas can spit as well, but I have never had an alpaca spit at me. They have very definite personalities. Some of them are shy but sweet. Some are very social and outgoing." As though on cue, Saturn had turned and gone nose to nose with Barbara Burton. Pictures were taken.

There were few of us and many alpacas: tan, gray, brown, copper colored. When we had come down the road and the landscape had suddenly shifted from hardscrabble to well-maintained, with split-rail fencing and stands of silver birch, Sarah had wondered aloud whether the Sunday afternoon tour would be crowded. But there were only about a dozen of us on it. It was chilly, autumn chilly rather than winter, but the cold weather felt like a new thing, the way it did at the beginning of every cold snap, and we were all bundled up. One of the two dads on the tour said he thought the small number of visitors was because of the weather, but it actually said on the website that reservations were necessary because only a limited number of people were allowed at any one time. There was a picnic table near the barns with warm cider and donuts, but not too close, one of the farm workers said, because the alpacas would try to eat the donuts.

"Please do not feed the alpacas," a sign said. "We like them fluffy but not fat!"

The girl at the donut table was a college student majoring in what she called ag studies at the state university, and I couldn't miss the fact that she talked about Barbara Burton the way the young women had talked about my mother at the Bar Association dinner. She had learned so much. It was such an interesting place to work. She was considering applying to vet school.

"My husband is a large-animal vet," I said.

"Oh, I wish he had come with you! We have a large-animal vet here all the time. Not that the alpacas get sick very often, just for maintenance, check-ups, immunizations, those kinds of things."

"Insemination?"

"No, Barbara believes in doing things the old-fashioned way. You can hear the males even from the house. It sort of sounds like throat clearing but louder, and for a long time. Sometimes it happens during a tour, and we steer the kids away. But the babies are so, so cute. You're really lucky today that Barbara is the one doing the tour. Usually it's one of us, and she's taught us so much that we know how to answer most questions, but she's really the expert on so many things."

Sarah was still at the fence line listening to Barbara discussing the background and behavior of the alpacas. "This is fascinating," Sarah whispered. "They're related to camels. I had no idea."

"They don't get cold in the winter, for obvious reasons," Barbara continued, running her fingers again through the thick coat of what was now a different animal, more wheat colored. "In fact they love cold weather. Winter seems to be their favorite season." I bit into my donut and the alpaca turned its long neck in my direction, its liquid eyes wide. I stepped back and could swear I saw a look of disappointment cross its blunt and oddly friendly face. Donut denied.

"She's begging," said Barbara to me. "Do not beg, Electra." Still the alpaca stared until I ate the last bite. Then she blinked.

"Follow me to the barn where we process the fleece," Barbara said, slipping through the gate.

"Can they jump over?" said the same little girl.

"They've never tried," said Barbara Burton.

"I think they're happy here," the child said.

"They are," Barbara said.

We wandered the place, past corrals of more alpacas, through the barn where the fleece that had been sheared in the spring was sorted and stored. Two barns were stacked with hay bales for the winter months, Barbara said, when snow was too thick on the ground for the alpacas to graze, and another barn was used as a workshop. An hour into the tour the children began to whine, and one of them threw up her donut and cider in the yellowing grass, which had gotten crispy in the cold. The small crowd began to thin.

"Would you judge me if I went up to the store?" Sarah said. "Apparently it's over at the far side of the house."

"Are you kidding? If we came here and didn't go to the store, we'd never hear the end of it from Jamie. I'll meet you up there in a minute. I'm just having a moment with this alpaca." A small russet alpaca with a wild tuft of hair on its crown had gone face-to-face with me at the fence and continued to look deep into my eyes. Its expression was comical and somehow curious, its head turning from side to side as though trying to figure me out.

"You've picked a good one," said a voice at my side, and I turned to see Barbara Burton smiling at me.

"They're funny animals, aren't they?" I said. "I can see why people like to have them."

"I often think that they have me," she said.

"My husband feels the same about most animals. He thinks the term 'cat owner' is ridiculous, given the temperament of cats." The alpaca was looking from me to Barbara and back again.

"Her name is Hester Prynne," Barbara said, stroking the alpaca's long neck.

I laughed. "There's an Alice, too," Barbara added, "after Lewis Carroll, and an Agatha Christie. We have so many that sometimes we're pressed for names, but of course every year there's attrition. I've bred alpacas for twenty years, and the lifespan is between fifteen and twenty. So I lose them on a regular basis. Luckily I have a lot of land, and the ones that die can enrich the earth for the ones that come after."

This was definitely the mother that Stephen Burton had told me about, the one who would stand outside bathing in the light of the full moon and habitually referred to the goddess, although through most of the tour she had sounded more like Mark, an animal husbandry expert explaining her herd.

"Where did your friend get to?" she said.

"She went to the shop. Your sweaters are legendary."

She shrugged. "Yes, I know," Barbara said. "And ridiculously expensive. But they pay for all this, and they provide jobs for dozens of people in the area. Most of them used to be farmers, but there's no money in farming anymore. It's too uncertain. We're also useful for smaller alpaca farms. They send their fleece to us, and we pay them for it. There's a big demand for the sweaters, despite the price tag. I'm sure your friend will find something she likes."

"I'd better join her," I said, reaching out to run my fingers over

Hester's neck. "My friend's not the kind of person who would necessarily buy one of your sweaters for herself, but she's exactly the kind of person who's probably right now buying one for me."

Barbara nodded. "She has that aura," she said. "She's a good woman."

"She absolutely is."

"My granddaughter thinks you're a good woman, too," she said, stroking the alpaca so that our hands bumped against one another's, and seeing the look on my face, she added, "I know who you are, Miss Goodman, and what you're seeking."

"I'm surprised. Maybe a little embarrassed, too. Do you feel like I'm spying on you?"

"Not in the least. You've been kind to a young woman whom you have no reason to accommodate. I'm happy to have the opportunity to thank you. I love Talia, and I worry about her, and she seems to have found some solace through meeting and corresponding with you."

"But she had no idea I was coming here."

"No. I pay close attention to the lists of those coming on the tour. There are activists who believe that keeping the alpacas here is wrong. Some of them think they should all be repatriated to South America."

I laughed. "I'm sorry, I know that's no laughing matter, but I'm picturing a cargo plane filled with alpacas."

"And, by the time it landed, alpaca feces." We both laughed.

"I saw your name on the list. I recognized it right away. I welcomed the opportunity to thank you for your kindness to Talia, and to tell you what I'm sure you already know: You and I are not related. I am most certainly not your mother."

"I know who my mother is."

"So do I. No psychic phenomenon, just an internet search. She seems like a formidable woman."

I nodded. The alpaca did, too. "Do they imitate?" I asked, in part to change the conversation.

"A few of them do. Most of them hum, often in unison. One will start and then the others join in. Some mornings I wake to what sounds like a hundred kazoos." She smiled. "It's a good life. You're welcome here anytime. And I'm happy to provide any help I can in your quest. Everyone deserves to know where they come from so they'll know who they are."

"I think I've finally concluded that a mistake was made, but I appreciate that. And I suppose if it's been helpful to Talia it wasn't a mistake at all, in some karmic way." I couldn't quite believe I'd just said that. What Barbara Burton had must be contagious, although obviously she hadn't passed it on to her very conventional son. To cover my chagrin, I asked, "Why alpacas?"

"Someone gave me one."

"As a gift? An alpaca?"

"He's a careless man of wild enthusiasms. He'd purchased one from a neighbor and then had no idea what to do with it. I liked it instantly. And of course if you have an alpaca you need another to keep it company. And"—with an almost balletic wave of her arm out over the fields—"voila." Hester hummed. "There it is!" I said. "What a funny little sound! No wonder you wanted one. They're pretty irresistible. They look like cartoon characters."

"Or cartoon characters are drawn to look like them."

Sarah was trundling down the steep rise next to the farmhouse carrying two large shopping bags. She waved and lifted them aloft.

"One more thing, Miss Goodman."

"Polly. It's Polly."

"One more thing, Polly. Among other things, I'm a healer. I have been all my life. Perhaps it's the sort of thing you don't believe in, but I can assure you it's true. So can many of the people I've worked with." She tilted her head toward Sarah, her dangling silver earrings clinking slightly, Hester humming behind us. "Your friend should see a doctor. And soon."

UNLIKE THE OTHER HOUSES AROUND THEM, THAT HAD BEEN bought and sold and even bought again, Mark's parents' house had never been modernized. It still had the original double-hung windows that were put in old houses, instead of the big sheets of plate glass that had been installed by many of the neighbors to frame the view of the water. So his mother and I, sitting in the living room, were in a kind of drafty dark cave in front of a fire that barely took the chill off. The old windows didn't do the job anymore, but Mark's father didn't have the will or the cash to replace them. From October until April the fireplaces were always going here.

"You seem abstracted," Lou said, the only sound her knitting needles turning the skeins of alpaca wool Sarah had bought into sweaters for the little girls. She had told me once that one of the most important things a teacher of young children had to cultivate was the ability to read body language, mainly so you would know when they had to pee or throw up when they were unwilling to say so. Almost from our first meeting I had been sure that she had been a model teacher. She had been able to read me from the beginning.

"I hate February," I said, thinking about what Barbara Burton had said about Sarah, avoiding it by avoiding talking about it.

"Well, of course you do," she said, turning the needles. "The best that can be said about February is that at least there's less of it than the other months."

"I'm glad I'm not the only one," I said, putting my book down and throwing another log on.

All the worst things happen in my life after another year has just begun. I know lots of people who dread Christmas and New Year's Eve, who talk about how hard the holidays are if you don't have a family, or you have a family and they drive you crazy. But I hate

January, February, even March, when all the yellow glow has been leached from the air and even the sunshine feels watery and half-hearted. The worst things that have happened to me have happened to me in those months. That's when I found out about Benedict. That's when my mother told me about Edgemere.

I remembered one February scrabbling around in my makeup bag to do something to my face so it wouldn't look like the mask of tragedy and closing my fist around a razor instead of an eyelash curler. For weeks afterward I had one of those thin slits along my palm that bled again every time I opened my hand. It had happened the week after we found out that the little bean embryo had slipped its moorings inside me. I remembered skidding on a slick of ice on the sidewalk and going down hard, sobbing so loudly that one man passing by asked Mark if he should call 911.

"It's all right," Mark had told him, even though it wasn't.

Lou is good with sitting quietly without speaking. She's old-fashioned that way, a throwback to an era when people, or at least women, thought it was fine to be still. She's old-fashioned in other ways, too. She wears her silver hair in a braid pinned to the back of her head and uses Pond's cold cream every night just as her mother did. "She has no business looking that good," Emily had said to me once. All four of her daughters-in-law love her. Soon after Mark and I married, the two of us were sitting by the water, and she said, "You wound up with the easiest of my boys. He got just the right combination of being loved and being left alone."

I'd thought of what she said in the years since, as I'd gotten to know the four Bailey brothers. Thomas, the eldest, the one his parents learned to be parents with. The path blazer, the leader. Douglas, in Thomas's shadow. Michael, the beloved baby. And Mark, the third. She was right; his placement in the lineup had been a gift. When she first said it, I imagined it with my own two, three, maybe four.

All the other members of the family were out, leaving the two of us to sit by the fire while they went to spend the day at a ski resort an hour north. Even Emily had had to go, because Thomas wanted the girls to learn on the bunny slope while he skied the hardest runs. The contradiction between his plans for himself and his desire for his children didn't occur to him. Emily would wear the baby in a front pack. "I don't think I'll be forced to put him on skis until he's at least a year old," she'd said as they left. "I don't want to go skiing," Sophia whined. "You'll love it," her father said.

"We'll stay here and get dinner going," Lou had said. The whole house smelled of stew and woodsmoke.

"Should I turn the oven off?" I asked.

"Another thirty," she said. "What's the book?"

"Anne Sexton's poetry," I said. "I want to teach her in my poetry seminar." I watched Lou's brows go up a fraction.

The head had come to me two weeks before, the day after school started up again, the girls less vivid and joyous at the beginning of second semester, their bare legs shrouded in sweatpants beneath their uniform skirts. Their Caribbean tans were beginning to jaundice. The head fell wearily into the student chair across from my desk. "The Sexton," she said.

"Not again," I said.

I'd hit a speed bump two years before with a senior seminar on personal memoir. Sylvia Plath, *The Bell Jar*. A deputation of mothers had been wild with rage at the notion that their daughters would read a book in which the central character was suffering from depression. The head had asked that I substitute something else.

Apparently a smaller group was concerned about the Sexton, not because of the content—I hadn't even settled on a poem yet, although I was leaning toward the one with the line "I am tired of being brave"—but because surely the girls would discover that the poet had gone into her garage one day, closed the door, and run the car engine. She was wearing a fur coat when she died of carbon monoxide poisoning.

I raised my eyes to the ceiling and shook my head. "Aren't some of the first-years reading *For Whom the Bell Tolls*? Did the mom brigade miss Hemingway and the shotgun?"

"Polly, I hear you. This one is absolutely your call, and I'll support you. Just know you're going to get blowback. For some reason they don't seem to mind it so much if it's men. What about Emily Dickinson?"

"Oh, for God's sake, every girl in the world has to study Emily Dickinson. The AP Art History class is doing Mary Cassatt, right, because God forbid they should do Georgia O'Keeffe, because we know what her paintings look like!"

"I agree with everything you're saying, Polly," the head said wearily. "Assign the Sexton. But if you could avoid assigning 'Wanting to Die,' I would appreciate it." The head had once been an English teacher, too.

"I'm foolhardy," I said. "I'm not reckless."

"You're a great teacher," she said.

"You poor teachers have to be so careful nowadays," said Lou, going to the kitchen to put the kettle on. "Though I did have a kerfuffle when I read that book to the first grade about the two male penguins at the zoo who hatched an egg."

"That's a true story!" I cried.

"Polly," Lou called to me from the kitchen, "remember whose mother I am." Of course she knew it was a true story. Mark had actually known the penguins involved, although they were not up in the Bronx.

"I know two women who use the term *kerfuffle,*" I said almost to myself. Also *thingamajig*. I could remember stumbling upon Sarah and Lou sitting in Sarah's den during drinks after our wedding ceremony, chatting companionably about clematis vines. I didn't know Lou well then, but afterward Sarah had said, "Oh, she is a pip!"

After the head had left me, I began to leaf through the Sexton collection again, so annoyed that when I heard a tap at my office door I had responded, "Enter," instead of "Come in," all ready to rumble. A woman had peered in tentatively, perhaps hearing the irritation in my voice. I scrolled through my mental files quickly. They tended to look alike, the mothers, bobbed hair, turtleneck sweaters, flat shoes, big totes. "Carrie Berg," she said, putting out her hand, and then added, "Josephine's mother."

"Josephine!" I said with a lilt in my voice, and then, remembering our encounter on the street, how unlike herself Josephine had seemed, how I had vowed to follow up with a message and had completely forgotten, I said, my voice pitched lower, "How is she?" And her mother started to cry.

There was not much I could do except, like my mother-in-law did now as I played back the encounter, listen. For reasons her parents couldn't really divine, Josephine had begun to take the train back to the city every weekend to sit in her bedroom, door closed, listening to music. In December she'd come home from Cambridge and refused to go back to college for exam week. She had withdrawn from her classes. She had withdrawn from her Windsor friends. Her mother understood that last part. Her friends were all talking about school, about the courses they were taking, the clubs they were joining. Her father couldn't understand. Josephine was his bright light, his golden girl. Every class, from grade school to high school, from AP Physics to PE, had been an A.

"What are you going to do, wait tables?" he'd apparently shouted when she said she wasn't going to go back to Harvard at all. Because of course Josephine had had to go to Harvard, which was where her father had gone.

"Maybe," Josephine had said, and gone back into her room.

"How can I help?" I finally said as Carrie Berg blew her nose.

"I don't know. I don't know if anyone can help. I don't even know why I'm here, except that she just idolizes you. The way she talked about you—I think she wants to be you. Or wanted to be." And what could I say: Oh good lord, no she doesn't. I remembered with shame the way I had minimized what she must have been feeling that day on the street with my cheap and easy response: You'll be fine. I should know by now how useless—no, insulting, cheap, and easy responses are. *At least he's not in any pain,* about my mute father. *There are so many ways to create a family,* about not being able to create one. *You must be so proud,* about my impenetrable mother. All of us, especially me, should know better, talking in sentences stamped on samplers.

Except for Josephine. What had she said to me as she was leaving that last day? You'll never know what it meant. I didn't know. I hadn't figured it out. I'd had my own cheap and easy response, not just to her, but to the head when she'd come to see me about the assigned reading. If I'd taught Plath and Sexton to a wounded Josephine, would I feel responsible now for her pain?

"Her mother doesn't know whether a visit from me will make her feel better or worse," I said to Lou as she handed me a mug of tea.

"I wish she could speak with our Emily."

"Her mother said she's seeing a therapist already."

"Not so much for that. The same thing happened to Emily her first year at Brown."

"Emily? Incredibly competent, together Emily? I thought Emily went to Smith."

"She did," Mark's mother said. "After she left Brown. Let her tell you the story." Lou picked up her mug and stood as the sound of car doors slamming punctuated by children's crying wafted into the house. She nodded toward the framed photographs that mobbed the table surfaces. I'd studied them all over the years: Lou young and slender framed in a doorway, Lou pregnant with two little boys standing in front of her, Lou thick and dowdy, Lou now thin in that way of older women, as though their heft was being worn down by the years. But always with the braid pinned up on the back of her head. "Time passes," she said. "Things change. You think, Oh, this is a tragedy. And then time passes, and it's not. It's over. At my age, the edges of everything seem . . . softer, I suppose? Oh goodness, I sound like an old fart."

"I hate skiing!" Sophia screamed in the kitchen.

"Let's make you some cocoa, sweet pea," Lou called to her.

Would I have asked her what I should do about Sarah if the skiing party had not returned in bad humor? Barbara Burton had told me Sarah should see a doctor, and I'd evaded the question of whether to say anything to Sarah and, if I did, what. All I'd done is dance around it. In the car, on our way back from the alpaca farm, I had asked Sarah about her health. "I had a physical in September," she said brightly. On our last walk around the reservoir, a savage wind whipping around the paths and tearing at our jackets, I'd wondered aloud whether she still needed to have scans, now that she was four years out. She was down to once a year now, she said, and she was having one next month. "Do we have to do the last loop, or can we go have coffee?" she added, and I dropped it.

She'd seemed so delighted with our trip to the farm, and she seemed so well and happy that I didn't want to cast a long shadow over it with Barbara's peculiar valedictory message. Sarah had been glowing as she handed around the sweaters at Helen's apartment during our New Year's book club meeting, the one that didn't include a book, just resolutions. "Oh my dear God!" Jamie had said, unwrapping an oversized turtleneck in a reddish color. "Hester Prynne!" I'd said. "That's the alpaca that wool came from! I know her."

Sarah had laughed. "Polly made a friend, and she was almost exactly the color of your sweater," she said. "Helen, I hope you like the blue. Apparently they dye it with some herbs or seeds or something. It looked like your color."

My sweater was the Fair Isle, the same one I'd first seen on Talia.

"You spent a fortune," said Jamie, pulling her turtleneck over her head.

"That looks so good on you," I said.

"I had so much fun," Sarah said. "Alpacas look like cartoon characters."

"Or cartoon characters look like them," I said. "That's what Barbara says."

"Did you meet her?" Helen said.

"She ran the tour," Sarah said. "And while I was shopping, Polly was talking to her."

"She wanted to assure me that she is not my mother. Which I knew. Apparently she'd heard all about me from her son, and from Talia."

"She seems motherly on the website," Helen said.

Sarah hummed. Now whenever I heard anyone humming, I thought of alpacas. "Alpacas hum," I'd said to Mark as soon as I'd walked in the door after our trip to the farm.

"Yep," he said, looking up from a book. "Foxes laugh. They also scream during sex. Humans tend to think they're the only species that makes identifiable sounds. How was it?"

"Great. I really like alpacas. Barbara Burton is really interesting. Really interesting."

"No relation?"

"None," I said, getting ready to repeat what she'd said about Sarah. And then I didn't. I couldn't. I was paralyzed by the absurdity and the importance. Stayed paralyzed by it. Diagnosis as fortune-telling. Intuition as fate. Maybe if I ever saw Barbara again I would ask about infertility. Maybe she already knew, had sensed that about me. Or maybe it was just all nonsense, what she called on her blog her "healing vibrations." That had to be my conclusion, watching Sarah watching us so happily with our beautiful new sweaters. Nonsense.

"Motherly," Sarah repeated, sipping on some eggnog. "I don't think so, really. I don't know if she's what I'd call motherly. She seems like the kind of woman who wants to save the world. Some of the women I'm on boards with are like that. And don't get me wrong, they're wonderful. They step up on every committee and they give piles of money. But I think when someone cares about everyone, they might not be as good at just caring about you. Instead of an earth mother maybe it's better to just have a mother."

"Never mind that," said Jamie. "Did you buy yourself a sweater?"

"I'm embarrassed to say I did," said Sarah. "I couldn't resist. I figured I'll wear it forever. And I got wool for Polly's mother-in-law so she can knit a sweater herself."

ALONE IN THE KITCHEN, LOADING THE DISHWASHER AFTER Easter dinner, I had asked Emily what she would do. "What if a person who called themselves a healer said a friend of yours should see a doctor?" I asked, sniffing at a mildewed sponge and tossing it in the trash.

"A healer?"

"That's what she says."

"Was it the sweater lady? Sorry, but Mark told Douglas, and Douglas told Tess, and Tess told Lou, and Lou told me. Not what she actually said, just that she's the kind of person who would call herself a healer." Emily's skepticism on that last word was so great that it made the term sound ridiculous.

"This family," I said. "So what should I do?"

"Does your friend have a sense of humor?" Emily said.

"Mommy, come!" Sophia screamed from the head of the stairs.

"Go to Daddy," Emily called back.

"He won't!"

"The hell he won't," Emily said to herself, pouring out the rest of her wine. "If I have any more of that I'll have to pump and dump. Which is such an attractive phrase, isn't it?"

"Mommy!"

"I don't know, Polly," Emily said. "My inclination would be not to say anything, but you know how cynical I am about all the woo-woo things going around. When one of my patients starts to talk about biofeedback I have to stop myself from saying they might as well just put their money in the fire pit and strike a match."

Thomas stood in the doorway tapping his foot in a spotless running shoe. "Sophia says she's going to puke," he said.

"Tommy, honey, you have an MBA and a high professional tolerance for bullshit," Emily said. "I'm confident you can deal with it."

"She only wants you."

"You can't always get what you want. Want me to sing it for you?"

"I'll finish up, Em," I said.

"Polly will finish up," Thomas said. "They all had too much junk from their Easter baskets. All year they can't have any candy, and then Easter comes around and it's all jelly beans and chocolate eggs."

"Don't forget Halloween," Emily said, pushing past him.

"I worry about Emily and Thomas," I said to Mark as we sat in the waiting room at the fertility clinic. "They're very edgy with each other."

"My brother's edgy with everyone. He was edgy when they got married. I remember him throwing a fit because he didn't like the wine at the rehearsal dinner. My mother had to take him aside for one of her little talks."

"'Thomas Elliot Bailey, I did not raise my boys to behave this way.'"

"I think that's exactly what she said."

"I asked Emily what I should do about what Barbara said about Sarah. And, by the way, she already knew about Barbara because of you telling Douglas."

"Sorry, sorry. I always forget that instead of trickle-down economics we have trickle-down information. What did Emily say?"

"We didn't get to finish the conversation. Sophia was threatening to throw up."

"They had too much Easter candy," Mark said, glancing at his phone.

"Everybody in the Bronx okay?"

"The field trips have already begun," he said. "I feel for the teachers, but there's too much tapping on the glass in the reptile house. Then the little girls start to scream, and all hell breaks loose."

"You haven't told me whether you think I should say something to Sarah."

"That's because you've done everything but. You told me what Barbara Burton said to you at the alpaca farm. You also told me that you'd already asked Sarah about her checkups, and she said she'd had all the tests and they were all fine. It sounded like she'd done all the things that she would have done if you'd told her what Barbara said, even though you hadn't told her what Barbara said. Sarah was supposed to see a doctor. She saw a doctor. That was the point, right?"

"But maybe the doctor would look more closely."

"Sarah's doctors are the best in the city. Sarah's given that hospital a big gift. They probably examine her very closely. You can still say something to Sarah if it's bothering you that much, but it doesn't sound like she would do anything more than she's already done."

Yes, I thought, that's true, and Barbara Burton is an alpaca farmer, not a physician, and nothing bad can happen to Sarah. That's my deal with God or the universe or whoever is running things. I looked sideways at my husband in the clinic waiting room. I remembered being in a restaurant with him after he said we would marry, when I still thought he was crazy to say so, when the piped-in music had been "My Funny Valentine." Mark had begun to sing it softly: "Your looks are laughable, unphotographable." It's true, I'd thought, looking at Mark, but then he had reprised the line "You make me smile with my heart." That was truer.

And meeting Mark, marrying Mark, was all because of Sarah. Mark had followed me into the elevator after that fundraiser, had walked with me to the corner. "Aren't you cold?" I'd said, and he'd looked down as though it had just occurred to him that he wasn't wearing a coat. "No," he said, "I like the cold," instead of saying, "I left my winter coat on the rack in the lobby that they put out for parties." Next morning the doorman had told Sarah and she had come down and looked at the rack, one sad limp anorak at one end of it like a person who had shed his skin. Mark's wallet was in one pocket, his phone in the other. "How on earth did you get home, Dr. Bailey?" she had asked him. "I walked," he said. "Can you give me the number of your friend, the one who was wearing the white shirt? She said she was a teacher. An English teacher. I'm a good guy, really. I'll take no for an answer if she doesn't want to go out with me."

Mark looked back at me in the clinic waiting room and smiled. "Thank God you forgot your coat," I said.

"You're telling me," he said, as he always did.

Jeannine came out of Dr. Betz's office smiling that smile people have when they like you but they know you won't like what they have to say. An intensely sympathetic smile. "Hey, you two," she said. "Come on in."

Here's the thing about Dr. Betz, whose white coat was draped over her office chair: She's known for having The Talk. It's why some people told us their friends avoided her, chose someone like the doctor Mark had hated, the one who name-checked the rhinos and whose practice is famous for continuing. No matter how old you got, no matter how unsuccessful you had been, they would keep at it. Jamie said she knew someone who had gone through eleven rounds of IVF at that practice, the last one at fifty-two years old. "I don't think I agree with that," Sarah had said, glancing at me.

"Neither do I," I'd said.

Dr. Betz won't do that. At some point she sits couples down for The Talk. She's not firing you as a patient, even though that was how I tended to think of it. She wanted you to know that she might have reached the end of certain kinds of artistry, sorcery, fertility magic.

"Our options have been narrowing," she said as Mark twined his fingers through mine, and for some reason I thought of Barbara Burton. Wasn't there some tea, some tincture, that she could cook up to turn my womb into a safe place for nine months? I looked down and realized I was squeezing Mark's hand so hard that his knuckles had gone flour white. I released and watched the blood pink them up again.

Blood rushed into his fingers and into my ears, so that afterward Mark had to fill me in on some of the things I'd missed. We could try some more rounds of egg retrieval and implantation, but past experience and lab results suggested they might be no more successful than the three before. Embryo donation was probably out, although that was something Jeannine and I had already discussed. I'd been incredulous, but apparently it was a real thing, some nice couple in South Carolina or Ohio who'd frozen a half dozen and decided two kids were plenty would be willing to pass their remaining embryos along to us. "Look," I imagined them saying, looking at our profile, "a teacher and a vet! That's good!" Adoption before birth, Jeannine had said, but not likely for us, because embryos weren't necessarily the problem, their incubator might be. In other words, me.

"Some couples with your profile choose surrogacy and have excellent results," Dr. Betz said. "Some choose surrogacy and use a donor egg." What was wrong with me that I just couldn't manage to embrace that idea, that every time I started to think about some nice woman walking around in maternity clothes with our fetus inside, my mind did a sharp U-turn. It was the same with conventional adoption. "It's as though she was always ours," someone had said to me at a party the year before. "It was as though I recognized her the moment they put her in my arms." Could I? Would I? Those questions might be moot. We were running out of time and running out of money.

"Intellectually I know how well it can work," I had said to Emily, sitting overlooking the sound one day.

"This isn't an intellectual decision," she'd said, braiding Rebecca's hair. "You feel what you feel."

All I felt was empty.

"I want a cheeseburger," Mark said out on the sidewalk. "With bacon." Two, he told the waitress when we were in the booth at the brew bar on the corner of Lexington Avenue: two burgers with fries. And two chocolate shakes. And a side of onion rings.

"I guess I could have a shot and a beer now if I wanted to, now that I don't have to be careful anymore," I said.

"Maybe not today," Mark said, turning a spoon around and around in his hand.

"So we'll be those people now," I continued, my voice hard. "One of those couples who go through life as a matched set, like salt and pepper shakers, and their friends with kids envy them and say, You two, anytime you want you can go to Paris, you have no idea about private school tuitions, about the kids with the issues, you just get to live your life, do what you want. We'll be those people. We're even a trend, aren't we, I keep reading about it, all these people who aren't having children, and it says they don't want to bring kids into this crazy world with pollution and inflation and the economy, but maybe they aren't counting the ones who spent all their money trying and trying and nothing happened and who just pretend, Oh, it's fine, it's fine just the two of us, we'll go to Paris, I don't even like Paris."

"Oh my dear heart," said Mark sadly, reaching across the table and knocking over the ketchup bottle as he scrabbled to pass me a handful of napkins from the dispenser. I put my head in my hands and cried, years of disappointment running between my fingers. *Clunk, clunk,* as the waitress put the heavy restaurant plates down, with the mingled smell of hot meat and dill pickle, and then a hand on my shoulder.

I looked up. "Listen, honey," she said in the creaky-door voice of a veteran diner waitress, "it all comes out in the wash. Everything."

THE JUNE BOOK CLUB MEETING TOOK PLACE EVERY YEAR OUTside the city. At Jamie's house in the Hamptons, at Helen's in Sag Harbor, at the home of my in-laws, which was what I had to offer in the way of out of town. Naturally Jamie bitched about it for months, and then we all had a good time, and she acknowledged that we had at the end of the day, and then promptly forgot all about what a good time we'd had when it came around again. Helen had reminded her of that once, and she'd said, shrugging, "You girls need to allow me my petty grievances." We used that as a catchphrase now: petty grievance, we'd say when someone complained about something small. But it had to be small.

"I'll arrange a car," Jamie said.

"I'll drive mine," Helen said.

"I've driven with you. I'm getting a car."

"Fine by me," I said. "Except that when we talk in the back seat we have to be judicious. Every time we get a car I can tell we shock some poor driver. There was that memorable waxing discussion. I thought the guy was going to drive off the road."

"Whatever," Jamie said.

The house where Sarah lived in the country was not the one where Richard had lived when they first met. Apparently that one had been, in Sarah's words, terribly grand, endless rooms, terraced gardens, a pool. Soon after they married it had been sold. Richard thought it was because it was shadowed by his first wife in the mind of his second one, but it was really that it wasn't Sarah's kind of place. They'd bought a cottage that had once been part of a big estate, stone and slate, three bedrooms, none of them large, a few acres hemmed in by trees and state game lands. Cozy, Sarah always said. It was one of her favorite words. That's what she'd said about the Warm As

Toast sweaters as she handed them around: "They're so cozy." Jamie had snorted. "At those prices they'd better be cozy as hell," she said. "Cozy squared."

Pulling into the driveway to Sarah's house was like entering one of those gardening picture books my mother-in-law had sitting in her living room, that always made her sigh and say, "My lavender never looks anything like that." There were peonies everywhere, white and pink. In a month, I knew, there would be day lilies, and the trumpet vines climbing the trellis to the side door would be flowering red. Even Jamie, never the romantic, climbed out of the car and inhaled deeply. "Oh my God, that smell," she said.

"I love peonies," Helen said, and Jamie, snapping back to her default setting, said, "Find me someone who doesn't love peonies."

"I'm happy to send out sandwiches to the driver," said Sarah, standing in the doorway, a hand on either jamb, white pants, floral shirt. It looked like a casual pose. I tried not to imagine she was holding herself up.

"I told him to go gas up and get lunch," Jamie said.

"He now knows that Jamie's daughters started their periods," Helen said.

Jamie shrugged. "I'm not going to edit myself for the sake of a limo driver," she said, hugging Sarah.

"Do you edit yourself for anyone?" Helen said.

"You're too thin," Jamie said to Sarah.

"We haven't even gotten into the house yet and we've already started," I said, trying to divert Jamie, who was the kind of person who would squeeze your waist if she thought your weight was up or down.

"Wait until you see what Estelle made for lunch!" Sarah said.

It was always a cookbook for this meeting, and Jamie always said dryly that at least she could be sure that no one had read that book, although Mark usually used the ones I brought home, a fact I kept to myself. Four copies of *Middle Eastern Feasts for the Home Cook* were on the kitchen counter, along with a chicken-and-dumplings casserole and a spinach salad with lots of bacon and caramelized onions. The French doors to the back patio were open and a table set outside with checked napkins and patterned plates. So perfect and lovely and I would have been fine if Sarah had not cocked her head and given me a warning look.

"I think I have a gnat in my eye," I said with a quaver in my voice, dabbing with a dishcloth.

"Polly, all those hormones are making you nuts," said Jamie, who was heaping her plate.

"I'm not doing that anymore," I said. "We've stopped." Which led me to quaver in earnest.

I have to say this for Jamie: She can go from backhand to soft shoulder in a matter of seconds. Maybe she has to do that in her therapy sessions when the husband storms out and the wife breaks down. There's no other way to say it: She enfolded me. And she's a lot shorter than I am.

"I didn't know," she said. Pat pat pat. "My stupid mouth." Pat pat pat. "I wish you'd told us." Pat.

"You don't need to talk about it, Polly," Helen said softly, and for once Jamie didn't insist on knowing everything.

"I decided to take a break," I said when we were finally sitting outside eating. "And it looks like the break's going to be permanent. Dr. Betz is too nice to put it that way, but I'm running out of time."

"There are other options," Helen said, but Sarah raised a hand in the air. It was practically transparent, or at least I imagined so. The sunlight filtering through the maple trees at one edge of the property seemed to throw her blue veins into high relief, like a map of streets, the roads to Sarah's heart. Her good heart. I started to seize again, but luckily everyone assumed it had nothing to do with Sarah and everything to do with me.

"I think we all know that Polly knows all about any and every option available, and that she and Mark have considered them,"

Sarah said. "If they pursue one, maybe she'll let us know, or maybe she won't. If they don't, they don't."

"Agreed," said Jamie, and Helen nodded. Sarah smiled. "Lemon squares for dessert," she said. She'd cut all her food up into little pieces and then, as far as I could tell, pushed it into small piles and eaten almost none of it. Half a dumpling, a piece of bacon.

"I love this meeting most of all, I think," Sarah said, hugging us at the door when it was time to go. And as the other two walked out to the waiting car, enormous bouquets of peonies in hand, cookbooks under their arms—"I'm giving mine to the driver," Jamie had said as we were leaving—Sarah said softly to me, "That was a lot for you. Thank you for doing that for me."

"Thank you for doing that for me," she had said at the end of our walk the week before in the park, the paths alive with people, the lawns full of sunbathers. I'd cried then, too, only pulled myself together because I realized I was making Sarah feel worse. It was true, she was too thin, and we walked as slowly as we'd ever done, even when she was having chemo.

"Let's sit," she'd said before we'd gone very far, stopping at a bench in the shadow of a big tree on a path that ran downhill and seemed mostly deserted. She'd taken my hand in hers and said, "Polly, my dear friend, I am really, really sick and I need you to know it."

When I managed to speak, after two bird-watchers had passed by enthusiastically talking about an owl in the Ramble, I said, "I knew. I knew. And I didn't say anything. I was such a coward. I knew."

"I don't know what you mean."

"When we were at the farm. Barbara Burton said you needed to see a doctor. I didn't know whether to believe her, and after everything you've gone through I didn't know whether I should say anything. I agonized, I agonized, who was I to agonize? It was nothing but cowardice is what it was. I couldn't bear to think about it, or to say it to you, and maybe if I had, then, you would have caught whatever it was earlier. She told me, and I didn't know whether to believe her, so I didn't say anything. I'm so sorry. I'm so, so sorry."

"Oh, honey," said Sarah, smoothing my wet hair back from the side of my face, "she told me, too."

"What?"

"I put my name and email address on their mailing list when I bought the sweaters. She sent me an email, and then she called me. She said she was concerned that it would be too much for you. 'Imparting that sort of news,' is how I think she put it. So she told me, and I told the doctors."

Sarah shrugged. Her collarbones, oh, her collarbones, with nothing but the thinnest coating of pale silk skin over them. "Better safe than sorry," she said.

"She should have told me. You should have told me she told you."

"I'm telling you now. I had a PET scan, and it looked a little squirrelly, and they did another one, and then one weekend I woke up in Connecticut and told Estelle what I wanted for breakfast, and apparently I wasn't making any sense. She thought I was having a stroke. Luckily one of my doctors has a place a half hour away, and the hospital has a satellite nearby. I won't give you the full name because half the time I can't remember it myself, but there were a lot of the blue meanies bouncing around between my skull and my brain, muddling the signals so that my speech didn't make much sense, and I wasn't exactly sure where or who I was for a few days. They told me it's something that happens sometimes when someone's had what I had before."

"What I had before." That's what Sarah has called it since she got the all clear. "The blue meanies" is what Sarah had called them at the time. "I'm sorry, but that drives me crazy," Jamie had said once when Sarah was in the bathroom, and when she saw the look on both Helen's face and mine, she'd muttered, "All right, all right, this is me backing off."

Sarah sighed. "At least it wasn't a stroke. They did a couple of go-rounds with a tin hat and some heavy zapping with the radiation, and I made sense again. Although my memory is still a little shot. Let me see, what's your name again?"

"Really? You're going to joke about this?"

"You have to laugh to keep from crying, my grandma always said."

"Barbara Burton can actually suss out something like this?"

"I told my doctor that. He was highly skeptical, to say the least. He said correlation does not imply causation. But I did tell Barbara."

"And I bet she said there's some magical herb you can try. Lungwort or tansy or something, that will cure it all."

Sarah smiled. "She said she was sorry."

"She should be sorry. She should have told me she told you. Oh, never mind, I can't believe I just made this about me."

"It is about you. That's why we're sitting here talking. You'll miss me."

When I could speak again I said, "There has to be something."

"There isn't."

"There's always something."

"Can we forgo that part of the discussion? It's not helpful. Here's what's helpful: your knowing. There won't be many others. I'll tell the boys. Estelle knows, and of course my doctors."

"Mark?"

"Oh, of course, sweetie, that goes without saying. I wouldn't ask you to keep anything from Mark. But that's it. If I tell Helen and Jamie the book club meeting will become a pity party. I can't bear that. I know you'll have to put on your best poker face, but I'm counting on you to do it. We have the getaway at my house next week. I need you not to show anything. I know that'll be hard, but you can do it. And if I start to flag . . ."

"We'll think of something. I'll think of something."

But she hadn't. She hadn't flagged for even a minute. If you didn't know, you wouldn't know. Or so I thought. The car was overwhelmed with the sweet scent of peonies even though we had put them in the back, in the hatch. Helen fell asleep and Jamie was quiet, staring out the window, until the grittier end of the city came into view. Then she said, without turning her head, "She's sick again, isn't she?"

"What? Because of the weight loss? She's always been thin."

Jamie turned and looked at me. "You're a crap liar, Polly," she said, and turned back to the window. "Really crap."

ONE OF THE STRANGE THINGS ABOUT LIVING IN NEW YORK City is that you don't really clock the weather the way people elsewhere do. Every once in a while there's a snowstorm so big that even we have to notice it, although it turns from blanket to mush pretty fast, and in all my years at Windsor we've only had two snow days, and both were Mondays and we teachers thought it was probably because too many families couldn't drive in from their country houses. Occasionally some city agency will declare a heat emergency, and everyone will stay inside in the air-conditioning, and because of that there are sometimes brownouts. The animals at the zoo mainly stay in the shade, or in the water pools. Mark orders chicken broth popsicles for some of the big cats, and there are sprinklers in some of the enclosures. He says it's the zoo workers and the visitors who are the ones in greatest danger of heatstroke.

But even though we could both hear the wind rattling the cable lines that snake down the back of our building, we hadn't paid much attention to the thunderstorm alerts we got on our phones. We'd had a nice morning. Sunday midday and the opening of an art show by a former colleague of Mark's who painted animals, nicely, we both thought. I took the artist aside and put a hold on a portrait of a hippo that I thought my husband would like for his birthday.

"He always wanted to paint," Mark had said as we came up the subway steps. "He only became a vet because his father was a vet." And then, "Whoa, something's happening," he said, taking my hand as every bit of trash on the street seemed to swirl around us in a grubby tornado, as though we were in *The Wizard of Oz* and New York would become the Emerald City as soon as the wind died down.

But once we came in the door of our building, which swung crazily as we opened it, all seemed still. There was a distant boom of thunder, a silver light outside our windows that might have been lightning, but nothing to worry about until Mark's phone rang sometime later when we were both reading in the living room.

"Oh Jesus," he said. "Yes. Yes. Right now. Yes."

You don't really appreciate the kind of damage a storm can do when you live in the city, either. The buildings seem to inoculate the trees, even in the parks, although in parts of Brooklyn and Queens that's not as true. But I had never seen anything quite like what happened to Mark's parents' house when the enormous pine near one corner tore from its roots, rising from a hole in the earth like some kind of prehistoric monster, and crashed through the roof into one of the bedrooms and through its floor to the living room, where Lou and Skipper had been sitting after cleaning up the kitchen once Thomas and Emily had packed up the kids and left for Maine.

"I can't thank God enough that those children weren't playing outside," Lou kept repeating. "They could have been killed. I just thank God. I can't even think about it."

"We would have called them in when that wind picked up," Skipper said. Blood had trickled down his temple where a spar of broken branch that came through the old plaster ceiling had made a ragged tear along his forehead when he leapt from the sofa at the crashing sound. "I jumped right up to meet the damn thing," he said. "It was a freak accident."

"Dad, there's a tree inside your house," Mark said. "I don't think freak accident really covers it."

"Oh my lord, the sound, Polly, first the sound of the wind, it was like a train was coming right at the house, and then, I don't know why, there isn't a train line here for miles, but then I heard the crashing and I thought a train was coming right at the house, right into the house. That sound, I'll be hearing it forever. Oh my lord, thank God none of the rest of you were here, it happened in a second, just a second."

All four of us were gathered together in the kitchen afraid that the tree, which only came through the old living room ceiling a foot or two, might fall farther. The wind was still shrieking outside, although Skipper said he thought it was dying down. Mark had had to hold tight to the wheel as we drove, and still the car had shimmied across the highway, driven by wind and water both.

Bless Thomas, whose way of dealing with a disaster was to turn it into a business deal. By the time he and Emily had arrived at her family's place in Maine, he had already spoken to people—"at the highest levels"—at the company that insured the house. Apparently their emergency team would be on site the next day. When I went up the back stairs and peered into the hallways and then the bedroom that was full of tree, there was less rainwater than I would have expected. "The tree is kind of acting like the cork in the bottle," I said to Lou. "It's hard to tell, but I don't think it hit any plumbing pipes, and we have lights, so the electric must still be okay."

"Don't go up there again, Polly. It makes me very, very nervous. It was bad enough, seeing him bleeding in the living room, but if anything happened to one of you, that would be it for me."

"Dad, I could stitch this for you, but a couple of butterfly bandages might be enough," Mark said, his father's head tilted onto the back of one of the kitchen chairs. "It might leave a scar, though."

"Son, with how beat-up this old face is, I don't think anybody will even notice a scar. I sure as hell won't. Lulu, will you love me less with a scar on my forehead? Will it be a reminder of my foolishness?"

"I won't need any reminder," Lou said, but I think she was talking about the disaster, not Skipper's reaction to it.

There was a full first aid kit in the pantry. I'd always said it looked like it belonged on a fire truck or in an ambulance, but teacher of small children as she was, grandmother of the same, Lou kept it fully stocked. "Good job, Mom," Mark said, peering inside.

"I wish there was something in there for my nerves," she said.

"You wouldn't take it anyhow," Mark said, opening a sterile towelette.

"I'll make tea," I said.

I crept back up the stairs while Skipper was talking to Thomas on the phone. Luckily the linen closet was at the end of the hallway, far from what I knew I would always think of as the tree bedroom. I struggled with a stack of quilts as I came down the stairs. We could sleep on the floor in the den and give Skipper the recliner and Lou the couch. There were plenty of pillows. "Your mother loves a throw pillow," I had said to Mark the first time we ever visited.

"Thomas says he'll come and get us tomorrow and bring us up to Emily's parents' in Maine," Skipper said.

"I don't want to do that," Lou said. "I like Emily's parents all right, but that house isn't big enough for all of us, and the last thing I need now is to feel like a charity case." I could tell she was close to tears at the wreck of her beloved house, the idea of being a guest in someone else's. The displacement, the destruction. I'd seen her looking out the kitchen window. There had been six Adirondack chairs by the water. Two of them looked like firewood. Two had been blown to the tree line and sat on their sides. Two had disappeared. They were probably at the bottom of the sound.

"You can stay at our place," I said.

"There's not enough room to swing a cat in your place, Polly," Lou said sharply, and that's how I knew how upset she was. Lou was never sharp.

"I've never really understood the concept of swinging a cat," Mark said, and I knew he had heard the unfamiliar sharpness, too. But more than anything the cat swinging reminded me that I was supposed to bring Sarah breakfast in the morning at her apartment, and spend the day there, and that I needed to tell her that was impossible. Jamie had tormented her on and off for an hour after she used cat swinging in conversation once.

I sidled into the den and called Sarah in the city. Estelle answered. "Don't wake her if she's asleep," I said.

"That's silly," Sarah said on the extension. "It's not even six o'clock. I've been sitting here on the window seat watching this storm roll through."

"That's why I'm calling," I said, and I gave her the slightly expurgated version in case Lou wandered by and heard the word "disaster."

"I guess we'll find them a hotel room tomorrow," I said.

"That's ridiculous," said Sarah. "I have the perfect solution."

In the kitchen Lou was drinking tea, her hands shaking slightly. Skipper was on the phone with Douglas. "Your mother says absolutely not," he was saying. "Another county heard from with an offer of shelter," Mark whispered to me. All the others were being kept away. Maybe we were only tolerated because Mark had simply said to his father, "On my way," without asking permission. Or maybe, as I'd often quietly thought—and Emily had said more than once—Mark was the favorite.

"You both must remember my friend Sarah, who hosted the wedding at her apartment? She's at her place in the city, but she has a house about twenty minutes from here, and she says you absolutely must stay there until this place is habitable again. She says to tell you both that she's so sorry and she'll be very offended if you don't take her up on her offer." Actually, Sarah hadn't said that, although she would have. But I'd just thrown it in for effect.

"That would be a terrible imposition," Lou said.

"It's the perfect solution," Mark said. "Man, it is so the perfect solution. She's the best, isn't she? Mom, you loved her when you met her at the wedding."

"She was at Polly's fortieth, too," Lou said. "I really did take to her. She's easy to like. But offering to lend her house—it's just too much."

"It'll only be for a couple of nights, Lulu," said Mark's father, and I knew we were good.

Lou put down her tea and peered into the living room. From time to time I could hear creaking noises from above and hoped that the brothers' constant complaints about their parents' failing hearing was accurate.

"I don't even think we should be in here until someone takes a look at the damage," said Mark, whose hearing is acute.

The two of us went upstairs, Mark packing for his father, me for his mother. "Not too much," I said, "or she'll realize they're in for the long haul."

"All I can say is, there's nothing too good I can ever do for Sarah. She's a saint, especially given what's going on in her own life. She's just a saint. She's saved the day here."

I carried two duffel bags out to the car. Looking up, I saw that the tree had come in right next to one of the turrets on the corner of the house that Rebecca was always insisting should be turned into a room for her. "Sophia can have the other one," she always said, and "I don't want it. I think it's creepy," her sister always said.

I wondered what Rebecca would say now, the turret detached, hanging to one side like a hat on a peg. I wondered if I could get Lou out to the car under an umbrella in the rain so that maybe she wouldn't see it. I tilted the umbrella to one side as she slid into the passenger seat of our car. Mark was driving his father in their car, mainly so he could talk about how they would manage with the insurance adjustors, the repairs. Twice we had to detour because of trees down on the back roads, but when we pulled into Sarah's driveway there were only some stray branches rattling against the undercarriage of the car, and a willow by the pond that had a big limb askew, taking its time to topple. It had even stopped raining.

"Well now," Lou said. "Isn't this a sweet, sweet place? And isn't your friend so nice to let us stay here."

"She says the fridge is full. There's a generator that'll come on automatically if the wind kicks up again and the power goes out."

"And the trees aren't too close to the house," said Lou, standing by the car. "Well now," she said again when we got inside, looking around at the nice comfy couches and the long wooden table in the dining room. It was a little like what Lou and Skipper's house would have been like if four boys hadn't rampaged through it for years.

"We'll take the smaller guest room," Mark said. That's where we had stayed that week that Sarah asked us to housesit, which had really been a vacation for the two of us.

"No, no," Skipper said. "You two head home. We're fine here. Better than fine."

"I agree," said Lou. "I'll feel better with time to myself. I don't want to make you both feel bad, but I need to not have fussing." I opened my mouth and she said, "Polly, you will fuss, you won't be able to help yourself. We'll be fine. We'll go over tomorrow and see what's what in the light of day. All I need from you is Sarah's number so I can call and thank her so much, so very much. This is a port in a storm." She looked around. "Maybe we should buy a nice little place like this."

"Now Lulu," Skipper said, patting her back, "you've gone through a trauma, but don't get carried away. You love that old house, and Thomas says the insurance people will get it fixed back up so we won't even be able to tell what happened."

"I'll never forget what happened," Lou said.

I'm never staying in that tree bedroom, I thought to myself. I'm telling Emily to avoid it, too.

"You're just traumatized," Skipper said, and his wife drew back and glared at him.

"I survived those miscarriages," she said. "I sure as hell can get through this!"

Mark and I were silent for the first ten minutes of the drive back to the city. "I think we're the ones who are traumatized," I said. "I didn't know that. About the miscarriages."

"First I've heard about it," Mark said. "Plus my mother said *hell*. I don't know that I've ever heard her say *hell*."

"She's a *heck* person," I said.

"Exactly. Does she know about Sarah?"

"No," I said. "No one does, really. She says she doesn't want people to see her as a dead woman walking. Although you know your mother. She'd take one look and know something was up."

"She's a saint. Sarah, I mean. What a thing to do. They're twenty minutes away from their place but they're also safe and sound. Shouldn't she be using the place herself? It's July."

It was true. No one was in the city except for us. Helen wanted us to come to Sag Harbor, Jamie to the Hamptons. We were staying home and sticking to our weekend routine, walking by the Hudson and watching red-tailed hawks catch rats in Riverside Park.

"I'm going to go see Sarah tomorrow. I'll ask her about her plans, but you know the way she is. She'll say your parents should stay there as long as it takes. Maybe she'll visit them. She and Lou can use antique expressions together."

By the time we got to the Bronx the sun was shining, a perfect summer evening, as though nothing bad had happened. "Look," said Mark, and there was the incandescent arc of a double rainbow in the faded sky.

I TAUGHT TWO SEMINARS FOR ENGLISH TEACHERS DURING THE summer, one on curricula for girls, another on getting students interested in poetry, two days a week for each. But it seemed that in between those, I was spending more time in the country than the city, at Edgemere, at my in-laws' poor battered house, at Sarah's cottage. Sarah herself had apparently been driven up by Estelle one day to check that Lou and Skipper felt at home in her house, and there had been, according to all parties, what sounded like an endless back-and-forth about Lou and Skipper's moving out. "We can go back to our own house anytime," Skipper had said. "I won't hear of it," Sarah said. "We're taking advantage of your kindness," Lou told her. "You deadheaded the roses," Sarah replied. Like that, apparently.

On the way back to the city Sarah had had Estelle drive her over to the house on the sound. When Thomas had first seen it, he'd said, "Jesus Christ almighty," and Skipper told Mark (who told me, who told Emily, who said, "I'll talk to him") that he'd had to read Thomas "the riot act, son, had to" in case he rattled Lou any further with his reports of devastation. Skipper got in the car every day to check on the progress of the work crews, which, he said, was too damn slow, but what can you do? Lou cooked and weeded.

"She's taking such good care of the gardens," Sarah said. "As far as I'm concerned they can stay indefinitely. They keep talking about putting me out, but I have a lot to do here in the city."

"For example?" I said.

"Having breakfast with you when you're free," Sarah said. I tried to do that every week, too, and not to notice how she pushed the food around on her plate, not to look at her collarbone or her translucent hands. All her pretty rings were in a dish on her bureau, because they slid right off now.

"How is she really, Estelle?" I asked when I was leaving, and Estelle, a woman of few words, shrugged, her face seized by that spasm, cousin to a frown, that meant she was using every muscle in it not to cry.

It was a busy time for me, which was good because it kept me from worrying too much about all the things I had to worry about. One morning I had coffee with Lou on the cottage patio, went over to their house to listen to Skipper talk about the dry rot the workers had found in the roof rafters, and then finished the morning by driving an hour into the mountains to visit Josephine. She was sitting on a bench at the edge of the lawn, where the walking trails began, a book in her lap. She'd cut her long curly hair so that it was a kind of corkscrew frame around her face. "You're too thin," Jamie would have said to her, but I didn't. I didn't know what to say. "Your hair looks good like that," I said. Which was true, but what a lame opener.

"My mother said you were going to come," Josephine said. "I'm glad. You didn't need to, but I'm really glad to see you."

"What are you reading?" I said.

"John Ashbery's collection," she said. "For pleasure. I'm reading for pleasure." And she laughed, a laugh with something caught in the throat of it.

The Refuge bore more than a passing resemblance to Edgemere Place. Lawns, verandas, terraces, except that everyone was younger, some as young as Josephine. She'd been there a month and, according to her mother, would stay at least a month more, maybe two. Her mother drove up three times a week—two to visit, once for family therapy. She still looked stunned when she spoke of her daughter, of how somehow they had gone from listening to Josephine give the senior speech at graduation, the stained glass of the rose window shining pink on her wild curls, to coming here to see how the daily therapy was going.

"Let's walk," Josephine said. "That's a specialty of this place, the walk and talk. I actually prefer it to the alternative, to being inside. Who knew I'd turn into a naturalist?"

The usual way of starting any conversation is to say, "How are you?" When you know someone who has had a death, or an illness, or is spending weeks in a facility designed to deal with mental health, even fairly benign mental health—"no schizophrenics" Josephine said dryly, sounding, as she always has, much older than her age—you realize pretty quickly that it's a completely useless, even ridiculous question. So we walked without speaking, the temperature dropping as we moved beneath the tree canopy, until finally I said, "Talk to me."

Her mother had told me some, but Josephine told it differently. "Suicidal ideation," her mother had said, and when I repeated that to Josephine she sighed.

"Do you remember that class when you talked to us about nuance?" she said. "Why would you, you've taught so many classes. But I remember. You talked about how there was virtually no nuance in *Wuthering Heights,* and how, by contrast, Virginia Woolf was almost entirely nuance, so that sometimes she was impenetrable."

I nodded. It sounded right, although I couldn't recall the lesson, what I'd been trying to teach them, where I'd meant to lead them.

"My father told me that I'd be going back to school at the end of August. He said he'd talked to someone who'd talked to someone at Harvard, and because I hadn't taken a medical leave, had withdrawn academically, I could return as a first-year, a new student. A fresh start. That's what he kept saying. A fresh start. He didn't ask if I wanted to go back. He just said I was going. And I told him I would rather die than go back there."

She stopped and looked at me. "Is that suicidal ideation? I don't think so. Histrionic, maybe." Finally she laughed a real laugh. "I'm overintellectualizing, aren't I? I promise I didn't learn that from you. I promise I don't do it here. I don't hate it here. I'm learning a lot, a lot that I never thought of before. I already understood my father.

There's one way to live, to be, and he's doing it, and he believes I have to do it whether I like it or not. He believes that liking it is beside the point. But I'm learning a lot about my mother, too. Of course she's terrified. I think that's why she wanted you to visit, that maybe you could wave the magic Miss Goodman wand and fix all this. I have to keep telling her that I'm making progress. But I'm not even sure that's how I would describe it. I've been a certain kind of person, with a certain sort of idea of my future, for so long, virtually my entire life, that it's as though I'm having to remake myself from the ground up. My therapist is giving me exercises to teach me to be more empathetic. What kind of person needs empathy exercises?" Josephine said, sighing. "Tell the girls in my class: Josephine is learning empathy! They'll be stunned."

"You're being too hard on yourself," I said. "It sounds like you're doing the work, as my therapist liked to say."

"Tell the girls that, too. Miss Goodman goes to a therapist. That they really won't believe. They all think you're perfect. For a lot of them you were the mother they wish they had."

"Oh boy," I said.

"In group here, we're all much harder on our parents than on ourselves. That's a central topic, our parents. After listening to us talk, you have to think that there are lots of people who shouldn't have children at all. And there I go, failing my empathy test. I'm so sorry. Under the circumstances that's a horrible thing to say to you, of all people. And I would never say it about you. Maybe we were all making assumptions about you, but on the days when you came into class looking really happy, we would always hope you had a big announcement to make."

"It didn't occur to me that you were all that interested in any of us teachers personally."

"Oh, I think we were much more interested in you than you were in all of us. We used to talk all the time about your husbands and wives, who was gay and who was maybe gay, who was mean and who was bad at their job. Miss Hayward lived in the neighborhood and it freaked us all out anytime we ran into her in workout clothes going to run in the park. I think some of us were disappointed that none of the male teachers tried to hit on us, and then once you made us read *The Children's Hour* we were disappointed that none of the female teachers had. We didn't like it so much, the teachers who had children of their own. That seemed like cheating somehow, like we weren't enough. Amanda said once that maybe it was better if it turned out you couldn't have children because it would mean you would always care about us more. We all blanked her on that, we all said that was a horrible thing to say. But we knew what she meant."

"No one assumed I'd just decided against it?"

Josephine pursed her lips. "At the risk of sounding presumptive, Miss Goodman, no, never. To begin with, somebody's aunt who knew you from Windsor saw you and your husband in the waiting room at the clinic where she was going. Plus, you kind of have mom written all over you. I don't know whether saying that means I'm becoming more empathetic, or that it's an unempathetic thing to say, but it's true. Jessamyn, who was adopted, was always getting upset that you didn't adopt. Which would have made her feel better about being adopted. Which she felt horrible about."

"I think you can stop calling me Miss Goodman, Josephine, and start calling me Polly."

"That's never going to happen, Miss Goodman. Never. You're Miss Goodman to me forever."

"I wonder how Jessamyn's doing."

"She's fine. She loves Wellesley, loves her roommate, loves her classes, blah blah blah. I know all this because her mother told my mother, who told me. And maybe it's true. And maybe it's what Jessamyn tells her mother. Or maybe it's what her mother tells the other mothers. There's not a whole lot I take at face value anymore. Will my mother tell anyone where I am? Doubtful. I'm not sure what the cover story'll be. Every time someone's seen me in our apartment building, they've said, 'Home from school?' Having me here instead of there is probably good for optics."

"That's cynical."

"I know. I'm trying to unlearn cynical. But I guess it's like riding a bike. You never forget." She held up the Ashbery. "But for once in my life I'm reading for pleasure. I don't have to explore Ashbery's themes or figure out how I can slot him into some overview paper on modern poetry."

I laughed. "There are a limited number of people who read Ashbery for pleasure. I always found him a slog. Brilliant, but hard work."

"I suppose," Josephine said. "I can't unlearn all my old habits at once, can I?"

The silence was deep.

"Here's another thing you've probably forgotten," Josephine said. "Do you remember the quote you put up on the board in the classroom when we were first-years?"

I riffled through my mind, my memory, through all the quotes, all the years, feeling as though this was a test and I was failing. Finally I shook my head.

"It was Edna St. Vincent Millay," Josephine said, "and I was so dismissive. I didn't think much of Millay's poetry. God. I was fourteen years old and dinging Edna St. Vincent Millay."

"She's not John Ashbery."

"But that quote stayed with me. 'Beauty is whatever gives joy.'"

I nodded. Now I remembered.

"I got up there to school last year, and I was so miserable. That's the only word for it. I wasn't depressed. I wasn't sad. I was miserable. I think I always believed that that was when my life would somehow become real, when I got to college, that I would feel like I was at home, that I was where I belonged, that it had all been worth it, the enrichment programs, the SAT tutor. And not only did I not feel that way, it seemed like no one felt that way, like being miserable was the price we had to pay for being exceptional, that only fools were happy. I worked so hard to get there, and then I didn't want to be there, but I didn't know how to do anything else. This was the path. I could see it all in front of me, four miserable years and then I'd graduate, probably a magna, maybe a summa, and then I'd go to law or business school, because my father says a doctorate is a waste with so few faculty jobs and such low faculty salaries. And I'd become a partner in a big white-shoe law firm, like my uncle, or a partner in an investment bank, like my father, and maybe I would have children, but it would be hard with those jobs to spend much time with them, I know how that works. But you can't quit, because then who would you be?"

She'd spoken faster and faster, and harder and harder, and then she stopped and turned to me, the book furled in her fist. "There's no joy in any of it for me. Not a drop. Not a bit. One day at dawn I was walking by the river, thinking about how Virginia Woolf walked into a river, because I can't even despair without making a literary reference, and the sky started to get a little pink, and I felt so foolish because I thought, for the very first time ever, I want some joy in my life. If it's stupid to be happy then I need to figure out how to become stupid. I got out of bed every single morning there feeling miserable. I don't know why. I don't know why everybody else seemed to not feel that, or be okay with feeling that way. But I'm not. I don't want that. I know it can't be every day, but I want to walk down the street every once in a while and feel joyful."

"Yes," I said.

"Yes?"

"Yes."

"I don't sound ridiculous?"

"No," I said.

"It's possible?"

"Yes," I said.

"You're not disappointed in me?"

"Oh my God, no. Not at all."

"Can you stay for lunch?"

"Yes," I said.

The food was good. "Hey, Josephine," a girl in a white sundress said, smiling.

"This is more like what I thought college would be like than college was," Josephine said. "When people are miserable here, they don't act like it's normal."

"What's your favorite part?" I said.

"Don't laugh, but it's art therapy."

"Why would I laugh? Although I have to say, I didn't know you could draw or paint."

"Neither did I. Like I said, I'm learning a lot."

"I want to tell you something," I said, and I told Josephine about how my path had been a path toward a doctorate in English, and how I had found that joyless, and how so many people had thought I was foolish to give that up, to trade teaching college and graduate students for teaching high school girls, to trade something that commanded a certain respect at cocktail parties for something that many of the people at those parties thought was second-rate, even as they sent their daughters to Windsor or places like it.

"My father said that once, when I was talking about what an excellent teacher you were," Josephine said. "He said, if she's so good, why isn't she teaching at the college level."

I shrugged. "He's not alone in that perception," I said.

She came with me to the car when lunch was done and we'd taken another walk. Maybe she would take classes at Hunter College, she said, and live at home. Maybe she would live with her mother's mother and go to the local branch of the state university. Maybe she would stay at The Refuge longer than she had planned. Maybe, maybe, maybe.

"You let me know," I said as I hugged her.

"Joy," she said. "That's my game plan."

THE GROUNDS OF EDGEMERE AT THE TAIL END OF A BLISTERing summer, reservoirs elsewhere revealing their rocks, leaves yellowing on trees like a fake fall. But the lawns at Edgemere still looked just as they had during a wet spring. Green, lush, alive. That must be one powerful sprinkler system. I guess they couldn't take a chance on anything hinting at death and decay. All the times I'd been here, and I'd seen plenty of the second but none of the first, except for one time when I'd passed a room that looked like a hotel room before the guest arrived, bureau bare, bed corners tight and smooth. Clearly its occupant had left permanently. There had to be some back entrance to the place, where the trash and laundry came out, and the residents, too, at the end, but there was no sign of it anywhere in the front. That very worst part of Edgemere, the inevitable end of it all, was probably a little bit like something that happened from time to time at Windsor. You'd get a curt message from the head: Decca Walsh has withdrawn from the school. Locker emptied, desk bare. We knew better than to ask for a detailed explanation. The girls would whisper and then stop like a shut door when one of us approached.

It was too warm for the veranda, so my father and I sat in the library again. Claire had been taken to the hospital for an infection, the nurse had told me. "He must be so upset," I'd said, hands on the handles of the wheelchair, and she had smiled faintly and I realized that maybe my father hadn't even noticed that Claire was gone. Maybe, as he did with my mother, he thought she was just in another room. When I'd arrived he said nothing for a few minutes, then looked up and said, "You're here now."

"Yes I am," I'd said, taking his hand.

After a few more minutes he added, "Good. It's good when you're here."

For the rest of the hour he said nothing and I spoke, mainly about Lou and Skipper's house and what was being done to restore it to its former state. I described the storm and he nodded, talked about the slow pace of the workmen and he nodded again. We went to the dining hall and both of us had small dishes of ice cream. The nurse also said that he choked on firmer food these days, but soup and spaghetti ("cut up small," she said) and ice cream and pudding all seemed fine. "He's still able to feed himself," she said, and I tried not to shudder.

After our ice cream I took him back to the library. "I'll sit with him," said one of the aides. "We're old friends, right, Mr. Goodman." His real old friends didn't come anymore. One of them had died of prostate cancer. Two of the others still insisted that my father didn't belong there. "He was his old self the last time I saw him," one of his golfing buddies had said when I'd run into him on the street after lunch with my mother, and it was all I could do not to say, "The last time you saw him was two years ago, and believe me, a lot has changed since then." That was when a few of them still came by, but then they stopped. "They can see the future," my mother had said grimly when I asked about it.

When my father had first arrived, when he could still have a conversation, he'd told the staff he wanted them to call him Jack. "We're not allowed to do that," one of the nurses had said. "We think it's more dignified to address our guests more formally."

"I don't know why," he said. "Everybody calls me Jack."

"It's like at school, Daddy," I'd said. "The girls call me Miss Goodman as a sign of respect."

"Exactly," the nurse had said. "We work for you, Mr. Goodman."

"Then get me out of here," he'd said. He said it to me three or four times that first year, and every time it broke my heart. Now I'd do anything to hear him say it. It was like the shell was still there but it had been breached, riddled with tiny cracks, so that what was once my father was slowly seeping out of him, leaving him empty, the way I'd felt empty every time I discovered there was no baby.

"We'll be good," the aide said, taking his hand. "I tell him stories about Trinidad. And do you know, not long ago he looked up and said, 'That's an island in the Caribbean.' Not many people know that, that Trinidad is an island, or where it is."

"How long ago?" I said.

She patted his hand and said, "Not too long, right, Mr. Goodman? You said to me, 'That's an island in the Caribbean.'" That's what they did here, the staff, after a few years. They carried on both sides of the conversation.

I left the library, and when I came around the corridor, eyes blinded by tears, I ran right into my mother. She looked at my face and said, "What? What is it? What is it? Tell me."

"He's fine. Or as fine as he ever is. He's the same."

She exhaled loudly. "You really frightened me, Polly. If you could see the look on your face. I imagined the worst."

"You know what, Mother, that's because it is the worst. Everything is the worst. I just spent almost two hours with him, during which he barely uttered a single word. And my closest friend—" I tried to stifle it, but those few words were too much, and I started to cry, truly cry, the way I tried never to do in front of my mother, the way I hadn't done in years.

"Let's go in here," she said as a couple passed by and looked at me, clearly stricken.

It was one of those small rooms they always have at places like this. They'd had one at The Refuge. "That's where they tell your family you need electroshock," Josephine had said and, I suppose, seeing my expression, had added quickly, "Not mine." Thinking of that moment with Josephine, looking at my mother now, all I could think was how easy it must be to read my face. "You definitely wear it, whatever it is," Garrison had said once. "I almost don't even have to ask."

My mother reached into her straw bag and took out a packet of tissues. There was probably Advil in there, if I needed it, and maybe a sewing kit. Why couldn't I appreciate that instead of resent it? I wiped my eyes, blew my nose, and handed her back the tissue, but she put her hand up: No. That was why. I remembered once, when I was in kindergarten, going to a birthday party, bakery cake and chocolate ice cream, and throwing up afterward as she held a bowl. When I was done I was sure I saw a look of revulsion on her face. Maybe that was what all mothers looked like when they were holding the bowl—Emily, Lou, Helen, Jamie. But at five you don't think like that. I heard Garrison's voice again: You're not five anymore, Pol. Maybe I was always five with my mother.

"My friend Sarah has a complication of breast cancer that seems to be terminal," I said. "I'm not even supposed to tell anyone about this. She doesn't want anyone to know."

"My clerks call me the vault, Polly. I'm very good at discretion. It comes with the job."

"I know. Sarah probably wouldn't mind anyhow. I believe you two actually hit it off." That "actually" being the giveaway. When Sarah had said she'd had a very good conversation with my mother, I'd had no response except "When worlds collide."

"I remember well how she hosted your wedding at her apartment. She was the flower girl."

I smiled, my lips trembling. "Exactly."

"I'm sorry to hear this. She seems like a really lovely woman. She certainly is fond of you."

"I've just been so shocked by it. She had breast cancer six years ago, and we all thought it was gone. And I guess it was, and then it came back."

"She and I discussed it at the wedding. She was just preparing for her treatment, she said."

"She told you at our wedding?" Unspoken was: Before she'd even told me?

"She said she was so happy to make your wedding because she'd just found out, and all the preparations had taken her mind off of it. And of course I understood. I talked a little bit about my own experience."

"What experience?"

"When I had it. I thought it would cheer her, my experience, because it was so uneventful. They took it out. I was fine. End of story."

"What?"

"Lower your voice, Polly. You're shouting."

"You had breast cancer?" I whispered.

"Well, not like your friend, it turned out. I know you said at the time she had to have chemotherapy, and I didn't. In my case it was encapsulated, which is much less serious. And small. It was like a small grape, the doctor said. It sounded as though hers was more serious than that."

"I'm sorry, I'm feeling as though I've walked into a movie halfway through. When did you have breast cancer?"

"When you were in London for your junior year abroad."

"And you didn't tell me? Daddy didn't tell me?"

"It wasn't a big secret. I just didn't think there was any point in telling you at the time, with you so far away. It was encapsulated. They took it out. I scarcely have a scar."

"I'm rewinding the mental tape here. My mother had breast cancer. And I didn't know about it. I am just finding out about it, what, twenty years later?"

"Honestly, I'm surprised Garrison never said anything to you," she said. "I wouldn't have brought it up if I hadn't assumed Garrison had told you at some point."

"Never mind Garrison. Why wouldn't *you* have told me at the time?"

"Why?"

"So I could come home and help care for you."

"I didn't need to be taken care of. It came out. I was fine. I was back to work the following week."

"I could have been there for you," I said.

"To do what?"

"To . . . to . . ."

"See? You can't think of what you would have done because there was nothing you could have done."

"Do you know how crazy this all sounds?" I said. "I could have helped."

"How?"

"Just by being there."

"You would have hated every minute," my mother said, without heat or rancor. "I did the right thing for us both."

Finally I said, "I'm speechless. I have no words."

"Tell Sarah I'm sending her my very best," my mother said, standing. "I hope she recovers."

"She says she won't recover," I said.

"I'm sorry to hear that," she said. "I'm sorry for her, and I'm sorry for you. It's hard to lose a good friend."

I almost said, How would you know, and then I realized that maybe she did know, that if I hadn't known about the encapsulated grape, maybe there were endless other things I didn't know about Mary Goodman. Maybe I had always been kidding myself that I was the only woman who felt this way. Maybe everyone's mother was a kind of mystery to her daughter. Maybe everyone's daughter was a mystery to her mother.

"So that's it? We won't speak of this again?"

"I'm happy to discuss it further, Polly, but there's not much more to say. I had genetic testing and there's no danger to you. Frankly, I haven't really thought about it in years. It was a long time ago, it wasn't significant or debilitating, and that was that. I'm sorry that's not the case with Sarah. As I said, she seems like a lovely person."

"All right then," I said. "I have a question on an unrelated topic. Why did you want to have my ears fixed?"

She turned slowly at the door. "Polly, I have no idea what you're talking about," she said wearily.

"I heard you, you and Daddy, talking about getting my ears fixed."

"What's wrong with your ears?"

I held my hair back. "The way they come to a point," I said.

I could tell she was thinking, thinking hard. It was a look she had sometimes on the bench. "The wheels are turning," one of the clerks had whispered to my American History class when we observed her for an afternoon, when I wasn't sure if I was proud or mortified or both to be on a field trip to see my mother.

"It was your idea," she finally said. "You said some boy at school was making fun of you, saying you looked like someone from some science fiction series or something. At least I think that's what you said. You'd been so upset that I thought I should at least mention it to your father, and we both concluded that it would pass. I assume it did. You never mentioned it again. It's another thing I haven't thought about in years."

"One more thing."

She sighed. I saw it happen, her chest heave beneath her linen jacket, the color of daffodils. She always wears color when she's not working. She always looks good in color.

"I'm afraid they're going to move him to C wing," I said, and she wheeled around, her lips drawn into a line so hard that they mostly vanished.

"He's not talking, he barely lifts his head. I'm afraid they're going to move him to C," I added.

"I will never allow them to move him to C. Ever. I will not permit it," she said. I believed her.

"Can I come for dinner and spend the night?" I asked Garrison after my last class on Friday, the first week back at school.

"Ah, Pol, tonight might be difficult," he said. "You could use my place solo."

"Forget it. You obviously have a date. Or something."

"You know what, never mind. Come over. Having sushi with you is much better than what I had planned."

"I wouldn't want to harsh your buzz," I said.

"Honey, you are forty-three years old now. You can't wear a crop top and you can't use teen slang. It's not a good look."

I always seem to wind up at Garrison's place when I feel things falling apart. It's restful there and, to be honest, borderline rich, all expensive beige furniture and high-thread-count sheets. We never need to clean up after ourselves; he lives in a building with concierge service, and someone comes in every day to make the beds and do the dishes, although Garrison is out so much, to dinner or for the night, that there's rarely much to do. In our building if something goes wrong, if the toilet is running or an outlet sparks, Mark calls the super and maybe he comes and maybe he doesn't because he's only one guy and 7H flooded the kitchen again and it's coming through the ceiling vent of 6H and we'll just have to wait and think of the sound of the toilet as white noise lulling us to sleep. If anything goes wrong in Garrison's apartment he calls Raoul at the front desk before work, and by the time he gets home it's fixed. It's so typical of my brother, that what I would call his home is just a step or two removed from a hotel.

"My lord, you're good-looking," I said when he opened the door.

"Please let it last," he said. "There's nothing sadder than an old queen with a facelift."

"That's a horrible thing to say!"

"Just promise me you won't plan a party for my fiftieth. And, by the way, if you're here because you've left your husband, you can go home right now because you've made the biggest mistake of your life."

"You know I'm never going to leave my husband," I said. "He's left me. He's at a five-day international conference in Amsterdam about breeding techniques, and it took him two weeks to tell me the subject of the conference for obvious reasons."

"Come eat," Garrison said. "There's edamame and sashimi and spicy tuna rolls."

"The nutritionist says edamame can mimic estrogen."

"No edamame for me," said Garrison.

"I'll have a beer," I said.

"And we obviously have a lot to talk about," added Garrison, going to his fridge, which is usually full of beer, leftover cardboard containers of delivery food, and the occasional jar of olives for dirty martinis. The wine is in the wine fridge. The concierge keeps it stocked.

"Wipe the soy sauce off your chin and tell me exactly what's going on," Garrison said once we sat down.

That's the thing about my brother: He's always been willing to listen to me talk about things that play absolutely no part in his own life, and over the years, even when what I was saying made me seem foolish, he waited to reply until I was done. So I reprised the day with Josephine—"Smart girl," he muttered at one point—and then our meeting with Dr. Betz. He kept quiet during that last, just reached across his midcentury modern dining table and interlaced his fingers with mine. When I was done he brought me another beer even though I'd barely touched the first.

"Let's get you drunk, honey," he said, in the overdone drawl he uses sometimes to cut the tension.

"It gets worse," I said.

"Not possible."

"It's Sarah," I said, and he took my hand again.

The other thing about my brother is that while much of the time he maintains this casual kind of boulevardier effect—and oh how he had loved it the first time I applied that term to him—when the occasion requires, he becomes exactly the way we both insist the marshmallow should be when we're making s'mores: hard and charred outside, but inside just a mess of goo. I didn't even have to explain about Sarah, chapter and verse, before his handsome face had fallen.

"Damn," he said over and over. "Damn, damn, damn." He got up and hugged me, hard. "I'm ready to cry. I got nothing for you except sympathy."

"I know. And she's being so brave, and if I used that word in front of her she would absolutely kill me. I said to her, How can you be like this? And she said, Polly, I figure I can either live in the living or live in the dying. And I'm choosing the first one."

"And now I'm completely losing it," said Garrison.

"Mark's parents are living in her house in the country. A tree fell on their house and took out one of the bedrooms and the living room ceiling, and while it's being rebuilt Sarah told them they could live in her place."

"Polly! Why has it taken you so long for this data dump! You've had the summer from hell and I'm just hearing about it?"

"You're away a lot during the summer, Gar. Nantucket. Newport. You do a lot of house guesting."

"I do no more house guesting than the average charming man of my age and disposition. Which, admittedly, is a fair amount of house guesting. But still. I would have canceled in a heartbeat. You should have told me."

"I'm telling you now. I just feel terrible all the time. I'm afraid families are a funnel, and ours is running out. Plus I think I'm reaching menopause."

"No, no, can we please draw the line at menopause? Isn't that what the book club is for? My God, they must be gutted."

"I'm the only one she's told. She doesn't want what she calls a pity party."

"Well, I could promise not to throw one, but in this case I'd be lying. How old is she?"

"Fifty-one."

"Good lord."

"Exactly."

"Well, the only good thing I can say about all of this is that it seems to have completely gotten you past the ridiculous Roots & Branches obsession."

Actually, Garrison had gotten me past discussing it with him because, at a certain point, I realized that it was hurting his feelings. He'd been so relieved, when I'd told him about the impossibility that Talia Burton's mother and I were secret sisters and when I had come back from Barbara Burton's farm with nothing more than alpaca stories. The day I'd told him who Talia's grandmother was, over brunch, he was actually wearing a Warm As Toast sweater. "I have several," he'd said. "They feel like newborn baby." And then he'd winced. So many minefields when life goes sideways. So many. Josephine had told me she'd had to learn to stop using the words *crazy* and *insane* as what she called "colloquialisms." "There are people here who get very offended," she'd said.

I wasn't going to tell Garrison that I'd taken Talia Burton on a tour of New York City colleges. "She prefers that I not come," her father had written me. "Is that acceptable to you?" She'd been shy when I first met her at the train, then opened up over lunch near Columbia. "I have a really good therapist now," she said. "Do you know a lot of people who are in therapy?"

I tried not to laugh. "Honestly, almost everyone I know is in therapy," I said. And I told her a little bit about Josephine.

"Is it helping?" she said.

"I think so. I hope so."

She had a high school acquaintance at Barnard, a young woman named Abby, who showed us around the campus and talked about the glories of single-sex education for women. "I teach at the Windsor School," I said, "so you're preaching to the converted."

"My lab partner went to Windsor! Hennessey Bateman?"

"She was in my senior seminar," I said. "She was a bio whiz."

"She so is! I thought I was smart until I got here and met her."

"Wait," Talia said. "Her name is Hennessey? Her first name?"

"It's a family name," Abby and I both said at once, and then laughed. Windsor is full of girls with family names.

"How do you two know each other?" Abby asked, and it was my turn to laugh with Talia.

"I thought Polly was my aunt," Talia said, "but she's not. But my grandmother says that if I want her to be, she can be. My grandmother really believes in manifesting things. She says I can manifest Polly as my spiritual aunt."

"I need to hear the whole story tonight," said Abby, who was putting Talia up for two nights. Which I had double-checked with her father.

"You don't necessarily have to go with me tomorrow to NYU and Fordham," Talia said to me.

"I'll let Abby take you down to NYU, but I thought after Fordham you might want to take an insider tour of the Bronx Zoo."

"Yes!" they both said in unison.

"That would be amazing," Abby said. "How did you arrange the zoo thing?"

"My husband is the senior veterinarian."

"Oh. My. God. That is an amazing job," Abby said.

"Right?" Talia said.

It turned out Talia loved snakes, which delighted Mark. There's a special place in his heart for animals that are, in his words, misunderstood. He took Talia backstage in the reptile building. Abby and

I stayed outside. "I just can't with snakes," she said. "Like a lot of people," I responded.

"I hope she comes to Barnard," Abby said. "I didn't really know her in high school but she seems like a cool girl. She says she'd like to go to school here so she could see you. She says her grandmother told her to manifest herself here, which is wild, right? My grandmother doesn't do manifesting."

Manifesting, I thought to myself. Why couldn't Barbara Burton manifest for Sarah, damn her. I'd even settle for weird herbs, or crystals, anything that would make Sarah feel better, stronger, more like herself. "I do sleep a lot," Sarah had said the last time we were together.

"Can we still walk?"

"Absolutely. Just not as far. And I might have to sit down."

"Works for me," I'd said.

I'd told Sarah about Talia's visit, but I hadn't said any more about Talia to Garrison, and I still hadn't mentioned Stephen Burton's blue eyes, or his ears, especially the ears. I'd noticed Mark checking out Talia's unremarkable ears when we were at the zoo. I'd felt guilty about not telling Garrison about it, but I didn't feel so guilty now, knowing there were things he hadn't told me.

"So our mother had breast cancer," I said brightly as we packed up yet another container of takeout for the fridge.

Garrison inhaled audibly, then said, "That tone of voice always means trouble."

"You mean the tone of voice a person uses when she discovers that her entire family somehow failed to tell her something important about what was going on within it? That tone?"

"I'm surprised it took you this long. I figured I was going to open the door and you were going to hit me with this. Can we sit back down? I always feel like conversations in the kitchen are so domestic in the most fraught way imaginable. I've never understood why *Who's Afraid of Virginia Woolf?* doesn't take place in the kitchen."

"Wait, did she call you about this?"

Garrison pushed past me to sit in one corner of the sectional. He lowered his head and pulled at his lower lip, which has always been his tell for reluctance to engage.

"Okay, she did," I said.

"She seemed genuinely upset that I hadn't told you. I think she said she always thought we told each other everything."

"So you already know not to make the excuse that I didn't need to be told because I was in London."

"I wouldn't have said that anyhow."

"So the bottom line is that the three grown-ups got together and decided that I didn't need to know this. Or maybe it was just the two grown-ups, you and her."

"Well, that has always been the dynamic, hasn't it, Polly? Or part of the dynamic. The other part, obviously, is you and Dad in your own little world. Polly and Daddy. Nobody else existed for him. I mean, I stopped visiting him because he had no idea who I was. And then I realized he had never had any idea who I was. And you know, for a while I imagined it was because I was gay, and then I realized it had nothing to do with that. It would almost be easier if I could think, Yep, the guy can't deal with having a gay son. But it wouldn't have made any difference. All he could see was you. You know the only two words he said the last time I was there? Come on, Pol, you can guess. Guess!"

I didn't say anything. I was closer to Garrison than almost anyone on earth, and I thought he was to me as well. Over the years he'd occasionally made a snarky comment about my father and me. But somehow I had missed that the snark was a glossy cover for the caring, and the anger, and the grief.

"Pumpkin pie!" Garrison said. "Those are probably the last words I'll ever hear my father say to me. 'He says that all the time,' the aide said. And I said, 'Yeah, I know.'"

He exhaled, and I could see that he wanted to circle back to the snark, because snark doesn't hurt, doesn't pierce your heart. "So Mom should have told you, if not when you were away, then when you got back. And she didn't want to. She doesn't like drama. She's never liked drama."

"I wouldn't call telling your daughter you have breast cancer drama."

"But she would. There you go. There's the disconnect between the two of you. And by the way, it goes both ways. For the last year you've been obsessed with this bogus gene pool search you've been on, but you haven't said a word to her about it, have you? That's been at least as important, from your point of view, as what happened to her twenty years ago, but you haven't said a thing. You probably don't even talk to her about what you've gone through to try to have a baby, you and Mark. You talk to me, and lord knows you talk to Dad, even when he seems so checked out that you might as well be talking to one of those ficus trees they have in the lobby. But the most important parts of Polly Goodman's life stay hidden from her mother, and it's not because you think it would upset her to know them. It's because you don't want to do her the honor. The thing about you, Polly, is that you're lucky. You let life in. I know because I don't, and I'm fine with that. I never have. But you want, and you give, and you open your arms to everyone but her.

"So the question is, when are you going to admit that this is a two-way street? For some reason the two of you don't connect, maybe never have, maybe never will, and you need to make your peace with that and realize that it doesn't mean she's a bad person, it just means she's different from you. Maybe she's more like me. Maybe when you judge her I feel like you're judging me, too. I know you don't want to hear this, and it might be cruel to say it, but since we're letting all the genies out of the bottle, I always hoped that when you had kids of your own you would look at her and think, Boy, this must have been a tough thing for her to do."

He stood up. "I don't like the drama either," Garrison said. "I'm going to bed." I sat still until I heard his bedroom door close, and then I slipped out of the apartment and took the elevator down to the lobby. "Have a nice evening," the man at the concierge desk said as I headed back to my own bed.

JAMIE CALLED TO ASK ME ABOUT A CHARITY FOR GIRLS THAT wanted her to join the board and, I suspected, to try to wheedle me into talking about Sarah. "I know they only want me for the money," she said, "but I don't want to sign up if this is some bogus sit-in-a-sister-circle deal."

I had to laugh. You have to laugh, Helen had said more than once about Jamie. It wasn't only that she reduced everything to its least attractive denominator; the reducing always had such an element of hard fact.

"They're actually fantastic," I said. "They provide great enrichment programs for girls whose families don't have the resources, and they have a college advising program that's as successful as any place. Everyone I know says their mentoring project is as good as it gets."

"I'm not mentoring some girl. I have my own girls."

"No one's going to force you to mentor. But you should definitely go on the board. Let me put it this way: I would join their board in a minute. And you're right, they want people who can give, but the money is all really well spent."

"I'm surprised they didn't ask Sarah," Jamie said. Aha, I thought, then played my ace: "I'm pretty sure Sarah suggested they ask you. Because of the girls."

Jamie's two daughters had both seemed slightly mortified to run into me in the hallway at Windsor, now that they had moved up from the lower school building a block away. I understood what was going through their minds immediately: Like, oh my God, a teacher who's been in our house eating bagels and who's friends with our mom is at our school. Inevitably, if they wound up in one of my classes someday, their friends would suggest that their grades reflected their mother's friendship.

Jamie's girls were fraternal twins—"not even an IVF situation, just my luck" she had said once—and she had named them Margaret and Elizabeth, two old-fashioned names, which I respected, clearly a reaction to Jamie's dissatisfaction with her own. "I mean, Jamie?" she'd said once when I'd mentioned it at book club. "President Jamie? Senator Jamie? My mother gave me a cheerleader name." We didn't get a lot of the wilder modern names at Windsor, no Stars or Septembers, but there was the occasional Summer. Predictably, both Margaret and Elizabeth complained that they had grandmother names, and for a time Elizabeth had demanded she be called Zsa-Zsa, but no matter how many times she wrote it in her notebooks it never really caught on, even among her friends, and it eventually evaporated.

"How's Sarah?" Jamie finally said.

"She's away," I said. Which was true, if you counted a day in Connecticut as away. She'd had Estelle drive her up to the house again to make sure Mark's parents were comfortable. "I've never been more comfortable in my life," Lou had told her on the phone. But Sarah had gone that morning anyway.

"And how are you holding up? What's going on with your phantom family?"

"Still a phantom. I accompanied my not-niece on college visits here in the city, and she wants me to come in October to her grandmother's farm. She wants me to bring Mark, who totally charmed her, and was charmed by her. She likes snakes, and she knows the difference between monkeys and apes. Mark really wants to see the alpacas, too, so I guess we'll do it."

"Buy me a sweater," Jamie said. "You get a deal, right? I'll reimburse you. Also, I keep forgetting to mention, the twins say you have the meanest girl in the school in your first-year class this year. Is that true?"

It was true. Constance Conway, known to her friends as CC. To the extent you could call them friends. "I knew you would be able to handle her," the head had said.

In my experience there were two kinds of people who became teachers and stuck with it: those who were crazy about their areas of expertise, and the ones who loved the students, the variety, the possibility, the glimmer of a future that each of them represented. Because we were a girls' school, I suspect, we tilted hard toward the latter. Our star bio teacher, Dr. Shanevsky, was the first kind, and I sometimes got the impression that he couldn't tell one girl from another—"you know, the one with brown hair" he'd say, or "that girl who always carries a backpack." School legend had it that he had been hired as an interim when his predecessor had retired under murky circumstances, and simply stayed on, which was nothing but a good thing. He loved science so much that he managed to communicate that love to many of his students, even some of the ones who hadn't thought of themselves as science people. He had been at the school for twenty-seven years, and I'd heard at least a dozen young female doctors at assemblies and reunions say that they had wound up in medicine because of Dr. Shanevsky. You'd see his weird lopsided smile as one of them spoke and wonder: Did he even know who she was? Did it even matter? For the warm fuzzies we had Miss Tutolo, who taught PE and coached field hockey yet could barely walk down the hall to the gym without tripping. She called her classes and her team "my girls," although when I asked her about reading *The Prime of Miss Jean Brodie* she'd looked at me blankly.

I guess most people would say that I was a combination of the two. There were certain writers I prepared to teach, even after many years, with a sense of glee. Austen, of course, but also Willa Cather and Edith Wharton. Poetry, too. But boy, I also loved the girls. We always liked to say piously at education seminars and conferences that it was important not to flagrantly play favorites, and I liked to think I was good at that. But there were girls that just drew you in. There were the ones who were so genuine and nice to the other girls, as well as to the teachers. There were the ones who seemed to dance through life, happy happy happy, which always made me wonder what their mothers were like. There were the ones who were so smart, so thoughtful, so bringing everything they had to the classroom, girls like Josephine, an intellectual Roman candle.

And occasionally there was one in whom you so clearly saw yourself that you felt you had to shade your eyes so she and the others wouldn't see it, someone who in so many ways reminded you of yourself when you were young. That had happened to me nine years ago with a girl named Susan McCreedy, who was smart but never sure she was smart enough, who was confident up to a point but then constantly questioning: Where should she go? What should she do? I took a really disproportionate pleasure in the fact that Susan had not only become an English teacher, but that she was the seventh-grade English teacher here at Windsor. She was the one who had told me that CC would be in my first-year English class. "She's extremely bright," Susan said. "That's both the good news and the bad news. All I can say is 1984." Which is our shorthand, based on the novel's evocation of that thing each person fears most, to describe the girl who has an unerring, almost uncanny sense of which buttons to push in order to rattle, distress, upset, sometimes even destroy. I'd never actually had one of the destroyers, but I'd heard the stories. There had been one who graduated the year before I came to work at Windsor. She was now the White House correspondent for NBC News. The head said that every time she heard her begin a question, "How can you possibly justify . . ." it took her right back.

You could tell she was canny, that on-air woman, and CC was canny, too. Susan had told me that CC had what she described as an avatar, and I'd encountered it day two, right out of the gate. There was a discussion of summer reading, and one of the girls—Ellen? Ella? It always took a few weeks before I'd nailed all the names down—had read a biography of the Brontës. One poor hapless girl asked if Charlotte Brontë was Emily Brontë's mother. She was the type the teachers all recognized, too, the girl who so wanted: wanted to be taken seriously, to be part of the group, to be acknowledged, and yet somehow only ever managed the non sequitur, the response that seemed beside the point, or the one, like this one, that was just risible. CC had snorted and clapped her hand over her mouth, while Ella, that was it, Ella, said kindly that they were three sisters, and none of them had children.

CC's eyes brightened as though that last comment had given her a cue. She tilted her head and said, "My mother says there's definitely an advantage in not having children. She says it would have been horrible for her not to have me and my brothers, but that it can be much easier to have a career if you don't have children. But she thought being a mother was more important." Maybe it was because of what Josephine had told me about how the students saw me, but I swore CC was looking out from under her bangs at me as she spoke. And of course I couldn't argue with her mother's point of view. We teachers didn't do that. There had been a girl a few years back whose parents were part of a conservative Christian church, and had asked that their daughter be excused from biology classes that touched on evolution. This was a new one for the head, since most of our families at Windsor were progressive, or at least pretended to be, and she made the mistake of calling the parents in to meet with Dr. Shanevsky. "That's preposterous," he had said. "I won't allow it."

But the rest of us understand that while our job is supposed to be to teach the girls, it was also to manage their parents, their complaints and their expectations, which were uniformly high. I suppose my mother had been too busy managing her own school and work life to try to manage mine, and that that was something I should be grateful for. "Yes, Polly, yes you should," I could hear Garrison saying. "Would you really have wanted her to second-guess the basketball coach about how much playing time you should be getting?"

Which I'd told him parents did at Windsor all the time. Sometimes in the middle of a game.

To my knowledge no Windsor parent had ever sat down for a conference and said that their beloved daughter was kind of average. All the girls were considered by their mothers and fathers to be gifted. This made life challenging when one of them, say, didn't get into a summer science program or wound up with a B on a year-end report. "I have to be honest," a mother had said to me at the end of the last academic year about a grade that, honestly, was a bit of a gift, "this is such a setback. I don't know if she can get past this." The temptation was very strong to reply, I have a mixed-race not-niece whose mother hung herself in the woods behind the house ten days after Christmas. How's that for a setback? I wonder if she can get past that?

But of course I didn't. In my conversations with parents and with the girls, too, I try to remember what Lou said to me once when I was complaining: "You don't know what's happening behind the curtain."

I remembered that remark, too, when Josephine's mother stopped in at the end of one school day when I was still in the classroom, the whiteboard covered with notes. Who is the poet addressing? Do her observations grow out of what you know of her background? Assignment—write a poem in her style.

Carrie Berg looked as though she had lost twenty pounds since I'd last seen her. She wore black pants and shirt, and although black might as well be the official color of New York City, it still felt to me as though she were in mourning for her past life or, more accurately, for that of her daughter's. There'd never been a better example of how hidden behind the curtain real life might be.

"I never properly thanked you for visiting Josephine," she said, sitting at one of the student desks. "It was so helpful to her."

"Despite everything," I said, "you have to know that she's an exceptional young woman. She's intelligent and incisive and unique.

She's extraordinary, really. Her insights into what's happened to her and what she wants going forward are so impressive. You should be proud."

"It's very difficult. My husband and I have very different ways of approaching this. He's quite impatient with all of it. The therapy. The facility. The expense."

I'd been to the Bergs' apartment during Josephine's first year, at a welcome cocktail party for the new families with daughters entering the upper school. The expense of The Refuge was probably considerable, but I was sure it wouldn't strain the family finances.

Carrie Berg wore a gold disc at the end of a long chain, and she sat moving it around with her fingers the way I'd seen blackjack players do with the chips when I'd gone once with the Bailey boys to a casino. The disc had numbers on it that looked like a date, and if I'd had to guess I'd have guessed it was the date her daughter was born. It had probably become a habitual gesture, the turning it over and over, especially recently.

"Maybe it's wrong," she said, "but you have a child and you start planning this that and the other thing. The schools and the activities and all the rest, and you realize that they're a person, they have likes and dislikes, and maybe they're different from yours. I remember a year buying Josephine one outfit after another that she wouldn't wear, she said she hated purple and then she hated dresses and then she hated anything with flowers, and I was so exasperated, I finally said, Well, then you pick out your own clothes! And the minute I said it, this little voice in my head said, What's wrong with that? I felt like it really taught me a lesson, and I tried to stick with it. But there's a definition of success here, not just here at the school, but here where we live, or maybe it's everywhere. Her first time with you, you read that poem by Robert Frost, probably just as an introduction, because it was simpler than a lot of what came later.

"'Two roads diverged in a yellow wood,'" I said.

"'And I took the one less traveled by, and that has made all the difference,'" said Carrie Berg. "I was an English major at Wellesley. That's where I met my husband. He was at business school." She sighed. "He's not much of a believer in the road less traveled."

"I'm planning to see Josephine again next month. I have family and friends living not too far from The Refuge."

"You should know that my husband tried to have them take you off the list of approved visitors. He feels that you ratify what he calls Josephine's worst impulses."

"And you?"

"I made them keep you on." She handed me the bag she'd been carrying. "This is for you, to thank you."

I'm ashamed that my first thought was scented candle, followed by fancy soap. Those were the kinds of gifts parents brought us to thank us and sometimes, we suspected, to influence us going forward. I arranged my face and dug into the pastel tissue, but inside was a handsome leatherbound book, a copy of *Jane Eyre*.

"Oh, this is too much, much too much," I said.

"Josephine insisted," she said. "She said you would know why. I asked, and she said she would let you tell me."

The book had deckled edges and beautiful endpapers, marbled green and gold. "You know the novel, right?"

"Of course," Carrie Berg said. "Is there a female English major who doesn't?"

"There's also a novel called *Wide Sargasso Sea*. It's about the first Mrs. Rochester. Josephine was the only student I've ever had who was dissatisfied with the way the woman in the attic was treated in *Jane Eyre*. They're all so anxious to have her marry Rochester that they just gloss over the first wife and whether there's another side to the story. Josephine wanted the other side to the story."

"I'll read that," Carrie Berg said. "Let me know how your next visit goes." We stood, and she reached out and hugged me, and I could feel the internal vibration of someone trying to stifle tears.

When I opened the classroom door, there was CC Conway,

standing to one side, and I wondered how long she had been out there. If someday she asked me about *Wide Sargasso Sea,* I would know for sure.

"Oh, Mrs. Berg," she said. "I'm so sorry about Josephine. I mean, we all idolized her." Oh, that "so sorry" dragged out like a bird call at night. Oh, that past tense.

"And still should," I said sharply. "Did you want something?"

"I forgot my collected poems. They're in my locker. I just wanted to read a little ahead." CC turned to Carrie Berg. "Tell Josephine everyone is thinking about her," she said, sliding past us.

"I don't know her, do I?" Carrie Berg said as we walked to the end of the hall.

"No," I said. "Don't mention what she said to Josephine."

THE OCTOBER MEETING OF THE BOOK CLUB WAS OBVIOUSLY GOING to be a problem. We didn't meet in July or August, and we'd started skipping September years ago because of back to school, but the October meeting loomed. If Sarah didn't come, it would be the only time one of us had missed, which, come to think of it, was remarkable, even if for a year the pandemic had forced us to meet virtually, with whoever was hosting sending along food as well as books. If Sarah did come, there would be no mistaking how ill she was. I had told her what Jamie had said in the car. "Jamie is nobody's fool," she'd said. "When this is all over she's going to be furious at me. And at you. It won't matter for me." I hated it when she talked like that.

The book club was supposed to be at Helen's apartment, and she'd already sent out the book, a biography of Emily Roebling. I already knew something about her; several years ago one of our students had done a one-woman play for her senior thesis about Emily's unsung role in the construction and completion of the Brooklyn Bridge. At the reception afterward one of the dads who was on the Landmarks Commission said quietly, "I think it's an overstatement to suggest that her husband just sat by while she handled the whole project. But I wouldn't dare say that here." A lot of the dads seemed overwhelmed by estrogen in the upper school, but at least they knew the virtues of girls' education.

It was my in-laws who saved Sarah's dedication to secrecy. They were still living in the cottage. One month of repairs had become three, then four. The roof joists, the roof, the turret, the ceilings. Not to mention the radiators and the phone lines that had been severed and ripped away. And repairs on all of that had only started after the tree work, removing, cutting into sections, carting away. Thomas and his father had gotten into a battle about whether pine makes good firewood, although Lou said that argument was just a surrogate for how irritating Thomas was being, dropping in at the house and screaming at everyone there, inside, outside, on the backhoe, in the truck, about how much time the repairs were taking. Skipper had gotten into the habit of stopping at the general store in town to buy pastries every morning and bring them to the workmen, and every time Thomas went on a rant about the roofers or the plumbers, Skipper would say, "You catch more flies with honey than you do with vinegar," and Thomas would shout back, "Enough with the goddamn honey," and Lou would say, "Language." Then Thomas would huff off to his car and drive away. Or at least that's how Sarah had described it all to me. Because Sarah was now living in the cottage as well. Estelle had brought her one day just for lunch, and she had, according to Lou, "taken a turn." Somehow she'd been persuaded to stay. "I'm having the time of my life," Sarah said.

"We have to reschedule," I'd said to Helen on the phone. "We can't have book club without Sarah, and she just can't leave my mother- and father-in-law." Listen to me, lying so fluently, although putting it that way wasn't a lie exactly, was it? She couldn't leave. Apparently there were days when she couldn't get out of bed for much of the time, and she and Lou would sit all day and talk in the master bedroom.

"Is she really in the country with your in-laws?" Jamie said.

"Cross my heart and hope to die," I said.

"Oh, for Christ's sake, Polly, don't you start with those expressions too."

"My mother-in-law and Sarah speak the same language. She told me the other day that Sarah was a game girl."

"I'm not even sure what a game girl is," Jamie had said.

Lou had said that one day when Thomas had come with Emily and the kids, which was the only way that he could come from now on, his mother had told him, because he wasn't, as she said in her best first-grade teacher mode, "a positive influence." It had been one of Sarah's good days, and she sat in the garden in a wicker chair with an ottoman, wrapped in her Warm As Toast sweater despite the sunny early-autumn weather, and played tiddledywinks with the girls. "They've both fallen completely in love with her," Emily said when I called the house. "She had a cabinet filled with games and toys, most of which I've never actually heard of before. She's doing paper dolls with them, too."

"My nieces love you," I'd said the day I drove up.

I'd found Sarah and Lou in the garden pruning hydrangeas. Sarah was in the wheelbarrow, a long, striped cushion I recognized from one of the chaises behind her for propping and padding. "Right there," I heard her say as I came down the brick path. "No, no, jeez Louise, lower and on an angle. I'm going to turn you into a master gardener yet."

"You are a slave driver, Sally Ann," my mother-in-law said, circling the hydrangea. Blue flowers, red wheelbarrow, like the photograph on the cover of an artsy greeting card. Globes of blue, square of red, or rhombus really, I guess. I was never good at math. It would be something to paint, especially now. Blue flowers, red wheelbarrow, blue-and-white-striped cushion, upon it something that looked like a long, narrow sack that was actually Sarah, tan pants, tan sweater, pale hair and skin. Two steps on the paint palette from the white of a ghost.

"Polly!" Sarah had cried, trying to wiggle her way up in the wheelbarrow so she was less horizonal. "You're here!"

"Here," said Lou, handing me the shears. "She can boss you around while I get lunch. Bossy, bossy, bossy."

"She loves me," Sarah said.

"Bossy!" shouted Lou from halfway up the path.

"There's a William Carlos Williams poem about a red wheelbarrow," I said, because if I talk about literature I can momentarily avoid the hardest parts of real life, one of which was right before me cocooned by cushions.

"I remember that poem," Sarah said. "Aren't there chickens in it?"

The three of us sat around the outdoor table, just as the four of us had in June, eating corn chowder. Dip the spoon, lift it, dip it again: Sarah did what my mother-in-law always called playing with your food, but Lou didn't say a thing. The Roebling book was on Sarah's bedside table. She swore she hadn't read it. Her stepsons had both come to visit; the way Sarah talked, it sounded as though Lou had spent that day over at her own house, which was Lou all over. All those years teaching people with the vocabulary of a six-year-old because they were six-year-olds had really taught her to read the room. Any room.

When I'd pushed the wheelbarrow up the path to the house, it was almost as though there was nothing in it. "She's vanishing," I had said to Mark that night in bed, and he groped for my hand in the dark. "When do you think you'll go back to the city?" I had asked her. "I haven't really thought about that," she said.

After lunch Sarah lay on the sofa, and I told her about taking Talia on the college visits, and how she and Mark had gotten on so well, and how I was going to go back to Barbara Burton's farm. "We can go again together," I said, because that's the kind of thing you say when you wish it were going to happen even though inside you know it never will. Sarah smiled. "Barbara Burton has been so sweet to me," she said. "She sends me some things she's written, and links to meditations. She has me taking turmeric and ginseng and some capsules she made up herself."

"They smell terrible," Lou said.

I told them both about Josephine and Josephine's mother. I told them about CC Conway, although I left out the part about how I had snapped at her in class. My emotional temperature nowadays was all over the place, the way it had been when I was fruitlessly being injected with hormones, although now I thought it was because my hormones were ebbing, fleeing, leaving me for good. So when CC interrupted one of the other girls to say, "But Miss Goodman, don't you find Emily Dickinson so simplistic?" I had snapped back, "Is that your mother's opinion, CC?" and watched her turn as red as the cover of our collected poetry text. "Sorry, go on," I'd added, but she shook her head, looked down, and slid from the classroom when class was over before I could say something to her. Although I wasn't sure what I would say.

The head came into my office early the next morning, the halls echoing with her footsteps in the mostly empty building. She sat down opposite me in the parent chair and leaned her crossed forearms on my desk. "CC Conway," she said.

"She complained. Oh, excuse me, her mother complained. She's practically a student in my class, she's mentioned so often, her mother, who knows everything about everything."

"Polly, you're too smart to take the girls at face value. If this were a novel, what would be the plot twist?"

"Oh God," I said. "There's no mother. The mother's dead."

"Close. The mother she talks about is invented, or I suppose you would say is aspirational. The actual mother left right after the youngest was born. CC had just started kindergarten here. All Dad will say is that Mom had some postpartum issues and, in his words, concluded she was not cut out for motherhood. You can imagine the tone he used when he told me that. The children see her four times a year, in California, where she lives. There's a stepmother. I gather that she tries. The boys are better about handling things, apparently."

"I'm an idiot," I said.

"You don't have to like her. But try to understand."

"I'm trying to understand her," I told Sarah and Lou. "I'm visiting Josephine again in a few weeks."

"Oh, those poor girls," Lou said, sipping her tea.

I was sitting at the end of the couch, Sarah's little feet on my lap. We always teased her about wearing a size six. She'd fallen asleep, or so it seemed, although I watched her, watched her chest, such as it was now, to make certain she was still breathing. When I looked up,

Lou was watching me with an expression of such sympathy and understanding that I had to look away.

"When is Skipper back?" I finally said.

"He's usually back in time for dinner," Lou said. "You should probably head back before that. There's bad traffic from about four on into the city. Besides," she said, dropping her voice to a near whisper, "you don't have a poker face, sweetheart. Nothing inside or out will be harder for her than watching you suffer."

"I don't want to leave without saying goodbye."

"That's exactly what she doesn't want you to do."

"You're a godsend," I said.

"It's been a blessing and a privilege. For both of us, I think. I've told her things about myself that I haven't really talked about with other people, and vice versa. Here's something I know she's never told you that tells you everything about how much she loves you—she and her husband had planned to have a family. That's why she has that cabinet full of toys that she let the girls play with. I said to her, 'So you bought all those same things you had when you were a little girl yourself.' And she said, 'I never had any of those things.' She said, 'When I'm gone, make sure Polly knows they're there.' I don't mean to make you cry, but a friend who hides something that important about herself because they know it will hurt you is a good friend. She wished she could hide this, too, but she knew she couldn't."

"I wish she'd told me, about the other thing."

"Sometimes it's easier to talk about hard things with someone you know, but don't know all that well."

"I guess that explains therapy."

"Not exactly. Someone you don't pay."

"Why do you keep calling her Sally Ann?"

"That's her name," Lou said. "When she first started work, so she could pay off her student loans, she thought the kind of people she wanted to work for wouldn't hire someone named Sally Ann.

She thought they'd be looking for someone more like them. She thought Sarah would suit."

"I need—" and then I stopped. "I need to be here when—" I repeated, then stopped again. I'm pretty sure Lou knew what the rest of that sentence was, and she smiled and shook her head. "I think maybe this is a time when all that matters is what she needs," Lou said.

"This weekend," said Mark, taking my hand across the breakfast table and almost knocking over the coffee cups, "is going to be epic. Epic."

"I think you're going to really enjoy it," I said.

We've planned a trip to Earthshine, the two of us, to have lunch with Talia and her grandmother, and Mark is excited. He doesn't care about the sweaters. He's worn the same Cornell sweatshirt since he first got it in veterinary school; the hem of the sleeves is raveling, and the drawstring for the hood came out in the washer years ago. "What's wrong with this sweatshirt?" he always says when I mention that it's seen better days, and those better days were ten years ago. He does alternate it with one from the Bronx Zoo that has his last name and the number three on the back, which is his number on the staff softball team. He wouldn't know what to do with a Warm As Toast sweater except to lose it somewhere. When he'd glimpsed the price tag on mine, he'd said, "You're kidding me!"

"Sarah bought it," I'd said. "I would never pay that much for a sweater." He'd held it to his face and breathed in deeply. "No alpaca. All I can smell is you. Which is nothing but a good thing." But I could tell he was a little disappointed that the animal smell had been obliterated for the sake of commerce. The man loves animals in the way I love students, and with less reason, as far as I'm concerned. He's been kicked, headbutted, and bitten, and I never have, although when I said that one day to Lou, she'd said, "That's because you've never taught kindergarten boys." Still, he can thrill to anything from a lemur to an ocelot. On one of our early dates, when I was still trying to drive him away, he'd been delayed because, he said, of an anteater who had stopped eating and needed a thorough exam, and I'd scented one of those evasive guy excuses, albeit a pretty original one, the kind that comes before being told you're terrific, but.

"An anteater is not a large animal," I'd said before he could even look at the menu.

"Okay, first of all, anteaters are about the size of Labradors. You're probably thinking of an aardvark, which is smaller. Or maybe an armadillo. Second, I'm trained as a large-animal vet but I'm good for anything and everything." He'd picked up the menu, then put it down. "Also, emergencies come up in my job. Sometimes animals get sick fast and someone has to take a look even if it's the middle of the night."

"Like an obstetrician," I'd said, and he laughed. Why he didn't ditch me then, or a dozen other times, I still can't figure out. "If you're really lucky, I'll take you with me when one of the animals is giving birth," he'd said. It had actually happened three weeks after our wedding, and I'd wept as a giraffe had dipped her endless neck once, twice, three times, silent as her baby fell to the ground in the enclosure, its tawny spots clouded in the shroud of its sac until it had broken free. Three times it fell back, its twig legs scrabbling in the empty air as it tried to stand, and each time I gasped until Mark whispered, "No, no, it's fine, don't worry." The fourth time, it managed to stand, finally, beneath the sanctuary of its mother's belly. Mark had been on full alert for any sign of trouble—the calf's not breathing, the female's rejecting it—but once he saw that all was well, he put an arm around my heaving shoulders, and when I looked up I saw that he was crying, too.

"Never gets old," he said. I had thought of that moment so many times, too many times. Never gets old watching an entirely new living thing emerge from its mother.

In my better moments I thought that Mark never thought of it that way; in my worst, especially when I was bloated with hormones to no effect, I would think that he must, in the deepest recesses of his id, resent me. The problem was that there appeared to be no deepest recesses. That's not to say that he was shallow in any way; if anything, he felt more deeply than most men I knew. Witness his baby giraffe tears.

But the reason I'd fallen in love with him, once I realized he wasn't a con, a sham, a user pretending he was a giver, was that he was that rarest of all things: a contented person. "I've never been to an alpaca farm," he kept saying, the same way he might say "I've never been to the Sistine Chapel." He liked Rome, and London. It's that he liked other, more ordinary things just as much. On a Saturday morning he'd say, "Let's blow by the farmers' market," and to hear his voice you'd think the farmers' market was the Grand Canyon. Or an alpaca farm. All experiences came with a lilt and a smile. When I thought that I almost dismissed him because I suspected there was a Benedict beneath the surface, even all these years later I felt a frisson of fear. I remembered struggling to speak about him to the book club without making him sound uninteresting, even boring, and then one evening, in the middle of some stammering anecdote, Jamie had suddenly said, "Holy shit, Pol, did you pull a Diogenes?"

"The one with pebbles in his mouth?" Sarah had said.

"That's Demosthenes," Jamie said. "Diogenes was looking for a good man."

"It was an honest man, I think," I said.

"Same difference," said Jamie.

His mother said Mark had always been a contented child with nothing to prove. Thomas, she always said, had to show he was the boss, and Douglas had to show he wasn't Thomas, and Michael, when he later came along, was the baby and so was accustomed to being made much of and still expected that to happen. Each of their wives would roll their eyes when Lou said all this, as she did from time to time, but I was spared because she would say that Mark just sat in his walker and watched the older ones as though they were a tennis match, and laughed.

"So basically you won the husband sweepstakes," Emily said dryly one night when we were sitting by a bonfire, and the other two wives nodded.

"Don't fool yourself," Lou had said. "He was the most addle-brained little boy you would ever want to meet. He ruined some of my best pots and pans because he'd decide to make cocoa or soup and then wander away and forget about the stove and take a clock apart."

"Truly? About the clock?" I'd said.

"He went through a period where he took things apart all the time. Luckily he got on the robotics team in high school, and that seemed to take care of that. I mean, he was still taking things apart, but they weren't my things."

"The man can forget to get off at the right subway stop, and two hours later he's anesthetizing an orangutan and removing an abscess," I'd said, and Lou had nodded. "That's him," she said.

"Gonna file some teeth," Mark said to himself one morning before leaving for work, thinking about the alpaca farm again, as though tooth filing were one of those things every human being aspired to attempt. I had wanted to spend Saturday at Sarah's house in the country, and I suspected that my mother-in-law had asked her son, maybe in collaboration with Barbara Burton, to distract me with something else. The thing about family: Lots of times someone was doing something behind your back, for your own good, even when it didn't feel that way.

The last time I had been at the cottage, the weekend before, Sarah had been wrapped in a plaid blanket on the chaise on the patio, fast asleep. I had gone inside to get her another mug of herbal tea. "Doesn't she need to talk about how she feels?" I'd asked Lou, and Lou had said, "Don't you think that when people want you to talk about how you feel, it's for them and not for you?" It sounded so cruel. It sounded so true. Lou hugged me and made the tea.

We went back outside together and when Sarah woke up, she

reached out a hand to each of us and smiled. "Did you tell her about the transplanting?" she asked Lou.

"It's such a gift," Lou said. "The workmen are down to the interior work now, so I have somebody over at the house getting the garden back in shape, and we're transplanting so many things from here. In the spring the beds around the house are going to be beautiful."

"You have to be patient," Sarah said. "Some things will take a year or two to settle in." As though she could read my thoughts, she had squeezed my hand. A year or two. Every year it would come back, whether or not she was there to see it, that explosion of color. "You make beauty out of nothing," I'd said to Sarah once, when she was showing me a trumpet vine that had grown from a cutting.

"Oh, so what, Polly," she'd said. "You make women out of girls."

"Do I?" I'd said. "Or do I just make better-read girls?" And that was long before I'd sat with Josephine at The Refuge, a girl I'd trained meticulously to succeed in a life she now viewed with contempt and revulsion.

"Bring us news from the outside world," Lou said. "We spend all our time working on the punch list for the house and talking about pruning. We're both sick of looking at paint chips that all look the same."

I spoke about the poetry seminar, about Sara Teasdale and Elizabeth Bishop and the terrible poetry that the girls wrote themselves. "Everyone writes terrible poetry when they're sixteen," I said. "Except for Edna St. Vincent Millay."

"No Sexton?" Lou asked.

"Anne Sexton? Why not?" said Sarah.

"Suicide," said Lou.

"Really?"

"Mothers," I said.

"Oh, I get that," Sarah said.

"So Sara Teasdale instead," I said.

"Sara Teasdale was a suicide, too," Sarah said.

"What?" Lou and I said.

"It's true. I don't know how I know that, but I do."

"Isn't that strange?" Lou said. "All the things we know that we don't know how we know?"

"I know that I love you, Polly," said Sarah suddenly, squeezing my hand again, and "I know that I love you, too," I said. Then suddenly we both started to laugh so hard we couldn't stop, and Sarah started to cough, and I thought, Oh no, Sarah will die from laughing. Lou took the mug of tea from Sarah's hands and thumped her on the back.

"My goodness," Lou said. "That was an unexpected reaction on both your parts."

"You were thinking what I was thinking, weren't you?" said Sarah, still breathless, and she started to giggle.

"Jamie?" And we both started laughing again.

"Oh Jesus Christ on a cross," Sarah growled, "stop with the sentimentality, you're killing me here."

"You do a pretty good Jamie," I said.

"Doing Jamie is like doing Jimmy Cagney," Sarah said. "Too easy. Oh, she's going to be so angry at me."

"I'll manage her," I said.

"Thank you again for this," I said to Lou as she walked me to the car.

"It's been a gift for me to spend time with her," she said, wrapping her arm around my waist. "Truly. I'll treasure it always. And I've learned so much about horticulture. I considered myself a bit of a gardener, but I've realized I was an amateur working with Sally Ann." Sally Ann—the friend I didn't know beneath the veneer of Sarah. No, not veneer—Sarah wasn't that person. She was like one of the things she grew, I guess. Lou had met the shoots, the buds. I knew the flower.

WE WERE BOUNCING ALONG ON THAT RUTTED ROAD, MARK and I, the same one I'd driven with Sarah what seemed like a long time ago. This time there were acres of goldenrod, bright yellow when the breeze blew it one way and the color of butterscotch when it blew in the other. Or maybe they were two different kinds of goldenrod. I'd never learned much about horticulture myself.

"Epic," Mark said again, breaking the word into two syllables.

I was pretty sure that alpaca teeth weren't the only thing making my husband so happy. Part of it, maybe most of it, had to do with the sex we'd been having. It had been somewhat ordinary, which was to say that it had been pretty great, but it had happened without planning or caveats or science, just two people side by side turning to each other and moving from kissing to touching to coming together, in both senses of the expression. I had had a fair amount of bad sex in college, guys who thought, as one woman had written on some feminist site, that the clitoris was an archeological ruin in Greece, so I was a complete sucker, in both senses of that word, for Benedict, who was emotionally sterile but sexually adventurous. Sometimes he treated me like an inflatable doll—"Now you get on top," he'd command loudly—but he knew what he was doing. I probably should have known he was doing it with other people as well.

With Mark it'd been different from the beginning, because I'd never had sex with someone I loved and who loved me back, who had that look on his face as though he couldn't believe what he was seeing. But the rabbit hole of the baby chase changed much of that. There were so many pamphlets, and the directives within them reminded me of what I'd hated about grad school, how the medical aspects had killed all the fun and play of sex the way pure enjoyment had been drained from every book in the PhD program, every book called a text instead of a story, and analyzed, criticized. God forbid you should say about a novel *I loved it!*

There were so many pamphlets with so many rules: We should abstain before a sperm analysis, after an embryo transfer. And that didn't even cover the times I was so swollen that I felt as though prone I would pop, or so emotional that the idea of doing what so often led to a pregnancy but in our case wouldn't meant that I couldn't stop crying, which is never a good starting point for lust. "You know how all these conservative states are talking about abstinence education for kids?" I'd said to Jeannine one day. "I feel as though I get nothing but abstinence education." To her credit she'd nodded sympathetically. "I feel like there should be a book for all of you called *The Joy of No Sex*," she said.

"The love between you is the bedrock of this process!" one of the pamphlets said in italics. It was a little like the flyer about Edgemere my mother had given me, with the color photographs of people playing chess in the library, toasting one another in the dining room, walking on the gravel paths—pea gravel because it's harder to stumble on those tiny stones, and easier to push a wheelchair, too, although there were no wheelchairs in the pictures. "Say goodbye to the stresses and strains of everyday life!" the flyer said. "Take an endless vacation." Somewhere there was obviously an entire cottage industry of people whose jobs were to make difficult things sound wonderful. "Edgemere: your encore," Garrison said after our first visit. "Some focus group must have really loved that one."

Dr. Betz didn't have a slogan, for which I was grateful. I'd made them up in my head: Baby maybe? Or maybe not. "One of the pamphlets has an exercise to enable the two of you to talk about the benefits of the limitations imposed by the process," I told Jeannine. "About how wonderful it is to discover other forms of intimacy. It's as though they think you've never heard of oral before. Or cuddling. There's so much about cuddling. Thank you for never recommending cuddling to us."

"I've seen you when you were at your most combative," she'd said. "If I'd mentioned cuddling you would have gone berserk."

In the last few years, when we could and did have sex, the way we'd untethered it from pleasure and tied it to science and medicine somehow made me estranged. It's hard to let yourself go when you feel as though you're watching yourself, looking down from the corner of the ceiling. The problem with having an empath for a husband is that I knew he knew, but I didn't want to talk about it in case he didn't. Or thought I didn't. Or something. Marriage. Like calculus only without the answers.

I'd finally started to come down off the ceiling the month before. I wasn't sure why, but I'd just cleaved to my husband, maybe to find one good, sweet, uncomplicated thing at a moment when everything seemed otherwise. Or maybe it was just muscle memory: This is what it was like before, when insemination went from his body to mine with a burst of feeling, not from a gloved hand to a pipette with nothing but a great weariness and fear. This was what it was like before, when Mark was holding me and not just my hand.

He smiled at me again from the driver's seat. "I bet these guys will be eating pumpkins like it's going out of style," he said, the golden waves giving way to rows of gray split-rail fence lined with chain link as the farm came into view. A large cream-colored alpaca ran across the top of an empty field, picking up speed and all four of his hooves, as though he were levitating. "He's pronking!" cried Mark.

"This is going to be the best day of your life, isn't it?" I said.

"Well, not the best day. The best day was the day I met you. But it— He's pronking again! Here comes another one!"

"They were pronking!" he said as soon as he opened the car door and saw Talia and Barbara.

"Oh goodness, they do it constantly," Barbara said, hugging him. "I have the happiest alpacas on earth. Though I never know whether that's the right verb, and I gather you agree." Barbara had written an entire blog post about her relationship with the alpacas, and also about her border collies. She called the dogs her co-workers because she sometimes used them to bring the alpacas into the barns.

"People always confuse them with llamas," Talia said.

"Well, obviously incorrect, but let's be tolerant," said Mark. "At some level, it makes sense. People confuse seals and sea lions all the time, even though they're very different. Sometimes they even throw in walruses, though once you've met a walrus you can't confuse it with anything else."

"I learned so much when he took me around the zoo," Talia said to her grandmother. "Pandas are not bears. Neither are koalas."

"This girl gives me hope," Mark said, and Talia ducked her head, her curls falling around her face, her smile shining like the sun just coming up along the edge of the horizon. "I'm so glad you're here!" she said, and I was pretty sure she meant Mark. She led him into one of the enclosures and started to rattle off names: Minerva, Persephone ("but we call them Minnie and Percy"), Zeus, Odin. One enclosure over I saw Hester Prynne. "If I thought she'd take to city life I'd give her to you," Barbara said as she came up behind me. "You've obviously taken to her."

"I could walk her in Central Park and everyone would stop and talk to me," I said.

"I have no doubt," she said. "How's Sarah?"

"The strangest thing has happened. Mark's parents moved temporarily into her house in the country while their house is being repaired, and somehow she wound up moving in with them. They scarcely knew each other before, and yet it all seems to be working well for all of them." I turned and leaned against the fence. I could feel Hester Prynne snuffling curiously at the back of my neck. "But if you're asking in the more global sense, Sarah seems to be dying. Which apparently you knew, and wanted me to tell her, and then told her yourself instead. It's like an O. Henry story, except it's not at all entertaining." I'd planned to be confrontational and managed only to sound plaintive. Turning back, I found that the alpaca had the end of my scarf in her mouth, and I laughed, and then stopped laughing and put my head down on the fence crosspiece. I felt splinters beneath my forehead.

"My mistake," Barbara Burton said softly. "I thought you would speak to Sarah, and that Sarah would speak to you. Sooner, rather than later. I'm so sorry that I caused you such concern." She swatted Hester gently on her nose, and the alpaca humphed audibly and dropped the corner of my scarf, limp with saliva.

"Perhaps you know that I've spoken to Louise," she added, although I didn't. "She's such a sensitive person, but no nonsense, too. I can't imagine anyone more soothing to be with during an illness." Which was true. I'd come down with the flu suddenly once when we were all at the house and Lou had tucked me up in bed and brought me chicken noodle soup and sherbet for three days until she concluded that what I needed on day four was pork roast and wild rice. "Thomas is sick, too," she'd said, sitting across from me. "I feel for Emily. Even as a child—Mama, I'm dying! Dying!" I'd laughed, my fever gone. I knew Lou made Sarah laugh, too.

Mark and Talia came over to us, and I introduced my husband to Hester Prynne, who made raspberries between her thick lips. "Oh, look at you with your heart-shaped nose," he said. "Aren't you a beauty?" Mark tilted his head to one side, then looked back at Barbara, his eyes narrowed. She nodded.

"We think so," she said.

"Want me to take a look? Unless you think your vet would mind."

"Oh, she was so excited you were coming!" Talia said. "She said you're famous because of a video of you with some camels."

I started to laugh. "Stop," my husband said, but he was smiling.

"The zoo posts it every May," I said to Barbara Burton. Mark, standing between two camels, singing "Midnight at the Oasis" as one camel lifts the baseball cap from his head and proceeds to chew on it. "Take a bite out of summer!" the slogan reads.

"Camels are related to alpacas," he said. "Alpacas are camelids."

"I knew that," said Talia as Mark went into the enclosure and began to run his hands gently over Hester Prynne's convex side and then below to her lower belly. Then I understood. He and Barbara thought the alpaca was pregnant.

"Come with me," Barbara said. "I have someone I want you to meet."

There was a long, steep hill to the uppermost barn, its walls painted a dull red, with a green metal roof. Inside it was obvious that this one wasn't used for the animals, only farm equipment and tools, the sharp smell of metal overlaid with the smoky scent of some kind of oil. The whole place felt as though it were faintly vibrating with the sound of machinery. Off the vaulted main area was a door to a long workroom. That's where the sound was coming from. Inside was a man at the bench with his back to us.

"Andre!" Barbara shouted. "Andre!" Finally she put a hand on his shoulder, and he turned off whatever he was working with and swiveled toward her. "These are beauties, Barbie," he said. "You're going to get top dollar for these. What did you charge for the last batch, two hundred a pop? You can jack it up for these. That fool who bought the place down the road from me, he was ready to junk those big black walnuts he took down. He said they made a mess with the nuts and the leaves. I said, 'Pal, I'll drag those away.' Six big bowls, three out of each trunk. I'd ask three hundred fifty if I were you."

"Andre," she repeated. "This is the woman I wanted you to meet."

"What?" He turned toward the door. He was like a stereotype of an old man with a certain history, from a certain place and time, in the same way Barbara Burton was. He had longish gray hair pulled into a ponytail behind, receding in front. He was wearing a tie-dyed T-shirt, a pair of ancient jeans with some sort of oil embedded in them, probably forever, and steel-toed boots. I figured that in summer he wore Birkenstocks. He took a cloth from the bench and wiped his hands, then stuck one out. The callouses were thick beneath my palm. "Andre Bettman," he said.

"This is Talia's grandfather," Barbara said, and when I saw the look on her face there was a kind of clicking sound in my head, that sound the dominos make as they fall over one by one. But I looked at his ears and they seemed like ordinary old man ears, like my father's ears, large and fleshy with big lobes. He turned back to the bench.

"Take a look at these," he said, rubbing oil into the surface of one bowl in a line of six, all somewhat different but all the same. He had refused to pretty them up entirely, given them smooth sides and bottoms but rims that were bark all the way around, rough and ruffled and true to the tree they'd come from. I'd never seen anything like them, and that's what I said. "See, Barbie," he said. "Your people will buy these so fast it'll make your head spin."

"Can I leave the two of you for a minute while I check on how Polly's husband is doing?" Barbara said. "You can continue listening to what a genius woodworker Andre is."

"They really are beautiful," I said. "I may buy one myself."

"Oh, she'll give you one," he said, continuing to rub away at them with the oily rag. "She doesn't give a damn about money, and Tally has taken a real shine to you, apparently. And your husband. Barbie thinks between the two of you, you may have gotten the girl off the fashion thing, which she thinks is no way to make a living. Although hell, she's made a pretty good living out of it, but she doesn't take that part of the farm seriously. She says selling sweaters is just for the sake of the animals."

"Do you work here?"

"Oh Jesus, no. I have a place a couple of hours away. I just bring her my things to sell. If we're in the same place for more than an hour or two we're at each other's throats. I once stayed for lunch and it went south so fast I never even got to really eat." He pulled a metal stool across the cement floor with the sound of fingernails on a blackboard, which I've heard so many times. "Sit," he said. "I've got to get a couple more coats of oil on each of these before I take off. I've got a job tomorrow framing in an extension for some people whose big house isn't big enough for them."

"So you don't just do this?" I said, nodding toward the bowls.

"Hell no. You can't make a living with this. It's a sideline. The rest of the time I just do carpentry, make kitchen cabinets, things like that. It's a living."

"But it must be satisfying, right? I mean, if I could look at cabinets I'd built, I'd take a lot of satisfaction from that." I was working so hard to be polite, detached, making small talk with a stranger. It was a kind of out-of-body experience.

"It's a living," he repeated. "I couldn't work in an office."

Andre Bettman had a tattoo on his forearm that I recognized as the Pleiades. The sentence *Who are you and what am I doing here?* kept rocketing around my brain as he oiled the bowls, and I kept trying to ignore it. He was wearing glasses that looked like the ones John Lennon once wore, and a braided leather bracelet. The stereotype was complete.

"So Barbie said that you're a teacher," he said, not looking at me.

"She doesn't strike me as a Barbie," I said.

"We met each other when we were kids. I guess you use more nicknames when you're kids, right? I mean, your students must do that."

"No," I said, being difficult, and accurate.

"She said it's a private school, where you teach. For girls. I'm a big believer in public schools myself. Tally goes to a public school. She wouldn't know how to deal with boys if she went to school with just girls."

"Single-sex education for girls has been shown to help with self-esteem and confidence," I said. Even to myself I sounded like the worst sort of academic. "But it's not for everyone," I added, trying to redeem myself.

"She's going to be able to charge an arm and a leg for these," he said, still rubbing at the bowls.

I was ready to go. I stood up from the stool. I took my hand out of my pants pocket, ready to say Nice to meet you, to head down the hill, to say to myself in the car on the way home, What was that? To say to Mark, The guy had perfectly ordinary ears, and to lie back against the car seat and close my eyes while Mark tried to figure out whether he should mention that that kind of thing often skipped a generation.

Andre Bettman could have done the same, put the tools away on the pegboard, swept the wood shavings off the bench and the floor, thrown the oily rags into the rusty metal barrel set aside for them in one corner. He could have said, Good to meet you, too, thanks for being nice to Tally.

Except he didn't. Except that as I rose, he turned and said, "You look just like your mother." And I sat back down, hard.

"How do you know my mother?" I said.

"Well, I don't know her now. I haven't seen her in, what, maybe forty years or so."

"I'm forty-three," I said.

"Yeah, I heard that from Barbie," he said.

"How do you know my mother?"

"Yeah, I think that's her story to tell. I told Barbie I wasn't sure this was a good idea, but that even so it was Mary who would have to give you the lowdown."

"The lowdown?"

"Whatever."

"Are you my father?" I said, and as I said it I couldn't believe it, couldn't believe it was true, couldn't believe I'd even said it.

"Jesus, of course I'm not your father. I've never even seen you before. I just met you for the first time. From what I recall, you have a perfectly fine father. I think he was the first guy I ever met who wouldn't let you ride in his car if you didn't buckle your seatbelt. As I recall we had a fight about it. I don't like mandates."

"Then how come a DNA test thinks Talia and I are related, that she's my niece? The only way she could be my niece is if her father is my brother, and the only way Stephen could be my brother is if you're my father."

"Half," he said. "Half brother. And those DNA tests, I mean, who gives a damn. You look at those animals out there, and if you tested them they'd be related to each other all over the place, and they have no clue. It's all just seed and egg."

"But humans aren't animals."

He blew air between his lips, dismissive. He had blue eyes. He was good-looking, but not in a way I respond to much. I guess *craggy* is the word people would use. If he were as old as my father, he'd aged well.

"Sure we are," he said. "We think we aren't, but we are, some of the people I've known over the years." He turned back to the workbench, turned away, as though he were done talking. As though we were done talking. So I left. I didn't say Good to meet you. I didn't say anything at all. I walked down the hill and it was like my mind had been scrubbed of thought, as though I'd emptied it all out of one of my pointy little ears so I wouldn't have to think, not yet. I hate ponytails on men. Hate them, hate them.

Talia was standing in one of the enclosures holding a smallish alpaca, one arm slung around its long neck, the other cupping its chin. Somehow when I had imagined filing its teeth, I pictured something small, like an emery board, but Mark had a big webbed belt around his waist and a flat tool at the end of a gooseneck that made a noise like a dentist drill. The alpaca danced a little in place, but Talia held it firm. "Great job," I heard Mark say to her. "It's always good to have an experienced assistant." He lifted the alpaca's lips and put his fingers inside the big mobile mouth, the alpaca the color of sand, the color of Sarah's sweater, the color of the sweaters Dr. Betz always wore. Maybe Dr. Betz shops at Warm As Toast, I thought, because if I thought about sweaters I didn't think about Andre Bettman saying I looked like my mother, which I've never thought was true, no matter how many times people said it.

Barbara Burton was standing at the fence rail, leaning on it with her arms, until she turned and looked back toward the barn. Then she walked toward me. "Let's go inside," she said.

"Why did you do that?" I said, the sound of the file making my words almost inaudible. "Why in the world did you think that was a good idea, to have me meet him like that? Your own husband?"

"He was never my husband. He doesn't believe in marriage. Or monogamy. He's the original rolling stone. But Tally likes him, and she needs all the family she can get."

"I have enough family, thank you. I didn't need you to force any more on me. I can't understand why you thought that was a good idea."

"Genes don't make a family," she said, putting her hand out to me. I backed away from her. "Genes don't make a father. But when you have children it's important to know the puzzle parts, just in case."

"I don't want to talk to you about this anymore," I said. "I want to go and watch my husband work."

I'M STILL NOT SURE HOW I GOT THROUGH THE REST OF THAT afternoon. I wanted to leave, but I didn't want to disappoint Mark or Talia. As we drove back through the goldenrod, dimmer as dusk approached, more mustard than gold, I realized that I could remember very little of what had happened after I had come down from the barn where Barbara left me. There'd been a very late lunch, some kind of soup with vegetables from the Earthshine gardens, brought out in mugs to the area where Mark and Talia were still working side by side. There was a discussion about the gestation period of alpacas. I think Mark said it was almost a year. I think.

"Are you all right?" he said in the car.

"No," I said.

Sometimes our minds protect us, but not enough. I noticed this in the last few years, or maybe even long before, when I'd found out about Benedict. You walk along with this pain in your head, thinking about the things you know, the things you've discovered, the things you've lost, and all those things run around and around in your mind, like a stone in your shoe when you can't stop walking. And then everyday life saves you. You walk into the coffee shop on the corner, and for just a minute or two it stops, your train of thought headed onto a spur: iced or hot, scone or muffin, weather talk with the girl behind the counter, with the person in line behind you. Maybe snow. Maybe rain. Maybe storms. You go to the laundry room and there's one of your neighbors and she asks if you have detergent, she's just run out, and you hand over your plastic bottle and she asks if they will ever get new machines, you can't get a decent-sized load in there, and you agree. The head of school comes into your office and says apologetically that there are some new forms they all have to fill out, and you both say, Not again, and she asks about a student who's been struggling and you say things have taken an upturn with that one.

There are those tiny moments of relief, when my mind goes elsewhere. And then I go right back to thinking about Andre Bettman turning from a workbench with a rag dark and musky with oil in his calloused hands, saying I look like my mother. That man. My mother. My ears. My eyes. Andre Bettman, of course, had blue eyes. Not the ears, but the eyes. They were even the same shade of blue as mine.

Sometimes my husband protects me, but not enough. He holds me in bed and he listens to me talk, talk and rage, and he doesn't say a word until morning, because he knows the things we say in the dark feel more weighted than the ones we say at the little table in our little kitchen. He speaks quietly, the way he always does when he says hard things, the way he has had to do over the last few years: The clinic called about your hormone levels, the number of eggs.

"You knew," I said, looking at his face. "You knew. Did Barbara Burton call and tell you? Did she backchannel this, too?"

"No," he said. "I just thought this would probably be the way it would turn out, ever since you told me about Stephen Burton's ears."

"Why didn't you say anything?"

"I couldn't say anything for sure. Besides, Polly, you knew, too, as soon as you saw his ears, or you wouldn't have even mentioned them to me. You're a smart woman. There were only so many roads to the end point here. You knew where it all had to end."

"I can't believe you're saying that."

"You didn't want to connect the dots because they all led to your mother, the one person you can't deal with. And now you have two choices. You can bury this and pretend it never happened, which we both know you won't be able to do. Or you can talk to her."

I stood up and took my mug to the sink. "I need to go to work," I said, even though it was a half hour earlier than I usually left. I'm a creature of habit: black linen pants and white T-shirt in the summer, black wool pants and a white sweater in the winter. I always walk to school, except in the harshest weather, across Ninety-sixth Street and through the park. It's the worst way to live at a moment like this because there are no distractions, and so the stone in your shoe is all you can think about. That, and what your husband, who somehow is never mean and rarely wrong, just said, about how deep inside you knew the truth but you buried it because you didn't really want to know it, would have left it buried if Barbara Burton, for some reason of her own, hadn't set up that meeting with Andre Bettman in the barn, hadn't decided the truth would set you free, when instead it just set you reeling.

I'm a creature of habit, but I have a job that changes every year, every term, every day. New faces at the desks, and new problems or issues for each. The head taught me a lesson when she called me out on the way I treated CC Conway. Josephine taught me a lesson when she opened her heart. I am going to try to learn those lessons and bring them to the small corner of the world where I teach. That's a job that takes me, for just a little while, away from my persistent thoughts and into a place in which I am most easily at home.

Despite Josephine's dismissal, I'm teaching Millay. I have to. This short poem always scores with the girls. I remember one year walking behind a group of seniors who were rocking side to side, arms around one another, reciting it aloud. Dr. Shanevsky had rocketed out of his classroom. "This is extremely disruptive, young ladies!" he'd cried, and they had stopped like statues, arms dropping to their sides.

But as soon as he closed his classroom door they began again, this time in a whisper:

My candle burns at both ends,
It will not last the night,
But oh my foes, and oh my friends,
It casts a lovely light.

"Thoughts?" I asked this year's poetry class, and hands shot up. "She's totally out of control and loving it," one of them said. That's what they like about the poem. Some of them think of themselves as burning candles, and all of them wish they were. The classroom windows rattled with a blast of cold air, then another. I asked them to write an essay, not on the subject of the poem, but on the feeling it evoked in them. I knew from past years that some of them would nevertheless deconstruct Millay, but that some would come close to talking about letting go, being free. I would discuss with Josephine the next time I saw her, I thought as I went back to my office. The class had blessedly, momentarily, driven away my thoughts about what had happened at the alpaca farm, about what I would do next, but they came back as I moved away from my classroom and the chatter of the girls. At least those thoughts had, for a short time, driven away my thoughts of Sarah and how she was being disappeared by her disease, even as she smiled at her garden fading away in the afternoon light.

Outside my office window the gingko tree had two brave leaves remaining despite the winds—small, ruffled half circles that looked like yellow butterflies. Instead of foliage you could see the street now, both sides, and on the opposite pavement I saw Mark standing, his hands shoved deep in the pockets of his winter coat, and I blinked, as though for a moment I thought it was a mirage. It was cold outside, and he wasn't wearing his hat, and my first thought was, naturally, that he had lost it on the train, or left it at the zoo, or dropped it behind the chest of drawers in our bedroom. I looked down at my desk to see if he had called to remind me of a meeting with him I'd forgotten, the kind of thing we once did when we were going from Windsor to the clinic.

Instead there was a message from the head's secretary. "Call MIL," it said, and for just a moment I wondered whether that shorthand ever stood for something other than mother-in-law, and, if not, why Lou would be calling me at school. I stared out the window at Mark, and I kept staring as I called Lou, and the kindness and care in her voice was terrible to hear, and the look on Mark's face as he finally looked up and saw me staring out the window was terrible to see. Because I realized that while I was teaching the Millay, Sarah had died. Died in her sleep, out in her garden, despite the cold.

"Don't be nice to me yet," I said to Mark in the cab.

Sympathy has an odd effect on me. It makes things worse. I was fine, that one time in the clinic when everything went wrong, until Dr. Betz put her gloved hand gently on my leg. Then I started sobbing and couldn't stop, tissue after tissue after tissue. Same now. The head asked if I wanted to take the rest of the week off, and I said no immediately, needing the routine, the distraction. Mark took me the next night to the zoo, where they were test-driving the special effects in a new World of Darkness, and spoke of nocturnal animals instead of loss. Garrison called and asked if I wanted to get takeout at his place. "I'm so, so sorry," he said when I declined. "Whenever I was around her, I thought of an expression that I think went out with the Victorians. She was a kind of modest person, which in this city stood out like a neon sign. She was good and generous, the kind of person who never looked over your shoulder at a party for who she could talk to next."

"I know," I said.

"I'm here, Pol," he said. "I'm always here."

"I know," I said.

"I'm driving up to her house on Saturday," I told Mark.

"Do you want me to come?"

"I don't," I said.

"I get that," Mark said, and that almost leveled me, because sometimes I couldn't believe that I'd wound up here, with this guy, who also never looked over your shoulder for who he could talk to next. And whom I would never even have known if it hadn't been for Sarah, and the party, and her possession of his coat the morning after, and her decision to pass along my phone number.

I'd only met Sarah's stepson Carter a few times, but I'd liked him, and liked him even more because Sarah had never used that term to describe him. Carter and Dickson, those were her boys, although they were already young men when she married their father. Not her sons; that, she said, would be disrespectful to their mother. We all remembered the day she'd arrived at book club, glowing, to report that Carter and his wife had told her she was welcome to call herself Granny after their first child was born.

"That's huge," Jamie said. "I knew a couple once who were divorced, and the dad's new wife insisted she be referred to as Grandmom with the kid's kids. Someone keyed her car. No points for guessing who."

Jamie, Helen, and I had met for dinner two days after Sarah died, in the back room at a small neighborhood restaurant. "Let the record reflect that this is not a meeting of the book club," Jamie had said, tears running down her face. We had both underestimated Jamie, Sarah and I. She wasn't angry at me. Neither was Helen. They understood what Sarah had wanted and planned. I wanted to drive up to the cottage immediately, but Lou had talked me out of it. "She's not here, sweetheart. She made arrangements," she said softly.

"No funeral," I told the other two. "No memorial service. Nothing."

"That's so Sarah," said Helen. "She never liked being the center of attention."

"I'm going up there this weekend," I said. "Carter asked me to meet with him at the cottage." I wanted to help Lou and Skipper move back to their own house, too. And I hoped Sarah had left me some kind of keepsake. Sarah's being Sarah, I was sure that she had. I figured I already had something splendid, the flowers that would grow around the Bailey house, that would remind me every spring and summer. But I knew I wouldn't need reminding.

I was fine until I got to the head of the gravel drive that morning. And then I wasn't. It took a while to bring my breathing back to normal, to convince myself that I could get away with saying I had a cold. As I pulled up in front of the house, Carter was standing in the doorway, smiling, and suddenly I remembered that there were cameras hidden in the stone pillars at the end of the drive that sent out an alert when someone pulled in. Sarah thought it was silly, but Richard had insisted, worried about those times when his new young wife was there alone.

"I just had to take a moment," I said, hugging him.

"Take all the moments you want," he said. "I've had more than a few myself."

There was a bouquet of some sort of white flowers on the small table in the hall. My mother-in-law, I imagined. "Your in-laws are over at their place," Carter said. "They took a few things home, and Lou said she figured you might want to spend some time just walking around on your own. They're really great people, aren't they? They kept saying it was such a gift to stay here while their place was repaired, but they could have gone home a month or two ago. Sarah said Lou was seeing her out. I think she'd figured that Lou might be the only person who could keep you at arm's length. Anyhow, there's coffee in the kitchen, and I want to go through some paperwork in my father's old den. Wander away but call me if you need anything."

I walked through the house quickly, looked for a moment into Sarah's pretty blue-and-white bedroom, the quilt folded at one end of the bed as though she would slip beneath it that night, another spray of white flowers in a ceramic vase on the bedside table. I knew I wouldn't really find her here. I knew to go through the French doors to the garden. Despite the cold snap the week before, there were still so many flowers, almost none that I could name. The roses and day lilies were gone, and in their place tiny purple stars, pink things like daisies, a few hydrangeas, but instead of blue, white with a touch of green. Holly bushes, a weeping hemlock. Things that could be seen among the snow. I remembered an October book club when Helen had said idly that the temperature that night was going to fall to the twenties. "Oh no!" Sarah had said. No hard frost yet, but any day now.

At the end of the brick path that led between the flower beds, there was a small tree, the soil at its base a raw umber brown, its trunk ringed with chicken wire so the deer wouldn't rub against it marking their territory. A magnolia, Lou had told me. Sarah had grown up with magnolias, she said, or I guess Sally Ann had. Sarah had given Lou the number of the nursery where she had chosen the tree months before. Two days after she died, the nursery people dug the hole twice as deep as it needed to be. The ashes went in, then the tree. I knelt down and patted the ground with both hands. I wanted to say something, but when I opened my mouth, no words came out, just a kind of low wail that died in my throat. I walked backward up the path so I wouldn't have to turn my back on the tree. I got a cup of coffee and stood at the French doors in the kitchen, staring at it, finally sitting down at the table.

I was there for a long time before Carter returned holding a file folder under one arm. "Too much coffee today, way too much," he said to himself, but he poured another cup anyway and sat down at the table across from me. "My brother is on his way back from Tokyo. He wanted to stop by tomorrow, if you don't mind. Feel free to say no, but there's a seascape over the desk that our father particularly loved. Sarah let us take most of his things after he died, but we left that there so the wall wouldn't look so bare. I asked Dickson, and he'd like it, too. We could trade it back and forth."

"Don't ask me," I said. "Take whatever you'd like. She always said the second-best part of marrying Richard was you two. You know how much she loved you both."

"And we her. And she you. Dickson's wife once said that you were the daughter she never had. And Sarah said, 'Younger sister, Betsy, younger sister. I'm not that much older than she is.'"

"I just hope somebody will be as happy here as she and your father were."

"What?"

"Whoever buys the place," I said, looking around me and then down that long path to the little tree that would someday be a big tree blooming. "Or are the two of you going to hold on to it?"

Carter shook his head. "Goddamn, Polly, she didn't tell you? I'm sorry, pardon my French, as Sarah would say. She didn't tell you? This place is yours. She deeded it to you months ago."

"What?"

"And all its contents. That's what the documents say."

"You can't just give somebody a house."

"Actually, you can. There was some legal reason to do it before she died, and not as part of the estate, and I think there were some tax ramifications, which she also took care of. But this is your house now."

"Oh, Carter, that can't be right. You and your brother—"

"No, no, Polly, we agree with this. Our father left us so much. He sat us down and said, 'Thirds. A third for each of you and a third for Sarah.' And as soon as he said it, she said, 'Do you boys think that's fair?' He could have left her everything, and believe me, it was a lot. A third was a lot. She left us the apartment in the city, which you can imagine is very valuable. The rest of her third she left to charity, except for a trust to handle expenses for this house, taxes, homeowner's insurance, things like that. She wanted this to be a gift, not a burden. Be happy here, you and the vet. That was her dearest wish."

"I don't know what to say," I said. "I've never owned anything."

"Well, now you do."

EDGEMERE AROUND THE HOLIDAYS IS A PLACE THAT HAS TO thread the needle. Festive, but not religious. Someone figured that they had to acknowledge Thanksgiving, Christmas, the New Year, but not in ways that would annoy any of the families or rattle any of the residents. The decorations are up from the middle of November to the middle of January. There are artificial pine garlands on all the mantels and around the doors, with small white lights. No blinking lights, because that apparently can cause what the staff call "an episode." The tree is silver with blue glass ornaments, which I guess is an attempt to veer away from Christianity. It has a little silver picket fence around the outside edge of the tree skirt, because three years ago someone in a motorized chair plowed into the tree and brought the whole thing down. "What kind of damn fool does a thing like that?" my father had said when we gathered on Christmas Eve his first Christmas there.

"We're all having dinner at the house tomorrow," my mother had said then, her hand on his leg.

"Ham?" my father had asked.

"Of course."

That didn't happen year two; visits to the house made him rage or, worse, weep. Sometimes, in those early days, I took him out driving for around an hour or so. "I once hit a deer here," he'd say on a narrow country road, or "I handled the insurance for them" as we drove past a house that had changed hands twice since the Herlihys lived there. Sometimes I wondered whether what he was saying was true, but one day we drove past the supermarket parking lot and he said, "That's where I taught you to drive." And it was.

But now it was year three, and there was none of that. Garrison had visited the week before, and when he called me I asked if our father had spoken while he was there. I hoped he had recognized Garrison, said something that made him feel, even for a moment, that he was more than an also-ran, an afterthought.

"I was talking to one of my co-workers, who has a mother in a memory care facility," he said, "and she said that the doctors told her that people with dementia frequently become more of what they always were. Which in her case is apparently pretty terrible, because her mother was not particularly nice before, and now she's even less nice."

"But at least she speaks, right?"

"But that's my point, Pol. Dad was always a man of few words. Remember that mug he had on his desk, with his pens in it?"

I remembered. It said "World's Best Listener." Someone who worked in his office had given it to him.

The staff said they thought he had been more silent without Claire around, that her occasional statements had led to his, and vice versa. Claire, one of them had told me, had had some medical issues. She wouldn't tell me more. Couldn't, she said. I hadn't seen Claire's daughter for a while, and I tried not to conclude that Claire had been moved to C, or worse.

"Do you remember that mug on your desk?" I said to my father. "World's best listener. You're still the world's best listener." His head now was permanently bent so he was looking down in his lap. Most of the time the only thing that moved were his hands, his fingers twining around one another.

"I'm going now, Daddy," I said, angling my head toward something like eye contact. I won't say exactly where I am going in case, in some back room of his mind, where a light still flickers, it rings a bell. Besides, what would I call it? Your house? Her house? Our house? None of those feels exactly right.

My father doesn't seem to know exactly who he is. I'm not sure exactly who I am. So I'm finally going to the one person who has never seemed to have any doubt. There's part of me that's terrified, which is what I told Mark, and there's part of me, that I won't acknowledge, that's triumphant. The honorable Mary K. Goodman fouled up in a big, big way.

I hadn't actually been to the house where I grew up, where she lives, in a little over a year. I see her at Edgemere or meet her at the restaurant on Main Street in town where the owner calls her Judge and brings over her salmon and salad without asking what she'd like. He does the same for me now, too, because once I'd made the mistake of saying, "I'll have what she has," and after that it had been gospel. It's fine. It's good.

I let myself in and could hear my mother in the kitchen pulling something together for lunch. The house felt oddly unlived in, like a place where someone comes to sleep and eat but doesn't really spend much time, doesn't put feet up on the ottoman to read a book or watch television in the den. She probably spends many more hours in her chambers than she does in her living room. Garrison told me they were going to make her presiding judge, whatever that entails.

"I hear you're going to be presiding judge," I said when I went into the kitchen, sniffing the air. Minestrone. The cheese and bread are already laid on the cutting board with a little dish of olives. It's a company lunch. I am company.

"That's just a rumor," my mother said, ladling the soup into bowls. We sat opposite each other at the oval table by the low kitchen windows, the seats where we always sat, the other two empty. Outside some birds were pecking at berries on a bush.

"It was always nice to have all these windows," I said, thinking of our apartment and its kitchen view of nothing.

"I gather you now have a kitchen with a lot of windows, and a high-end stove and marble countertops. And several bedrooms and bathrooms. Along with a good deal of land and landscaping."

"I showed Garrison some pictures," I said, reaching for the cheese knife. "I'll invite you both once we get settled."

"That's an extraordinarily generous bequest. And I'm sure it's all properly handled. I know the firm that's always represented her."

"I still can't believe it," I said.

"Will you spend the holidays there?"

"I'm not sure yet," I said. "It might be too soon."

"I'm truly sorry," my mother said, sounding as though she meant it, and that opened the door. I inhaled, and began.

"So," I said, "to make a long story somewhat shorter, on my birthday last year my friends in the book club—"

"The book club that doesn't read the book."

"Exactly. For my birthday they gave me one of those ancestry kits, where you send in a swab and they tell you if there's anyone out there related to you, any family you didn't know about."

What I could tell, by looking at her face, is that while Garrison had told her about the house, he hadn't said a word about Roots & Branches. She wasn't prepared, wasn't armored against this. I saw something on her face that I'm not sure I had ever seen before. She looked frightened. The other moms looked frightened when I was a kid, but never her. I fell and broke my arm on the climbing gym, and she had that habitual expression on her face as we settled into the ER cubicle: This is a task and we will handle it. It's the same look she had on her face in the newspaper photograph when that assemblyman's wife had hurled herself toward the bench after her husband's sentencing. I suspect it's the same look she had when she had that bad mammogram and the lumpectomy after, or when the doctors finished their tests and said, "Certainly he is somewhat younger than the usual dementia patient, but there's no doubt." My mother doesn't scare. But she's scared now.

Her face was still, but there was something in her eyes that seemed to me to say, Stop, no. But I didn't stop. I walked through the entire thing: the not-niece who thought I might be her mother's sister, the nice father of the not-niece, his mother and her alpaca farm, my visit there with Sarah, my visit there with Mark. I didn't mention that I'd later been in touch with Stephen Burton, whose mother had told him about my meeting in the big barn while his father oiled the black walnut bowls. "Maybe we should meet again?" I'd asked in a message. "Welcome a conversation about Talia and how she'll handle it if she doesn't get into Barnard. No wish to discuss the sperm donor," he'd replied.

Barbara Burton had sent me one of the black walnut bowls. They're gorgeous. I'm going to give mine to Emily. I can't stand to look at it.

"Which eventually brought me to Andre Bettman," I said, and my mother blinked twice.

One of the birds had stopped foraging for berries and was pecking at the siding of the house. Finally my mother said, "What do you want from me, Polly?"

"Well, the truth about my father would be a good beginning, although it would be about twenty or thirty years too late."

The fear disappeared, replaced by anger. "Your father is Jack Goodman. No man ever loved a daughter the way he loved you. He doted on you from the day you were born. He always talked about you like you were the best thing that had ever happened to him. He even said that once to me, actually: 'That little girl is the best thing that ever happened to me.' The doctors said that commonly, the spouse is the last person someone in his condition recognizes. I didn't say a thing, because I knew they were wrong. You"—and she pointed at me with her index finger—"are the last person he will recognize."

"Good diversionary tactic, Your Honor. Let's get back to Andre."

"What did he tell you?"

"He said it was your story to tell."

She let air out with an exasperated sound. "Of course he did."

"You could start by explaining to me how an itinerant woodworker and Mary Goodman wound up in the same place at the same time."

My mother turned her head and stared into the distance. She did that sometimes on the bench, and I'd once told Garrison I thought it was because she looked good in profile. "Oh, for God's sake," he'd said, "she's done that when she's thinking our entire lives."

Maybe she does it when she's thinking deeply, because there was a long silence before she turned back to me. "I was twenty-two when your brother was born," she said. "The girls I went to City College with all had jobs and apartments, and I had a baby. This may be difficult for you to understand, but I would take him to the park and sit on a bench and think, How is this my life? What have I become? Your father was just building his business, and he was gone for ten or twelve hours every day, and it was just me and the baby."

She stopped and exhaled loudly, then said, "I was invisible."

As though some storm had passed, she continued, "Then we moved here, when he was two, and I met Roberta. You probably don't remember her and I don't even know her last name now—I believe she's been married and divorced twice. What used to be the old Park Theater started a summer program, amateur theater, but decent, actually. She started volunteering there and she asked if I wanted to help her. The kids ran around backstage while we pulled costumes and props together. It felt a little bit like having an actual job.

"Andre was building the sets one year. He was friends with the man who ran the theater program. He was completely fraudulent. It was as though the sixties had never ended. He used the term *man* a lot. He referred to people as cats: That cat doesn't know how to use a drill, things like that. He wore overalls and tie-dyed T-shirts."

"He still does," I said. "And he has a ponytail."

My mother shook her head. "I'm not surprised," she said. "I'm sure he took enormous pleasure in trying to humiliate me in conversation with you. Sitting on the bench is exactly the sort of job for which he would have contempt. Fight the power and all that."

“That wasn’t my impression. I got the impression that he was both trying to protect you, and remembering you fondly.”

“Did he argue with you? My God, he loved to argue about anything and everything. Politics, of course, but plays and movies and foolish things. I remember a pitched argument about solar power before anyone was talking about solar power, and another one about imports from China. He loved to argue with me about the emptiness of the suburbs, about feminism. Office work—that was something he laughed about. The look on his face when I said my husband ran an insurance agency. Jack drove him once to pick up some supplies, and he argued with your father about seatbelts. He was always a devil’s advocate, so half the time you didn’t know whether he believed what he was saying or was just taking a debating position. I liked it. It made me feel intelligent. Your father never argued with me about anything. Yes, Mary, he would say as though I were a child. Over the years I learned to appreciate that, how steadfast he is. But not in the beginning.”

“Do I have to actually say it, or will you finally?”

“Roberta and her then-husband took the children to Ocean City for a week. Garrison was at a children’s play group in the park. I took care of the costume closet, which was really a small room on the second floor of the theater. That’s where I slept with him. It’s incomprehensible to me now. Actually, it was incomprehensible to me then. He never showered. He smelled like he never showered. The first time, he didn’t even speak. He opened the door of the room, stepped in, and just grabbed me. I don’t think a word was exchanged from beginning to end.”

“So it wasn’t consensual?”

She shook her head again, this time as though she were coming awake. “It was totally consensual. Her first day back, Roberta took one look at me when he came into our room and said, ‘Mary, Mary, quite contrary, I don’t blame you a bit, but don’t get caught.’

“I can’t explain it to you. He had that thing that you can’t explain or define. You meet someone who may not be attractive or nice or intelligent, but he has that something. There's not even a name for it." And suddenly she leaned forward, her eyes narrowing, and said, "But of course you know all about that, Penelope. You married that. Your first husband was nothing but that. Anyone could see that he wasn't a good person, that he would be unfaithful and perhaps even mean. But whatever it is, he had it. And you fell for it. And Andre had it. And I fell for it too. Every night, when your father, *your father,* because he is your father, would walk in the door and kiss me, I would feel so guilty and I would vow to myself, Mary, it's over, no more. And I would keep that vow for a day or two, and then it would all fall apart."

"Someone described him to me as a careless man of wild enthusiasms."

"That's insightful and completely accurate."

"How long?"

"Five weeks," my mother said. "July and August."

"And then you stopped?"

"I wish I could say that that was the case. But it stopped because one day I came in to work on the costumes for the last play. It was Ibsen's *A Doll's House,* which I'm sure is a bit of irony that you'll appreciate. And he was gone. He'd finished the sets two days before. He didn't even tell me he was going or say goodbye. Two weeks later I started vomiting in the mornings, just like I'd done the first time. Your father was ecstatic, so happy. 'Let's have a houseful, Mary,' he said. He thought I loved our life as much as he did. And I loved him, I always have, I always will, even now that so much of him is gone. And how he has loved you. A daughter, he'd say, my best girl. He talked all the time about how you looked so much like his mother, how it was uncanny, the spitting image. I couldn't see it myself, but it made him so very happy, as though his mother had been reincarnated. It made him love you even more, love you so much."

"And that's why you didn't."

"Didn't what? Love you? Of course I did. Of course I have. But you made it so hard—judging me constantly, talking about how Jennifer's mother went on the field trip and Jessica's mother made her birthday cake and all the things you resented about me because I made a life for myself. You and your father and your constant judgment."

"Oh please. My friends. My boyfriends. My college major. My job, my apartment. Judgment is your job, not mine."

"Penelope, you and your father are the worst kinds of judges. You judge with a smile."

"Well, that remark certainly makes clear how very much you love me and, for that matter, him. I just have one last question: At what point did you finally realize that Andre Bettman was my father?"

"He's not your father. Genes don't make a father." It was exactly what Barbara Burton had said when we stood in her field. It was what Jeannine had once said about adoption.

"I'll rephrase: At what point did you realize for sure that I was the product of your affair with Andre Bettman, not your husband?"

She looked to the side again and tears slid down the slope of her face. She looked old suddenly.

"About fifteen minutes ago," she said.

MY MOTHER WAS SPENDING CHRISTMAS DAY AT EDGEMERE. "I would like to take some time to process our discussion," she had said in an email, and "Agreed," I had replied. My brother usually spends Christmas in a place that seems as far removed from it as a place can be. "I'm leaving for Vietnam for a week tomorrow," he said. We exchange gifts in early January. That's when I would tell him my news. I wasn't sure I would tell him about the conversation with our mother.

Mark and I spent our first night in what was now our country home on Christmas Eve. We slept in one of the guest bedrooms, just as we once had when we were housesitting, because I still thought of the biggest one as Sarah's room. Lou and Skipper drove over with a big wreath for the front door, pine boughs and red-plaid ribbon. "There's an entire cabinet of Christmas things," I said. "Dishes, ornaments, platters. Everything. There are four ceramic Santas and a creche."

"That's handy," said Lou.

"I haven't taken any of them out yet."

"Well, you're coming to us for dinner tomorrow anyway," she said, but I knew she knew that wasn't why.

Two weeks beforehand I'd asked Jamie and Helen to come to the cottage for the day. I'd always been nervous about the way in which Sarah and I were closer with each other than with each of them, and I wanted them to feel included. I stood in the doorway, where she had stood in June, and they came toward me, and for just a moment all of us clung to one another and shook with sobs. Of course after a minute Jamie pulled back and said, "All right, that's enough of that" as we all mopped our eyes, and when we got inside and sat down at the kitchen table, added, as she had before, "Let the record reflect that this is not a meeting of the book club."

"Let the record reflect that the book club is done," said Helen, looking from one to the other of us, and we all nodded.

"We'll still see each other all the time," I had said. "But it can't be the book club anymore."

"How many years has it been?" Helen said.

"Lucky thirteen," said Jamie. "Not that I'm superstitious. But I'm relieved that no one said, Oh, oh, Sarah would want the book club to go on."

"By which you mean me," I said.

"If the shoe fits," Jamie said.

We had salads and soup, and outside the French doors a soft snow began to fall, hissing faintly at first and then silently edging the tops of the evergreen shrubs with a veil of silver-white. There had been another hard frost the week before, and a man Sarah used for the heavy lifting in the garden had cleared away the dark gunk of stem and leaf where, incredibly, the plants had once bloomed and would surely reappear. In Central Park, when we walked in the early, shivery spring, Sarah would stop and say, "Look, Polly! Daffodils!" She had kept a journal of what was where in the garden outside and when it flowered. I thought about mentioning the magnolia to Helen and Jamie, and then I decided not. Too soon, I thought. The magnolia still looked like a big gray stick with smaller gray sticks atop it, and when I walked down the path and stared at it, squinted at it, I could hear her saying: Wait until May. Wait until May. My whole life would be different in May.

Two weeks ago I had made an appointment to see Jeannine. "I want you to do something for me, and it's going to sound crazy," I'd said when I sat down in her office.

"That's one of my areas of expertise," she'd said, smiling, and when I'd told her what I needed, she'd smiled even more broadly, left the room, came back and put one hand on my shoulder and, with the other, handed me a plastic cup. "Take this into the bathroom," she said.

Too soon, I thought again when I looked at Jamie and Helen and thought about telling them. Maybe it's a good idea to leaven grief with joy. But it felt like a betrayal of the sorrow to me at that moment.

"I also wondered if each of you would like to take something, a painting or a photograph or a vase or something," I said.

"She already did so much for each of us," said Helen. "She endowed a scholarship in my name at Vassar."

"She made big gifts to all my charities," Jamie said. "I had no idea. To be honest, I had no idea she was that rich." Helen and I both started to laugh, but every time we laughed we teetered on the edge of tears. I knew that in some way the three of us would never recover from this, and from the role Sarah played in each of our lives, with her gift for stealth generosity. I was sure that even before all these bequests, there had been things she'd offered to do for Jamie and for Helen and even for Mark that I'd never known about. "Don't thank me, Polly," she would always say, whether it was for a tureen of soup or an offer to see us to another round of IVF. "I love doing it."

"She gave fifty thousand dollars to Windsor," I said. "And fifty thousand to the Bronx Zoo for veterinary services." I hadn't known about either until the head came in to tell me about an unexpected bequest, and the development director had come in to thank Mark, who at first was thoroughly confused. When we'd visited the cottage he'd walked from room to room just shaking his head, and then he'd put his arms around me and said, "It's incredible for us to have this. But I'd trade it in a minute for you to have Sarah back, especially now. Especially at this moment."

"And she would say that now was the perfect, perfect time for us to have this house."

It was so easy now to get in the car on Christmas morning and be at Mark's parents' rebuilt home in no time. You could still see all the places where their house had been put back together—"like Humpty Dumpty," Skipper liked to say—because the new siding was a different shade of brown than the old, and the new copper flashing was catching sparks even in winter sun, while the old had turned to a mossy green. Lou said she was still suspicious of some of the ceilings and complained that on a wet day she could smell fresh paint.

"Mom," said Thomas, "the house looks like nothing ever happened. Given the damage, it's amazing. Be grateful."

"It's just inside me," she whispered in the kitchen, basting the turkey. "He doesn't understand that that sound, and the way it looked, the tree through the ceiling—I still see it and hear it. It's inside me, maybe forever."

"Of course it is," I said.

Rebecca wandered into the kitchen. "Have you seen my mom?" she said.

"Come help me cut carrots," said Lou, pulling out a chair at the long pine table, and Rebecca fell heavily into it. "All right," she moaned. "But next time it's Sophia's turn."

Emily popped through the den door as I walked by and grabbed my arm. "Please take me to see your house," she said. "I'm dying to see it again, and the girls keep asking about the paper dolls. Dinner isn't for another three hours. We won't stay long."

Sophia emerged behind her. "Can I come?" she said.

"You're watching the movie," Emily said. Through the door to the den I could see David standing behind the coffee table staring up at the TV screen, his mouth open, two tiny pearly teeth glowing in the reflected light. He'd just learned to stand, late apparently. "And was I concerned?" Emily had said. "Hell no. Of course now he won't sit down." Mark was sitting on the couch behind him, a leg on either side of David's droopy diaper butt, providing guardrails just in case and staring at the TV as well. "It's a nature video," Emily said.

"Can I come?" Sophia said again.

"This is a girl trip," her mother said, crouching beside her.

"I'm a girl."

"It's a big-girl trip. Big girls and a bottle of wine."

"You told Daddy Aunt Polly wasn't drinking wine anymore."

"So Aunt Polly can drive, and you can stay with Uncle Mark and Daddy and Grandmom and Grandpop."

Sophia hurled herself to the floor and began to cry. "Got the keys?" Emily said as we moved down the hall and the sound of wailing faded. "Sophia, honey," we heard Lou call from the kitchen.

"We are blessed in our mother-in-law," Emily whispered.

The road had been plowed and sanded after the snow the week before, and grit rattled around in my wheel wells. "I'm so excited," Emily said again. "And not just about the house." She mimed zipping her lips shut. "Are you in middle school?" I said.

"No, but those girls will be someday, and when they are, I'm coming to stay with you every chance I get." She stared out the car window at the passing trees. "I love that bowl you gave me," she said. "Lou says there's a story behind it."

"There is, and I'll tell you all about it sometime. But not yet."

"You do you," Emily said.

"I still really feel like you handled that so poorly," I'd said on the phone to Barbara Burton.

"I'm sorry," she'd said. "What I learned from what happened with Talia's mother is that everyone needs to know where they come from. I don't mean who they need to love, or cleave to, or follow. But having a mystery in your family tree can eat away at a person."

"I was fine," I had said.

"That may be true. Or it may not. But I didn't do it for you. I did it for your children."

A branch had fallen across the drive just inside the pillars, and I swerved around it and thought about how, tomorrow, I would go out and pick it up and throw it into the tattered brush, and then I wondered if that was the right thing, if there was some routine for dealing with downed branches. There was so much to learn. In the middle of the night last night I'd come awake at a faint sound from below. "Did you hear that?" I'd whispered, and Mark had rolled toward me and lay still and finally said, "That's the furnace coming on."

"Is that normal?"

He'd laughed. "Go to sleep, Polly, my love. You need your sleep."

There was still some snow here and there on the slate roof, edging what Mark had said were called snow catchers, metal brackets with eagles atop them. So much to learn.

"Oh Polly," Emily said, putting her hand on my arm. "It's so perfect."

She walked around from room to room, stopping to open closets and look out windows as though she were a real estate agent. She even went down to the basement. "This is a new hot water heater," she murmured, almost to herself. Finally she circled back to the living room and looked at the ashes in the old fireplace. "You made a fire, but you didn't hang your stockings," she said.

"Our stockings are at Lou and Skipper's house," I said.

"It's perfect," she repeated, sitting on one of the couches. "I thought so when I visited Lou and Skipper here, and I think so even more now that I've had a chance to really look around. Everything about it is wonderful. And in a couple of years you'll be able to think of it as your house."

"Really?"

"I think so. A swing set on that grassy area to one side of the flower beds will make all the difference. I can tell you the best one to buy. Maybe all the sisters-in-law will chip in and buy one for your shower."

I stared at her, but my hand wandered down. It seemed to be possessed at this point by some reflexive urge to cup my belly. It had begun when I was sitting across from Jeannine, after she'd run the tests, when she'd said, "Can I call the doctor in? This will make her day. She loves it when Mother Nature takes over from her."

"Polly, I don't mean to be crass," Emily went on, "and if you want to keep this a secret we can both pretend I never said anything. But your boobs are twice their normal size. Thomas insists you got breast implants."

"What?"

"I know, I just laughed. I mean, on my list of people who would pay for a D cup, you're pretty far down. You might be last. Plus you said no to wine and blue cheese. And Mark keeps looking at you like he's having a religious experience."

"I'm due in April," I said. "Honestly, I thought I was going through menopause. For all those years I thought the only way I could get pregnant was in a doctor's office, so I was barely keeping track of things, and when I skipped I thought, Well, I'm under a lot of stress and I'm forty-three, this is what happens. Then I had some bleeding, which threw me. It wasn't until I couldn't zip my favorite pair of pants that a lightbulb went off. Which is pathetic, right? I was already four months pregnant when I figured it out. We just don't want to make an announcement until we feel as though we're going to go the distance."

Emily leapt up and hugged me, hard. "Oh, you are so going to go the distance with that rack on you," she said.

"It's so weird. I've wanted this for so long, and now I'm afraid. I feel like maybe I'm like one of those women who spends months planning a wedding and doesn't think about the morning after, or the week after, or the years after, when she's married. Never mind, don't pay any attention to me, it's hormonal, right?"

"No, actually, I know exactly what you mean. Everyone says, Let's have a baby. No one says, Let's spend the rest of our lives creating a fully functioning human being."

"You could have told me that before," I said.

"We all have to keep it a secret so we'll have company. We don't want to scare you off."

"Well now I'm really afraid."

"It's the hardest job there is," said Emily. "And everyone makes mistakes. But you won't make as many as most people. And boy, I am so happy. I can't wait to tell Thomas."

"Well, we wanted to wait a few more weeks. And if you tell Thomas, he'll tell Douglas, and Douglas—"

"Never mind," Emily said. "I know. Even better—I'll keep it a secret, and then when you make an announcement, I'll say I already knew, and Thomas will be so pissed. But I do have to tell you, Lou asked me whether I thought you were. She thinks the alpaca lady already told you. Or maybe she said the alpaca lady already told her."

"So are we fooling ourselves? I thought there were only four people who knew." Jeannine and Dr. Betz, of course, and that night after I went to the doctor's office, Mark. For the rest of my life I will remember the look on his face: the moment of shock, the moment of joy, the tears that he could not squelch. My dear husband, who had spent years pretending that this moment would not be the happiest of his life, his kind and thoughtful subterfuge collapsing with the way in which he kissed me, a kiss that was nothing but pure love. Sometimes I would get texts from him now that were just smiley faces, bursting fireworks, long lines of xoxoxoxoxoxo. "You can stop bringing flowers now," I'd said, so the next night it was a box of cookies, the night after that cake and a stuffed kangaroo from the zoo gift shop with a little joey in its pouch. It was only a matter of time before he pulled a onesie from his backpack.

Now Emily knew, and maybe Lou. Barbara Burton had sent me sage and anise, and when I'd looked both up I saw that they were herbal supplements for pregnancy, so even though I hadn't told her, I probably had to add her to the list. Soon I'd tell Helen and Jamie, and the girls at school would start to talk in the lunchroom: Did you see Miss Goodman this morning? Is that just a big shirt? Can she be? Isn't she way too old? I would send a message to Josephine so that she wouldn't hear it through the Windsor grapevine. Preparing to leave The Refuge for her grandmother's house, she had sent me a quote from Gandhi: "Joy lies in the fight, in the attempt, in the suffering involved, not in the victory itself." I understood why it spoke to her, but with the victory itself inside me, I thought otherwise at the moment.

I couldn't wait to go to lunch with Garrison when he was back, and to feel his happiness across the table. I would meet my mother at the restaurant on Main Street, or maybe I would invite her to the cottage as a gesture of something. Not forgiveness or understanding. Maybe a truce? I had no idea how she would respond to this news. Jamie's mother had been one of those people who said, "I'm too young to be a grandmother." And there was Emily's mother, of course, who loved being a grandmother in a way she had never loved being a mother, and Lou, who loved it all, every bit of it. As Emily and I drove back to the house I decided to pull Mark aside before dinner and tell him I thought we should make an announcement. I would let him say the words so I could see that look again on his face.

Naturally, after I'd told Mark I'd told one other person. There was a sheen of ice on the road to Edgemere, and my car had shimmied sideways, and there again my hand had gone down protectively. But I'd straightened the wheel and continued to the parking lot and been happy to see that the ice there had disappeared, beaten down by rock salt.

"You and your mother keep missing each other!" said the floor nurse when she saw me. "She just left. Your dad's in the dining room."

He was sitting at the table with one of the aides. "Look who's here, Mr. Goodman!" she said, and he lifted his head and stared at me for a moment, and it was like someone flipping the pages of a dictionary looking for the right page with the right definition, and then he reached the one he needed and the light came on behind his eyes, the light that, as sure as if he'd said it, said, Hello, pumpkin pie.

"He's just finished eating," said the aide.

"I think I'll take him to the library," I said. Pushing him was like pushing nothing, he'd gotten so thin, and it reminded me of Sarah in the wheelbarrow, the wheelbarrow that was now in a garage that was improbably mine. The blanket over his legs caught for a moment in one of the wheels, and I stopped and freed it. I couldn't help it; I thought about how it was like pushing a stroller.

The library was empty. I set him next to the gas fire for the warmth, and because maybe, just maybe, there was a chance he could still read the words "Joy in the Morning" engraved on the mantel. I pulled a wing chair close to him and, folding one of my hands over his, clasped atop the blanket, leaned in close and whispered in his ear, "Daddy, I'm going to have a baby. You're going to be a grandfather."

ABOUT THE AUTHOR

ANNA QUINDLEN is the author of many bestselling books, including the #1 *New York Times* bestselling novel *Rise and Shine,* the #1 bestselling memoir *Lots of Candles, Plenty of Cake,* and *A Short Guide to a Happy Life*. Her other novels include *Blessings, One True Thing,* the Oprah Book Club selection *Black and Blue, Still Life with Bread Crumbs,* and *After Annie.*

ABOUT THE TYPE

This book was set in Caslon, a typeface first designed in 1722 by William Caslon (1692–1766). Its widespread use by most English printers in the early eighteenth century soon supplanted the Dutch typefaces that had formerly prevailed. The roman is considered a "workhorse" typeface due to its pleasant, open appearance, while the italic is exceedingly decorative.